ONE TWO PUNCH

An Uneasy Future Bundle

PAULINE BAIRD JONES

PBJ

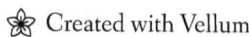

A floating city. An Epic Hurricane. An evil entity bent on destroying all who stand in its way.

Welcome to New Orleans New, 2061.

With a category five hurricane heading for New Orleans New, Homicide Detective Violet Baker and her alien partner, Joe, put aside detecting to help with the emergency. Their task? Evacuate some dirt-siders who don't understand the concept of a twenty-foot storm surge.

But their mission quickly gets complicated by a mysterious murder and the sabotage of their skimmer.

Joe knows who to blame for the murder and the sabotage. For longer than he dares admit, he's been on the track of an evil entity bent on destroying his world and Vi's.

Stranded in the path of the storm, secrets will be

revealed and enemies faced. Can they defeat evil and get that well-deserved happy ending kiss?

If you like mystery mixed with sci-fi, humor, intelligence, and action, then grab this new series by Pauline Baird Jones. But batten down the hatches for a crazy ride!

CORE PUNCH

A kiss may be all they have life expectancy for.

When an intergalactic cop exchange program serves up an alien partner for NONPD Detective Violet Baker, she can't help wishing the handsome alien would be a little less Joe Friday about keeping the pleasure out of their business. Yeah, he's kind of purple and she can't pronounce his name to save her life, but he's almost the only guy in the New Orleans New police department that she's not related to.

Dzholh "Joe" Ban!drn has come a long way hunting the evil that has infiltrated Vi's floating city. When he meets his charming partner, he discovers another reason to stamp out evil. If only he wasn't keeping so many secrets from her....

When an epic hurricane heads their way, they are sent dirt side to New Orleans Old (NOO) on a rescue mission. But murder and sabotage strand them in the heart of the raging storm.

As they fight for their lives, Joe realizes that the evil he's hunting is actually hunting them....

🦋 I 🦋

His partner liked to call it the Big *Un*easy and Dzholh—Joe—Ban!drn decided Violet Baker had a point. New Orleans was more often uneasy than it was easy. Joe studied said city while his partner, at the controls of the police skimmer, adjusted their course so they'd skim beneath, and avoid tangling with, the water umbilical. In his travels, he had seen floating cities on other planets. Cities that spun, orbited, and hid when threatened. Prettier cities. Why did this one feel special in its unease?

That they'd managed to raise so much of the old city, grafting on much that was new without a loss of its larger-than-life personality, was a feat he'd have deemed not worth the effort if he hadn't seen it, if he hadn't lived in it these past six months. Was it familiarity that made the old city seem valuable or was it the incoming hurricane?

Wu Tamika Felipe was—according to the news vids—the biggest storm to close in on the city since Chen, the storm that had almost wiped the original city off the map some fifty Earth years ago. Chen had been the catalyst to save what was left by raising it. Officially, dirt side was called New Orleans Old or NOO and the new city was New Orleans New or NON. To the locals, it was still the Big Easy or Nawlins.

Joe could understand why any city that endured severe flooding had been lifted up and out of the danger zones once the technology became available from his people. Most Garradians preferred a dirt side landfall, particularly after a prolonged time in space, so he found it puzzling that most of the major US cities and many European ones had followed suit. Even some of the smaller concentrations of population had opted for raising or had moved up into the lifted cities in the years that followed.

I believe it was a combination of something called the Green Movement and a fear of overcrowding and over-whelming the food sources, his nanite, Lurch, commented inside his head.

You believe? It was unlike the venerable nanite to be less than certain.

There is a lack of factual data. A problem that occurs when scientists consider their science settled.

Lurch had existed long enough to observe much science come unsettled. It was possible that this storm might unsettle the notion that floating cities were prefer-able to dirt side living. WTF would be the first trial-by-hurricane for the technology and, most particularly, for the ancient parts of the floating city. Not that the dirt side remains of the old city would fare well during the incoming storm. The storm surge would be, according to the experts, unprecedented.

Lurch snorted, the action registering as mild gastric distress for Joe. He could not blame the nanite for the snort. *Unprecedented* had experienced much usage in the news vids since the storm hit category five status. One might conclude that there had never been a category five storm, i.e., without precedent. Only most broadcasts had been detailing with considerable relish all the previous category five storms. Including the destructive force of Cat 5 Chen.

Apparently there are those who do not know the meaning of unprecedented.

It was a valid conclusion based on available evidence. Though the lack of understanding was not endemic. Those who did understand the meaning of unprecedented had made efforts to educate vidcasters through all means available to them. The public mockery had not changed anything that he had observed. Perhaps it was like trying to turn a meteor? Velocity, once achieved, being hard to redirect?

Perhaps you can create an equation for it after the storm?

The mental nudge was deserved, Joe acknowledged, though he doubted the storm's passing would provide much quiet reflection, if the pre-storm briefings taking place around the city were any indication. Those in charge of managing the city were optimistic in their public statements. But private briefings showed awareness of the incoming ass kicking—Baker's succinct summing up following several hours of briefings. His partner-in-crime-solving had no difficulty being direct.

Detective Baker has expanded your vocabulary.

Joe felt the nanite's approval of said expansion. Joe did not point out that his vocabulary was more than adequate or that it had already been expanded to include millions of alien languages when the nanite moved into his head. One did not tell a nanite what it already knew.

But you weren't using any of my additions.

At least Lurch did not call them upgrades.

Joe had learned much from the homicide detective in the past six months, an education that extended beyond expletives, he would have noted if it did not already know this, too. Baker was an excellent law enforcer and a good detective. And unlike many of the Earthlings he encountered, she also smelled quite good. This was desirable since he often shared the confines of a skimmer with her. And bad since he often shared the confines of a skimmer with her. Her pleasing scent could be a bit distracting. Also in the distracting column was her habit of tonal humming and rhythmic shifting, something she called "seat dancing" to music only she could hear, which she'd been doing while Joe reflected.

"I hope this doesn't take too long," the detective in question, or rather in reflection, muttered, breaking off her humming and dancing. She handled the aging skimmer confidently as they curved into the shadow cast by the hovering city.

Joe murmured agreement even though agreement was contextually obvious. Of course they needed to expedite their transit. They'd dropped down from NON in the relative calm between two feeder bands. Neither of them had any desire to be dirt side when the next feeder band arrived, or if the stalled hurricane decided to start moving again. He had learned during his six months in this place that Baker's people mistook silent agreement for inattention. Hence the silence-filling murmur.

Despite the imperatives of time and storm, he looked forward to dirt beneath his feet again, though *green side* might be a more appropriate description. Other than the ribbon of the river cutting through, there was only green to be seen in every direction. If green had been the goal of the Green Movement, they could legitimately claim success. Almost one could believe the area looked like it had when the first explorers arrived. Except amidst the green—and coated in it—were the remnants of the long abandoned city. The occasional chunk of moss and vine covered formerly high-rising overpasses popping up here, and over there one could pick out an irregular course of abandoned streetlights wrapped in the green vines that had moved in when men went up. Between the old lights, grasses pushed against chunks of broken asphalt. Lines of trees wound through the landscape, possibly marking old transit lanes and remnants of parks, because naturally the trees couldn't be raised. In the "preserved" section, there were a few actual buildings visible, though preservation didn't include de-vining them, Joe noted. The only places where efforts had been made to contain out-of-control nature were the ancient cemeteries, which was somewhat ironic, now that he considered it. They were small, isolated squares and irregular rectangles dotting the tangle that was NOO.

Little cities of the dead, the locals call them.

The crypts did have the look of buildings, the impression increasing as the skimmer dropped down just shy of the tops of the trees edging what had once been St. Charles. Did he see the glint of the tracks from the streetcar line? Or did his mind conjure it because he knew they must be there? Did the shadow of the floating city trace patterns onto the ground, or highlight things already there? It still perplexed him that the raised city had been patterned as much as possible on the original. The upper city even followed the curves of the river below, though there was no visible purpose in preserving the old boundary. Now there were more transit bridges crossing the "river" than had been present back then, because one did not have to build or pay for them, but not nearly as much as there legitimately could have been over the essentially empty space. To the north of the city, a faux Lake Pontchartrain remained a recreational zone for pleasure skimmers and gliders. Like the river, transit bridges were limited and controlled. "River traffic" was also restricted to approved vessels, such as those transporting goods and materials and passenger ferries.

They did not wish their city to change.

Joe could understand the resistance to change. The desire to keep things as they were. The willingness to do what one must to save that which mattered the most. But this desire to preserve might be coming back to haunt them now with the storm coming. The newer buildings should weather the storm adequately, or so the city leaders hoped, but there was an undercurrent of concern about Cat 5 wind impact on the old structures. Much was made in the news vids about the longevity of these structures, but lifting had subjected them to stresses unforeseen by the people who constructed them.

"Okay, let's fire up the sensors and make sure our dirt-siders are where they were. And pray the idiot thing works today."

Joe attempted activation—though minus the prayer. The habit of praying over technology puzzled him. His people had their gods, but they were, as far as he knew, indifferent to technology working or not working. He did as requested, his gaze glancing off Vi—Baker. Joe had permission to call her Vi both inside and outside his head—the NONPD was as informal and random as the city they protected—and he did so when formality would draw more attention than it deflected. But inside his own head he tried to keep it impersonal and professional. With less than stellar results. Even a glimpse of her profile ignited a duality of responses. A queer delight at the sight of her and surprise at that delight. Perhaps it was her lack of perfection that intrigued him? His people had engineered pretty faces into near ordinariness. Vi's—the name slipped through his guard—people had begun genetic engineering some time back, but he did not think her parents had availed themselves of the service. Her imperfections were a delight in a sea of the bland perfect. Her height fell somewhat below the standard considered optimal, and the variations of her female form fell into the slight range. That she was not "well endowed" seemed to cause her annoyance on occasion, but Joe found her shape pleasing. Her voice was clear and agreeable, with just a touch of a husky undertone when she hummed or sang or was tired. The nose tipped up a bit and one side of her upper lip was a tiny bit crooked. He decided it added to the dangerous charm of her smile.

Her most unusual feature was her eyes. They were violet, like her name, and intense, intelligent. They were also uncomfortably piercing. He'd seen hardened criminals shift in discomfort from the full force of her gaze. At times such as this—he tried to think of a proper description—but it was difficult. She was as unique as her city. If one looked in her eyes in an attempt to parse, one lost the, um, plot. Her gaze was a weapon of mass distraction.

He'd seen even hardened criminals become dazed, confess to crimes, or propose marriage. This amused him less than it did Vi—Baker. One criminal, a member of an organized crime family, had had the effrontery to ask her out to dinner during an interrogation session last month.

She'd looked amused. "Brave of you, Afoniki."

She did have many relatives within the ranks of the NONPD.

"Is that a yes?" Afoniki had persisted.

Vi had laughed. "You have a death wish, bubba."

Vi called everyone bubba.

Except you.

Lurch was correct. Sometimes he wondered why. At their first meeting, he'd introduced himself and held out his hand in the approved Earth manner, well in control of faculties and body temperature until he caught the full force of her gaze. Vi—Baker he reminded himself firmly—had blinked. Twice. His heart had stuttered once, then again when her hand slid into his like it belonged there. It seemed like her lips tried to form his name. And then...

"Nice to meet you, Joe," she'd said instead, with a cheeky grin that disrupted his heart rhythm once more.

The name Joe had stuck like glue. So had the heart arrhythmia. But only when he was around Vi—Baker.

Vi—Baker gave the sensor what she liked to call a love tap—it was not a tap he'd have linked to love, though he would not have been averse—he clamped down on the thought. The screen flickered once, then again, and finally began to boot up. There were better, more reliable systems widely available, thanks to their trade agreements with Joe's people, but the NONPD seemed to live in a permanent state of financial crisis.

"Why are there—" a slight pause while he edited out Earthlings and replaced it with, "—citizens lingering on the surface when they must have been made aware of the danger some days ago?" He'd seen vids of transports evacuating humans from the surface over the last several days, when WTF's storm track had indicated an intention to not only place the city on the wet side, but perhaps send the eye in for a visit.

"There are a lot of reasons why people cling to dirt," she said, giving the sensor another love tap, one that made the screen flicker again, but it did begin scanning the surface. "According to my Paw Paw, it goes back to the Voodoo Queen, Marie Laveau. She's supposed to protect the city. The fact that she hasn't always come through...well, we can forgive and forget. And we believe it won't happen until it does because we are the city that care forgot."

She flashed him a quick grin. Joe fought his way through the force of her smile. Finally managed to produce a question. "And the other reasons?"

"There are fears that if they leave they won't be allowed back."

Joe frowned. "But there are many dirt side industries."

"Oh, the farmers and fishermen aren't worried about getting back, but the Corps quit doing much maintenance on the old levees, maybe thirty years ago? So the river is creeping in, changing course, taking back land." She frowned, the expression as intriguing as her grin. "The thing is, some people don't actually work down there. They live there because it's who they are, that's how it's always been and always will be."

"It will not always be if they die down there," Joe pointed out, though it felt both obvious and unnecessary. And how did they live if they didn't work?

They live off the land.

"Logic doesn't always trump emotion. Or tradition." Her lips pursed a bit wryly.

He wondered why the wry.

She's a Baker, Lurch pointed out, with its own version of wry. It felt much like an internal itch between his shoulders.

Joe considered this, adding up the many—make that very many—Bakers who served in the NONPD, including their Captain.

Do you think she did not wish to be a police officer?

The idea interested him. He had not planned on this law enforcement side trip. But he could not be sorry. His gaze drifted toward her once more. Her shoulders began to twitch. Not quite seat dancing, but heading that way. Since they were in the skimmer, he knew she was listening to music through her gear. Though that was officially discouraged, it wasn't outright banned because this was NON. One might as well ban crawfish or *beignets.*

Or letting the good times roll...

Her dance stopped when the scan finished. "Looks like we got four dirt-siders to collect—wait—what the—"

"It is a cold spot." Joe mentally echoed her surprise.

"Cold spot?" She gave a tiny shake. "Not possible. The heat's been building in for days ahead of the storm. It's so freaking humid, I almost bought diving gear on my way to work today."

Vi—Baker had made this threat many times since

summer arrived. She also claimed he'd grow gills if he stayed long enough. Almost he believed her.

"Malfunction?" She gave him a hopeful look.

Joe considered this and shook his head. If all the spots had rendered cold—but they hadn't. "Unlikely."

She muttered something that could have been a curse. "Can you get me co-ords? We'll have to check it out."

"Should we not perform our primary mission first?"

"Our cold spot is in the old city. If the feeder bands keep dumping water like they have been, it's more likely to be under water before we can get back. It fills up fast in a normal rain, now that no one is pumping the water out. And we're assuming our dirt-siders will cooperate with their rescue."

It made sense to secure the body, if it was a body, that lacked the ability to be uncooperative. "Should I report our course change?" He asked because he was supposed to, not because he believed she'd agree.

"That will take longer than checking it out."

Vi often stated that forgiveness was easier to receive than permission. She was most skilled at getting forgiven.

She adjusted course and speed, then eased the skimmer lower. The fact that Resources Management hadn't upgraded their regular craft to a more adept emergency transport told him all he needed to know about the priority of this assignment. Or the risk assessment. Vi had seemed annoyed about it, but had shrugged it off pretty fast.

With so many relatives in positions of authority, I

suspect the detective has learned to be pragmatic about her assignments, Lurch noted.

The venerable nanite often hovered between wry and pragmatic, and this thought was no exception. It was, perhaps, a function of living longer than human memory, not to mention its dependence on humans for survival.

We all depend on something for survival.

"Let's buzz the spot first," she said, "maybe we won't have to stop."

Joe attempted to activate their lower vid recorder, but it did not cooperate, even with the application of multiple love taps. Vi muttered something unflattering about its progenitors.

"Side vids are working," he said.

"Okay, I'm going to make a low pass with a high bank angle and see if can get something on those side vids for you to look at."

It was a move with some risk. The big storm was pushing a strong wind ahead of it. The trees were dense in the area, and the wind created turbulence over the trees. He saw a break and realized it was one of the little cities of the dead. Their cold spot must be in or near it. There was less plant congestion around it, which might help.

"Let's see if this piece of excrement has anything left," she muttered, adjusting her bank angle. "Let me know if you see it on the vid. I'm only going to try this once."

He watched the vid as they flashed past. He stopped the recording, zoomed in on the object.

"Well?"

"It is a body," he said reluctantly. It could not be alive and be that cold, so the conclusion was acceptable, despite lack of confirmation. "Inside the cemetery enclosure."

"Dead in a dead space. Someone has a sense of humor." Vi keyed in a query on possible landing sites, while the skimmer made a wide, slow turn to bring them back over the area. "Looks like we don't have a good place to land inside. It's against regs anyway. Only unrestricted access through the walls is on this side here." She tapped the screen. "Like furthest from frosty that we can get. Great. I'll go for that lawn in front of our gate. At least I hope that's a lawn and not a ship sucking swamp."

She finished her turn, reducing altitude as she brought the skimmer down as gently as was possible with an aging, in-atmosphere craft descending through a turbulent atmosphere. Which was to say, a most bumpy ride, concluding abruptly when a down draft thumped them against the spongy ground.

"Sorry about that," she flashed him a wry grin, then looked out the front viewer. "Let's hope it didn't shake loose something that we'll need later."

It was a legitimate concern. The craft seemed to shed functionality almost daily.

She pulled up weather data and studied it. "WTF is still stalled. That's odd. I don't remember Nash predicting the storm to stall this long."

Nash Roberts V was a weathercaster with a cult-like following that Joe found inexplicable. He had not been around long enough to verify Roberts' accuracy, but the locals swore he could do more with something called a whiteboard and a marker than all the fancy tech currently available. Joe didn't comment on her comment because he'd learned one didn't. You could mess with many things in NON, but you didn't mess with Nash.

"A stall is good for us. We should be able to what we gotta well before things get dicey here."

Joe opened the hatch and looked out. The lawn—was that the correct word for the narrow expanse of dense grasses severely outnumbered by weeds?—was very wet. He lowered one booted foot, hoping it would eventually find solid ground down there. His foot sank to the ankle before it did.

This used to be a street or you might have sunk up to your armpits.

He brought his other foot down. When it also encountered support, he stood. From this vantage, he noted water flowing sluggishly through the weeds and grass. According to their weather data, it was too early for the storm surge. Had the rainfall caused this? It was difficult for him to process that much water falling from the sky. On the other hand, NOO was a steadily subsiding bowl, and as Vi had noted, no one tried to drain it anymore. As uncomfortable as their emergency gear was in the dense heat, he was glad for it. The flooding had most likely displaced the predatory animals that existed down here, though some were amphibious in nature, so perhaps they were emboldened more than displaced.

I believe poisonous snakes can swim, Lurch confirmed

with specious innocence. *And the fire ant problem has exploded since humans moved up.*

But wouldn't the water disperse the ants?

They form into balls to survive. It paused. *You do not want to accidentally penetrate one. Even your suit will not provide adequate protection.*

Joe look uneasily around, wondering if the nanite was playing with him. Would his Glock 3000 stun them or anger them?

Vi had also clambered out. She tested the ground with her boots. "There's a kind of drop-off here. Watch your step. And for fire ant balls. You do not want to set them loose in the water while we're in it."

Joe felt a glow of virtue from the nanite. Why did it always have to be right?

She scowled at the chest-high wall of the cemetery. "Looks like that's our access point over there." She pointed at a breech in the wall. Moving with care, she headed for the rear of the skimmer and pounded the hatch control with her fist. It opened with its customary reluctance.

"Sure hope the body bag has recharged."

Like the rest of the skimmer, the charging mechanism had an uncertain functionality. He helped her extract the bag and then secured their CSI kit. Vi—he realized he'd forgotten to keep it formal, but gave it up because it was too hot—locked it down and input the cords into the body bag's guidance system. He tossed the CSI kit on top, then she sent it on ahead of them.

"Hope it makes it," she said, philosophically, watching

it rise over the wall, then cut across the top of the crypts. "Can you imagine what a pain it must have been to carry bodies out of, or into, places like this?"

He made a noncommittal sound. He did not have to imagine. He knew. "I hope we do not find out."

"No kidding." She bounced on her toes a bit, looking around with a dubious expression. "Who on earth would want to live on dirt? It's so dirty."

"Not all dirt is so moisture laden," he pointed out, amused. The upper city was not what he would deem clean, though its clock was about to cleaned—yet another Vi phrase that he found to be obscurely apt.

"I suppose not." She turned back to the hatch and extracted two dark bags with loose straps attached to them. He arched an inquiring brow. "Our 72'r kits," she said, showing him how to slide the straps over his shoulders so that it rested uncomfortably on his back.

"What is a 72'r kit?"

"No clue," she said, "but we have to carry them when we are not in official transport and are at emergency status. Regs."

Regs was the end to any and all arguments, he'd learned. It trumped understanding and logic.

According to historical records, Lurch told him, *it contains emergency supplies designed to sustain a single human for seventy-two hours. It also has additional emergency materials. I can provide a list of what is supposed to be contained in them....*

Unnecessary. Joe tried shifting it to a less uncomfortable position. And failed.

"Has anyone opened one?" Joe asked. "Looked inside?"

"Not in my memory."

Since she was well into her 20s, possibly closing on her 30s, this was a bit disturbing. How sustainable would the supplies actually be? On the positive side, if they hadn't been opened or used in her memory, they were unlikely to require them.

Vi made a disgusted sound, tugged at the neck of her emergency rig. "Could it get any hotter?"

The first time she'd asked this he'd attempted to answer it. Now he knew better. Though in his experience so far, the answer was always yes.

"If Captain Uncle thinks this is going to freak me out, he can think again."

"You suspect this is what you call a prank?"

"With my relatives, I always assume it's a possibility." She checked her portable unit, gave it a love tap. "We'd better get moving or our body bag will *crapeau* out without us."

Getting moving, they quickly learned, was easier said than accomplished. A couple of feet from the skimmer, the hard surface ended. Each step was a journey down into knee high water, then a tug-of-war with the sucking mud created by that water to extract their boots. Even the heavy grasses did not assist their progress as much as they should have. Their bulky storm gear added to their navigation difficulties, though he was not ungrateful for the protection it afforded as Lurch indicated plant forms that stung and others that caused painful itching and skin disruptions. He conceded that Vi had a point. Dirt side, while attractive, was unappealing as a place to live. Amazing that humans had endured it as long as they had.

Ahead of them, the cemetery looked even more like a miniature city. Stone walls made a sort of beachhead against a sea of glistening green. When the gate was reached, they found more hard surface beneath the grass, though it was not even in its disposition, lending itself to the additional concern of face-planting.

Old sidewalks, I would postulate. Even when they were widely used, they were somewhat inconsistent to navigate.

Inconsistent?

The city tended to sink in an uneven manner. It was built on a swamp and continues to sink even now.

Oh. What was it about this spot that had attracted their attention in the first instance?

The river. The water was their transit.

This dead city, in its way, was as interesting as the floating one. The cemetery had once been surrounded by something somewhat similar to the city above, so it would have had pedestrian paths, these uneven sidewalks.

"Are there vids of when the city was here?" he asked, surprised to realize he'd voiced the question aloud.

"Yeah" She half frowned. "My Paw Paw likes watching old vids, prefers something called spaghetti westerns, but he also likes seeing the city how it used to be, too. I can ask him for a list, if you'd like."

"I would like," he said, surprised that he meant it. It would have made this trip more interesting if he could imagine how it had been, had been able to "see" that old city here as they moved around.

Once through the narrow gate, the height of the grass diminished some, Joe noticed, and the ratio of grass to weeds modified to a ratio better for the grasses.

"The Catholic Church tries to maintain the cemeteries," Vi said, as if he'd asked. "They still own them, you know. Looks like they mow the grass every now and again."

Lurch could have provided much information on the NOO cemeteries, but it did not seem necessary to the circumstances, and Joe found info dumps distracting when not need-to-know. In any case, Vi provide more than sufficient distraction. He noticed she looked from right to left as she walked along the narrow row between the crypts, her walk lacking its usual determined grace, though that was the fault of the mud and heavy boots. He would not have minded the distraction she provided if she did not also boost the heat factor. He tugged at the neck of his gear. The intense humidity compounded his discomfort, and their gear provided no way for natural cooling to occur.

"Do you seek something..." The cold spot had to be some distance off.

"We have some family history here, or I think it was here. Just wondered if I'd see *the* crypt, but the carvings are so faded, there's no way to tell. If I'd known I was coming here, I'd have downloaded a map." She paused and looked back at him.

"*The* crypt?" Joe asked.

"Oh, this ancestor of ours wasn't buried here."

Joe blinked. "So *the* crypt is where this ancestor *wasn't* buried?"

"Yeah."

He considered asking for additional clarification, but his last attempt had not gone well. There were many things, he'd learned, that failed to bridge his alien divide.

She looked around her. "Weird ass place. Our Voodoo Queen is supposed to be buried here, you know. Wish we had time to put some *gris-gris* on her tomb."

Her grin almost knocked him back a step. He had to smile back. It would have been rude not to, but he felt uncomfortable when she didn't immediately resume her progress toward the cold spot.

"You have a nice smile, Joe." She tipped her head to one side. "You should let it out to play more often."

A nice smile? Was that a good thing? Nice felt luke-warm. Though there was little luke about his present warmth.

Lurch seemed to sigh. *Yes, my friend, it is a good thing.*

"I will endeavor to do so," he said, wishing he could match her casual tone. Something in her expression changed though he could not isolate and identify what. His smile faltered. She distracted him when he didn't look at her. Looking increased her distraction factor exponentially and tended to cause a rise in internal temperature, one easily noted by Lurch. Though it tried to respect Joe's privacy, it could not help but notice physiological reactions to outside stimuli. Or be amused by them, which tended to increase the effect. It was unprofessional of Joe to be distracted by her.

As Baker had said to a crime scene tech recently, "Eyes forward, Stigson. We're not here to get hot and bothered."

Stigson had kept his eyes forward, but heat and bother were inevitable with or without the personal aspect, thanks to the climate in this place. The heat index should have been sufficient excuse to the nanite when Joe experienced his temperature variations, but Lurch seemed able to parse which variation was caused by heat and what was caused by heated.

He glanced—casually he hoped, though feared he failed—to one side, then the other. "It is most quiet here."

And then it became more than a distraction from looking at Vi. It *was* quiet. Too quiet? The hairs on the back of his neck lifted. Or tried to. Sweat and the heavy suit kept them down, but it felt as if they lifted. The feeling of something ominous was most marked. And easily explained by the approaching storm.

"Even nature is getting out ahead of WTF." She grinned once more.

This grin was different, more like the ones others used when using the storm's acronym. He had wondered, but not asked. According to Lurch, explained jokes were no longer humorous.

Perhaps she sensed his confusion for she added, "The

Hurricane Naming Board got so caught up in being politically correct, they forgot to check the initials before they released the name into the wild. Once it was out, there was no taking it back."

This did not help as much as she'd perhaps hoped, so Lurch supplied the translation and further explanation, enough that Joe found that not all jokes lost humor upon explanation. He smiled involuntarily and got caught in her intent gaze once more. The air shifted and the wind picked up, reminding them that WTF was incoming and it was no joke.

Vi started a bit. "We should hurry." She yanked a booted foot out of the mud. "Try to hurry."

Did she look regretful? Or did he hope she did? It was not as if they had a future together. He was not sure he would have a future. Even his past had become murky, since Lurch moved into his head and launched him on this crazy quest.

Their progress resumed. It seemed harder to walk in the lanes than it had in the tall grasses, possibly because their boots sank deeper into the mud. These paths must have degraded more than those outside the walls, or they had been constructed differently. Some crypts were bordered by low fences almost obscured by weeds or grasses, others bumped up against the path. All were covered in green moss and black mildew, some were also covered in heavy vines. On many he could see outlines of names, but most were obscured despite the attempted upkeep. There was no question that their surroundings added to the growing sense of incoming trouble.

"Shouldn't be far now—" Vi stopped abruptly. "*What* the—"

Joe had a feeling she meant this in the actual meaning of WTF, not the storm name, despite the cutoff at the end. It didn't take the sight of the hovering body bag for Joe to know they had arrived at their crime scene. All he had to do was watch Vi switch to detective mode. She rolled her shoulders, and he knew her gaze would narrow and turn laser sharp. She had the best technology that the NONPD could afford, but her eyes, her brain were, in Joe's opinion worth more than all the tech.

Except me.

Of course, Joe agreed, though he wondered. Was it possible to know too much? So much one lost the ability to follow intuition?

That is why I have you.

I lack Vi's flair.

You lack experience. The ability to go with your gut. But you are learning.

Would he learn in time? Joe grabbed the kit off the body bag and initiated deployment to secure their scene. The electronic grid would protect the integrity of the scene, though "integrity" did not seem indicated in their present circumstances. The bag launched, tracking toward the body. Once centered over it, it "taped" their scene, the name a relic of a different time, according to Lurch. Then it released a variety of collection probes, including a vid module that would create the 3D scan of the crime scene. Within a minute, all possible portable non-naturally occurring materials had been collected by tiny drones, tagged and secured to the underside of the body bag. The red electronic tape turned gold, an indication that they could now enter their scene. He activated protective hand and face gear. As though it was not already hot enough.

At this point, they did not know a crime had been committed, well, other than the illegal body dump, he reminded himself, though without much hope. At least the tech would enable them to secure what evidence had survived the rain and wind before the storm drenched the scene again. He checked the time, then the storm's progress on his portable tech. Ran the numbers. It must be an illusion that the dark clouds looked closer than the tech showed them to be. The wind had increased, though without cooling anything. It flowed past, weighted with water and heat.

Vi activated her crime scene gear and followed him through the tape where she crouched by the body.

"This guy did not die in his sleep."

It was true the eyes retained a look of horror that was not comfortable to see. Joe's headset produced a list of just-collected debris. He was not sorry for the distraction from looking at those eyes. The only thing of interest was something called a Royal Crown Cola bottle. And a banana spider. The bot shouldn't have grabbed the spider, though the malfunction did not surprise him. And he was happy not to have to share space with the large arachnid. He looked around and spied the shredded remains of a huge web tucked under the crypt's overhang. There was not much other debris from the scene and little that appeared related to their corpse. The dead man huddled between two small columns as if he'd been sitting on one of the three steps leading to the imposing crypt, and then died, rolling onto his back, with his knees drawn up to his chest. He wore trousers, but his upper torso appeared to be bare. Joe touched one leg. Pushed on it. It gave a little, but was still somewhat frozen to his bare chest. That would explain why he'd shown as a cold spot. The intense heat would boost the contrast.

"Looks like someone emptied their freezer," Vi murmured.

"Emptied the freezer?" Joe felt some disquiet. And much confusion. The corpse wasn't solidly frozen, but it hadn't shown up on the sensors prior to their leaving District Headquarters. It had to have been dumped between their last scan and the activation of their sensor on approach. Perhaps a window of fifteen minutes? But the partial thaw indicated it had been here longer. Or been allowed to partially defrost prior to dumping?

"In the early days, soon after the city was raised, the bad guys experienced problems getting rid of inconvenient corpses."

Joe blinked, thinking through this "problem." He frowned. "They used to bury them." His brow cleared. "But soil is not deep in the raised city." Weight issues. The raised city boasted hologram trees because the soil lacked the depth for real ones—a move that had initially been very unpopular until the cost was totaled up and presented to the taxpayers of the time. The cobblestone paths in the French Quarter were also simulated.

"They used to freeze stiffs until they could dump them down here, but that was before we had better sensors. I haven't heard of a freezer dump for a long time." She frowned, considering. "Years."

He noted she did not use the words "good" or "effective" to characterize the "better" sensors. He'd have called them barely adequate, but there were higher priorities. He frowned. "Perhaps they hoped to capitalize on the confusion prior to the storm's arrival?"

"Then they seriously mistimed it. No confusion yet." There was a beep indicating an identity match. Vi's frown deepened. "He's a dirt-sider. A squatter."

Like those they'd been sent to collect.

"Perhaps he expired and other dirt-siders were fearful the death would cause them problems?" Joe offered the idea without much conviction.

"If they wanted to hide a body, they wouldn't freeze him. That preserves a body. If they wanted to hide him, they'd bury him. Bodies decompose fast in this heat, plus the critters would help them out. Anyway, I doubt a squatter would have access to a freezer. The power grid is patchy down here, especially around the NOO airport where they squat. They only maintain power around industrial areas and farms." She shook her head.

"Then someone wanted this body found intact." It was the only logical conclusion.

She sighed. "We'll need to notify HQ, but let's bag this bad boy first, get it back to the skimmer before our power runs out."

Using her portable unit, she maneuvered the bag until it hovered just above the body. "Pray we have enough power," she muttered. She punched a button and a web shot out on either side, slithering out of sight under the corpse. When the webs had connected, the body was lifted until it was snug against the bag platform. Vi rotated the bag, so that body rested on top of the platform. This brought the underside of the body into view. The bare back was covered with round pockmarks in an almost regular pattern.

"What the—" Vi began and once again stopped. She stepped close and examined the marks.

Joe couldn't move. He wanted to move. To flee. His body felt as cold as the corpse. But Lurch had locked him down.

Get under control. Lurch's voice was sharp in his head.

He could breathe, but that was all. He looked down until he was sure he had his expression under control, the one part of him Lurch couldn't help. *I am.*

"Curious," Vi touched one of the marks with a gloved hand. "It almost looks like something burned its way out." Her frown deepened. "I wonder—"

It took two tries for him to get the words out. "You wonder?"

"Do you remember Calvino's murder?" Joe shook his head. "It happened around the time you arrived, or maybe before? I forget. We didn't handle it. Was Federal because Calvino was a big deal in his crime family."

"I don't recall that," Joe said, his throat dry.

"It was kept pretty quiet, because no wanted a copycat, or so they said. A mini turf war erupted right after, too, which sort of took over the news. I only heard about it because my cousin was on the task force. What he described, it might have been this." She touched one of the spots with her gloved hand. "Curious. I can see why this MO freaked them out."

I missed it. Lurch sounded chagrined.

You had to search with care. Why—? Joe didn't finish the question. He was not sure what to ask.

*It is tired of waiting. So it takes advantage of the storm to test us. Testing **you** for signs of me.*

They—*he* had tried to be careful. Lurch was always careful. Joe thought he had been, too.

You have been careful. Hence the test. Lurch's tone modified to almost amused. *If it has been dirt side all this time, it might be frustrated enough to make a mistake.*

Joe had expected to feel relieved when it made its move. He could not resist a glance at the approaching storm.

It always had a flair for the dramatic.

❧ 2 ❧

Joe looked almost as stiff as their stiff, but Vi already knew he was a bit parsimonious with, well, everything. He was the total opposite of "Big Easy" NON, while still managing to be adorable. At their first meeting, she deduced he was not demonstrative because she was, you know, a detective. He nailed dead pan and mainlined sober. Was the quintessential Joe Friday—both the vintage and the many remakes. That's why she'd tagged him Joe, though she hadn't meant to say it out loud. At least she hadn't called him ET. She had tried to wrap her tongue around his real name. It hadn't wrapped and her throat made a sound like Maw Maw's cat hacking up a hairball. So when he didn't complain about the Joe moniker—and the Garradians didn't cut off diplomatic relations over it—she let it ride.

It was how she rolled. Though periodically Captain

Uncle tried to break her of her rolling habit. It was his job, she supposed. Because he was an uncle and not just a captain, she'd used her Look on him when he tried too hard. Sometimes she had to boost it with the innocent modification, but she tried to wield that power with care. Not that Captain Uncle would ever fall in love with her, but a captain with scrambled brains wasn't good for anyone. She didn't know why her Look worked, with or without the modification. Was glad it did, because it had gotten her out of some sticky situations. And some interesting proposals.

Well, it worked with one notable exception.

She studied that exception. Who was studying their stiff like it held the secrets to the universe. For him, it might. He was that smart. For her, she just wished their stupid emergency gear wasn't hiding his butt. His rear view was one of the few bright spots in a typical crime scene. Or an atypical one.

Which this seemed to be.

She sighed. If she'd ever imagined that she'd be dirt side in a moldy, muddy graveyard with a purple alien, a weird-ass corpse, and an epic hurricane incoming, she'd have called the mind shrinks to have a chat.

She studied what she could see of Joe's profile. His skin wasn't *so* purple. It was more of a hint than an actual tint— just enough to make him a hit at Mardi Gras. The rest of him was a hit any time. The Garradians were known for being real pretty, and Joe was *not* the exception, even in a post-genetic-modification world. Dang. Broad shoulders. Lean hips. Vid star features. Dark hair. Dark eyes. Awesome brain box. Not a relative. That was huge. In addition to Captain Uncle, she was related to about eighty percent of the NONPD. Not that not being not-related to Joe had benefitted her as much she would have liked. If she hit on him and it didn't go well, it *might* cause the intergalactic incident she'd managed to avoid to date. An intergalactic incident would make Sunday dinners at Grand Maw Maw's tense. On the other hand, dating ET would totally boost her cred with the cousins. Easier thought than done. She had no clue what he did with his off hours, which was sad. A detective should always have a clue.

And a detective should know better than to end up this deep in the mud. If the dirt-siders wanted to take on WTF, who was she to deny them their God-given right to be stupid in the face of the unprecedented precedented? Or would that be the precedented unprecedented? She was worse at grammar than she was at math. And she sucked at mud. Which sucked. Literally and figuratively. WTF wasn't here yet and she was sick of it, too.

Time was, according to Grand Paw Paw, when everyone had believed that man caused all the weather problems. Vi'd call it extreme hubris, but her generation had bought into the "man had solved all the weather problems" line of bull. Seemed hubris was catching. And everyone did know—or should know—pride went before the fall. She looked up at her city. Thinking falling thoughts was probably bad *juju* right now. She tried to redirect the thoughts, but it wasn't easy with Maw Maw Nature preparing to pull their pride out from under them. Vi could almost hear her cackling with glee.

She rose, feeling the increase in the wind tugging at her. She released her visor, hoping it would cool something off. It didn't. She frowned at the horizon. "That looks worse than the radar says it should be."

"We should return to the skimmer." Joe rose, too, his expression back in the "Friday" zone.

As if Nature's Maw Maw heard him, the wind kicked up some more and the black clouds began to curve in tight, like she was pinging on them.

"Yeah." Vi nodded, just in case the word wasn't agreement enough.

Being Joe, he didn't hesitate, retracting their crime scene tech as fast as it would let him. Storm aside, if they lingered too much longer, their body bag might run out of power. She did not want to haul it all the way back to the skimmer. Talk about old school. She took a last look at her crime scene, not happy it was gonna get drenched. She'd never liked relying wholly on tech, especially their *crapeau* tech. Would have liked to do her own search. But Maw Maw N and her pet storm were setting the pace today. That she felt their hot breath on her neck was a totally correct metaphor—something she tried to avoid at her crime scenes if at all possible.

Joe dropped the kit on the bag next to the corpse. In its current configuration, the corpse didn't take up that much room. She'd eyed it a bit wistfully. There was room for her to hop a ride, but it had never liked heavy lifting. Ouch. She tried to avoid linking herself with the words "heavy" in a sentence, but it was just that kind of day. She keyed in the return command and the bag rose, making the turn toward their skimmer. It sputtered a bit, but kept going. For now.

Without speaking they started back, though out of necessity, their path was less direct than the body bag's, since they had to stick to the paths. Was it her imagination that the mud seemed deeper on the return? Each sucking step seemed harder than than the last, draining both energy and breath. It let WTF gain on them, too. She glanced at Joe. Something was bothering him. She knew him well enough to know that, though she didn't know what or why he didn't tell her. He was a puzzle wrapped in an enigma wrapped in whatever was more mysterious than an enigma. She needed to quit wishing he'd do something, and then she needed to find a guy to kiss. Even if he asked her out, which did not seem likely, what was the point? The exchange program would end, he'd go home. People did. Especially alien people. She'd heard they considered Earth a kind of slum part of the Milky Way. On the rude side, considering how much the guys from their galaxy seemed to like alien-earth-girls match-ups dot com.

Their dragging, slogging struggle made their shoulders

brush together. Well, their emergency gear brushed together. How sad was it that she liked it? The narrow paths of the creepy cemetery were hardly a romantic venue by any definition, but a girl had to work with what she had. Even if she wasn't exactly getting anything for all her work. Except tired. Dang, dirt was hard work. Why did anyone want to live on dirt? It was infused with gravity. And dirt. They had gravity up in the city, but it wasn't so sticky.

Normally she'd be mulling their crime, wondering the whys, wherefores and hows. Today she was worried about finishing what they'd been sent to do and getting the *crapeau* topside again. Would they have time to collect their dirt-siders and get back before the bad stuff hit? Short answer? No clue. If she looked at tech, she thought, sure, they had plenty of time. Then she looked at the clouds looming to the west....

Their skimmer was not rated for anything over 50 mph, nor was it rated for high altitude flying. Probably wasn't rated for low altitudes either. The piece of *crapeau*. She didn't know how it would fare sitting out the feeder band in the mud either. Thanks to the news vids, she knew more about the storm surge than she had two weeks ago. It had been reported on more as a curiosity than a concern, though, since no one was supposed to be down here when it arrived. Even though the water seemed higher going back, this couldn't be surge, not when WTF was stalled off shore.

She tried to pick up the pace, but the mud and water

conspired against her. To add insult to misery, it began to rain again. She dropped her face shield. Almost she asked Joe if he thought it seemed worse, but he had the same data she did. Either the data was wrong, or she was wrong. Since this was her first hurricane, she was going with she was wrong. Even though her eyes disputed the data stream. What, she thought she was smarter than the sensors? Than the radar?

"Hope our dirt-siders don't give us any problems," she muttered. Why hadn't anyone spotted them sooner? Captain Uncle had been really not happy she and Joe were the only ones he could send down. He'd muttered some words that would have had Grand Maw Maw grabbing her bar of soap. He'd given her both a Captain and an Uncle look, the one that meant, get your butt back up here ASAP. Funny how guys never quite got over worrying about girls....

Based on data at the time, though, it had seemed more annoying than risky. But the rate the wind was picking up —they might find out exactly how well their aging skimmer handled in bad weather. She peered through the blurry face shield. Had the bag made it over the last wall—

It shuddered and drifted out of sight. Was gonna guess that was a no. She muttered some of the same words as Captain Uncle. With some difficulty they altered direction.

"Assuming we can get to our dirt-siders, I suppose we won't be allowed to," he paused, "subdue them?"

Joe tended to be pragmatic about individual rights, one

of the many cultural differences she'd been briefed on prior to being assigned as his partner. He'd been briefed on their laws and procedures or he wouldn't have asked the question. She gave it some thought. Technically they were only supposed to set their Glocks to stun when all others options failed. The standard for use was high when there were cameras everywhere, including the inevitable personal devices with advanced recording capability. But dirt-siders tended to be anti-tech. And the sensors had limited capabilities that did not include high-res video. They might get a pass on lowering the standard a bit.

She caught sight of the body bag, resting crookedly on a crypt just inside the wall. She might be getting annoyed enough by the sight to stun a dirt-sider who was slow to cooperate. She grabbed one end of the body bag, Joe grabbed the other, and they pushed up. Her boots retaliated by sinking deeper in the mud. Suddenly she had a new understanding of the term "dead weight."

"Let's see how much they weigh before we stun them," she advised.

THE RAIN FLOWED LIKE A RIVER OUT OF THE foreboding sky, reducing visibility to maybe a meter—it was hard to tell with it running down her protective visor—as they wrestled the loaded body bag into the rear of the skimmer. The wind had picked up, pelting them with bits of leaves and twigs, and water swirled around their knees, turning the ground around the skimmer into even more of a mire than when they'd landed. WTF seemed determined to justify its name.

Vi'd seen rain. NON had rain. It had always had rain. Raising it didn't get it out of the rain. Probably brought it closer to the rain. But she'd never seen this kind of rain. She tossed her 72'r kit in the back, leaned against the skimmer to catch her breath, while Joe shed his pack. Man, if it was this bad this far from the eye wall, they needed to make sure they were well up before it got any closer. She hit the hatch control with her elbow. She might have been thinking a few more Grand Maw Maw not-approved words. It took its time lowering. When the hatch locked in place, she headed for the cockpit, leaning into the wind and using the maintenance grips along the side to steady herself in the high water. She clambered over the vestigial wings, glad to be out of the water for that few seconds. The specter of fire ants and other nasty stuff hung over her as she fumbled for the side hatch control.

When it opened, wind and rain rushed in with her. She subsided into her sling with relief. Water cascaded off her and her gear, forming small pools on the floor. Of course, this hatch also took its time locking back in place. The wind and rain were worse from Joe's side, and it was a relief when his hatch locked down. If auto-dry had worked, she'd have used it. It didn't, so she dug out the towel she kept in her personal cubby and wiped off her face shield. When the towel was too wet to do any good, she tossed it back and retracted the visor. Muttering some more words

Grand Maw Maw wouldn't have liked. Another time she might have been worried that she knew so many. Since she didn't have time, she retracted hand protection, then applied her attention to the skimmer controls. Time to find out how screwed they were.

Technically, based on the skimmer's specs, they were "fine." The skimmer supposedly had all kinds of emergency tech, such as instruments-only flying and wind stabilization, oh, and emergency boost. Most of it had died long before the skimmer was gifted to Vi upon her promotion to homicide detective. The aging skimmer was the NONPD's version of a hazing. You did your time, didn't whine, did good work, and you got assigned something that actually worked fifty percent of the time. That was about as good as it got with their budget.

And based on the weather data her portable tech was picking up from the under-city data bouncers, they were also "fine" where the storm was concerned. In fact, it shouldn't be raining yet. She studied the sheets of water flowing off the view screen.

"Do you get the feeling our data isn't updating right?" she muttered, wondering why she was surprised something had gone wrong with this hunk of junk. She'd blame the skimmer slamming to the dirt, but their data had to have been off before that to be this off now.

Joe, working on powering up the skimmer, shot her a look that was almost human. "Yes."

Vi sighed. She hated being such a girl, but... "I think we'd better call for pickup. This piece of *crapeau* isn't rated for flying in this kind of wind." Assuming they had a clue what kind of wind it was. Captain Uncle would be pissed she hadn't told him about the course correction. They weren't close enough for her to use her get-out-of-trouble Look on him. And if the wind kept banging stuff into them, well, that wouldn't go well either.

"I concur."

The skimmer powered up enough to give them some data access, the screens updating with a rapidity that was almost impressive. Didn't even need a love tap—unless she counted the landing as one? If it been this nice before they left the skimmer on their frosty body hunt—she studied the data. Maybe she should be more careful with her wishes. Ignorance could be bliss.

"Unfortunate," Joe said, probably in response to her succinct, one-syllable sum up of just how screwed they were.

"They won't be able to send anything down in this."

Joe opened his mouth, but then nodded instead. She peered at him through the last rivulets of water running down her face. His brows were drawn together in a frown. Outside, visibility had worsened. She studied the weather data. So instead of hugging the shore, WTF's eye wall was actually closing on the city. She adjusted the screwed dial up to FUBAR, threw in some holy freaking *crapeau*. Captain Uncle's data must have been screwy, too. He'd have never sent her down here if he'd known WTF was this close. Now, when it was too late, she could see the radar data on the feeder band that directly concerned them. It was mostly red with slashes of ominous orange and yellow. The skimmer rocked as a particularly big gust buffeted it. She strapped in, though it felt a bit futile. It might help if they got picked up by a tornado, but even so, the landing was gonna be a bitch. The skimmer had not been designed for slamming against *terra* or *firma*.

It was darker, though the flashes of lightning intermittently revealed the rising water. The skimmer was supposed to be airtight. They wouldn't know right away if it actually was because of all the water they'd brought inside with them. And if they had to use engines and stabilization jets to hold position, how fast would that drain their power? She flipped off temperature control, just in case. They couldn't afford the fuel drawdown if they were stuck down here for too long. There wasn't available data on how this model of skimmer would perform in extreme conditions because its makers had thought there wouldn't be any. Ah, hubris. Looked like they were going to get to test it, not in its prime, but when it was old as dirt. She better understood that phrase by the way. Her boots were caked with a bunch of it.

"If we can ride out this feeder band—" Vi didn't finish with the obvious. The timing was only going to get more challenging as WTF moved closer. There were feeder bands coiled inside feeder bands coiled around an eye wall that was feeder bands on mooncrack. And while they waited for that, it looked like they might get to check out the storm surge. She wished she remembered more about storm surge, what it did and when. All she remembered was that it could "rise unexpectedly fast." And that the rise depended on where one was, something about tides and where the eye came ashore. WTF was moving in west of the city, which put them on the wet side. It was not good to be on the wet side of a hurricane. There'd been some blah, blah, blah in the news vids about how lucky they all were to not be dirt side this time. She didn't feel lucky.

Whatever, she had to phone home. She still hesitated. Captain Uncle was going to burn her already uncomfortably hot backside. She sighed. "Might as well get it over with."

His gaze shifted her direction. "I believe that would be wise."

Something in his tone made her uneasy. She activated a channel. Nothing. Didn't even get the not-connected hum. She tried a love tap. Another. Followed them with a hate tap. That was odd. Could always get a not-connected hum. Though this was the skimmer's first serious storm test. And there was that bang against terra soggy. "Do you think the storm is affecting communication?"

There was a lot of electrical activity out there. And the winds. Could WTF have already taken out the communications network up top? It wasn't a ridiculous worry. Grand Maw Maw had better tech than the NONPD. Oh, budget, the curse of all our lives....

He hesitated. "That is the most logical supposition."

He'd never made logic sound so dubious. She felt a chill despite the heat building both inside and outside the skimmer. She looked around, but there wasn't anything to see other than the rain.

"Do you know why the authorities waited so long to retrieve these dirt-siders?"

The question seemed a bit random, but Vi wasn't adverse to a distraction. "That's right. You weren't there when it came up." Vi rubbed an errant rivulet of water out of her eye. "They popped up on the sensor, rather like our corpse, between the last two feeder bands. Captain Uncle thought maybe they'd been using some temperature screening stuff and either changed their minds or it got damaged. If they are getting nervous it should make retrieval easier." She could hope. Hope was good. It was like bright and stuff.

"Curious." She arched a brow at him and he added, "That both the dirt-siders and the corpse were hidden from the sensors."

She frowned. "Yeah, but—" What did it mean?

"The weather is an unpredictable element," he said, as if following a line of thought all his own.

"Which could have been predicted to be unpredictable," she felt compelled to point out, though it shouldn't have been quite so unpredictable. "Do you really think both events were deliberate?"

"I have a suspicious nature," he admitted, like that was a news flash.

"But what's the end game?" she asked.

"Unclear."

"Sabotage isn't logical," she offered, a bit uncertainly.

Though it would be ridiculously easy to sabotage this piece of *crapeau*. Just give it a good kick. Still...too much about this felt wrong. And one thing she'd learned was to trust her gut when things felt wrong. "Logically, someone would have had to be out in this to un-screen our vic. And mess with our tech—which could have been overki—unnecessary." Unless they had some really cool something that could do those things for them. She added, though she wasn't sure what it meant, "The vic is a dirt-sider."

A squatter, someone out of the tech loop, in fact. A little person, barely on the grid. Who might have died the same way a crime boss had died, but wouldn't that be something a killer would want to hide? All of this seemed designed to draw attention, to make them suspicious. Okay, going with attention getting, whose attention was someone trying to get? They couldn't have known she and Joe would be the ones to come down. Could they? If there'd been anyone else, Captain Uncle would have sent them. Unless whoever it was had made it look like they were the only ones? Okay, getting paranoid. She'd pissed off a few perps in her day, but she couldn't call to mind anyone who would take this route to hose her. Or be smart enough to pull off the tech tinkering.

Joe?

His people might have the tech that could do this, but why? If they wanted to get him, why wait until he was in another galaxy? She shivered, despite the heat, stared at the heavy rain like she could see through it. Was someone messing with them? If they were, what did they want?

"We need to—" Vi stopped, managing to maintain her charm despite the scowl.

She did not like inaction.

Neither do I. Lurch felt most wry.

How could we anticipate this move? Joe wasn't even sure their tech problems had been caused by it. Their problems could be the inevitable result of aging technology. If it was Lurch's enemy, well, the hunter had become the hunted so quickly, he did not know how to react.

I believed I'd learned to expect the unexpected.

Joe frowned. *How can one expect the unexpected?*

It is a challenge. Humor lightened the nanite's tone for a second. It thought so intensely, it was like having heartburn. *My apologies.*

The burn eased some. A discreet expulsion of air also helped, though it tasted most unpleasant.

"We can't get to the city until the wind dies down," she said, "but the water is rising. From the rain or the surge? No way to know for sure with the tech acting up. This boat is supposed to be watertight, but, well, if this is the storm surge, it could surge us into a wide choice of objects not that far from our parking place."

It was true that flooding waters could be quite forceful. Enough to carry debris that could impact on their craft, even if they didn't change position.

They should not fly.

They could not safely remain dirt side.

"Perhaps we should attempt to hold position above the water? Fly low?"

"And burn up our fuel?"

Joe leaned forward and scrolled through the weather data. Even if it was not up to date, it did have some predictability to it. "The bands do not follow the same track inland, because the hurricane is moving ashore from east to west. Do you see that angle?" He pointed at the screen. "Assuming this is correct, or close to correct, the airport where the dirt-siders await rescue will be affected later than this position. That is also where any help will be sent, if HQ becomes concerned about our non-appearance and the sensors are unable to locate us in the storm."

He doubted anyone would be surprised to lose the sensors in the melee of the storm. In their various briefings, Joe had sensed a high level of expectation that many systems would fail.

"It's where we were supposed to go." Vi sighed. "I should have notified HQ that we were taking a side trip, though I'm not sure that would be much help right now."

Would they have been allowed to get through if they had decided to call in the change? He wondered. They might have received advanced warning about the storm and had time to escape, if it were involved in their current difficulties.

"But we can't fly there, not in this—" she stopped, possibly unable to find a description adequately negative.

Her people have let their hurricane knowledge languish for many years.

They are not the only ones to rest on their status quo. Joe felt Lurch acknowledge the hit.

"When we were making our approach, I could see the remnants of old transit lanes. If we modify our lift, stay above the waterline, we might find some protection from the most extreme winds while we use these lanes to work our way to the airport."

And if this is a hostile act, an attempt to force my exposure, it might frustrate that. Perhaps tip the status quo our direction?

It might even require it to expect the unexpected. Lurch felt amused.

"Can you follow them from memory?"

Joe smiled. "No, but your raised city is very like the city that was, is it not?"

She brightened. "We use our map of the raised city as a guide down here. I like how you think, Dzh—Joe."

Joe concealed a smile at yet another failure to say his name.

She turned from him and stared outside. "We can't fly blind at low altitude."

"It will be difficult," Joe acknowledged, wishing—but if he told her the truth, even if she believed him, it would put her at greater risk. "I can, perhaps, see further than you. Alien eyes." He half grinned at her. "If you transfer drive control to my station—you can navigate, since you are more familiar with the city than I am."

The strain in her face eased with a task to perform.

Lurch could have transferred control for him, and it could have done much to repair their failed systems, but care must be taken not to expose its existence if this were the trap they'd been expecting. If the skimmer had been tampered with, then triggers would be in place to expose the nanite if it attempted to assist with the tech. The best Lurch could do for them right now was enhance Joe's vision and reflexes.

"If it will transfer," she said, applying more of her "love" to the controls.

That depends on the game it wishes to play.

For a few seconds, Joe wondered if it had also disabled their engines. When they activated, he did not know whether to be relieved or worried.

It seems we play the slow game. For now.

For now, Joe agreed. Between the lash of the rain and the force of the wind, even the boost from Lurch only gave him a few meters of forward vision. The landscape was wild, the trees bending almost to the ground, then whipping around violently. It would be challenging to discern shadows from obstacles until they were upon them, and controlling the skimmer in the high wind created additional difficulty, even with automatic stabilization thrusters. The water had risen enough to begin splashing over the front of the skimmer and he felt it shift. Remaining there was filled with risk as well. It was now or never.

"It'll be slow going," Vi said, both looking and sounding frustrated.

"Yes. But better than not going." He hoped he was correct in this, as he eased up and began their initial lift.

Vi gripped his arm, causing a disturbance to his thought process. The bright look in her narrowed gaze did not help the problem.

"I have an idea."

$$\text{❧} \quad 3 \quad \text{❧}$$

"There's a sort of hack," Vi said, her body bent double as she struggled to get the panel off the underside of console. "One of my cousins showed me how to do it. We had this April Fools' thing going and we needed to track, well, someone." She reached up for a tool, caught his eye, and grinned. "First advice, first day, learn how your *crapeau* works so you can mess with it and not get caught."

Admirable.

Lurch was inordinately fond of rule breakers. The speed at which she was able to access the internals of the console indicated a familiarity with the technology that would not be pleasing to those tasked with keeping the equipment operating at "optimal."

"It's all spin," Vi had told him early on when he had pointed out the difference between assertion and reality. He'd arched his brows and she'd added, "Don't believe half of what you're told and that half, well, lower your expectations by another seventy-five percent. Why do you think I call this place the Big Uneasy?"

"This might not work, but if it does..." She applied pressure to the tool, before concluding, "...we might have a fighting chance."

Any chance was better than their current odds, Joe knew, studying the barely visible landscape, while trying to hold position just above the water level. Waves slapped against the underside of the skimmer, while rain poured past them at a wind-driven angle. It was not an optical illusion that it appeared to be "falling" sideways. It was disturbing. And somewhat disorienting. While he did not believe it was pure chance that resulted in their current predicament, like Vi, he had difficulty perceiving its end game. The situation appeared to be as fraught with peril for it, as it was for them. Could it be observing them from a safe distance? What was safe in this storm? The city above was also at risk as WTF moved in. One thing his people had learned, when technology tried to take on nature, nature usually won.

It might just want us dead.

There are simpler ways of achieving that.

I told you it had a flair for the dramatic. Perhaps it is toying with us.

That would imply absolute knowledge on its part that you are here. Could we, could I have made so costly an error and not know it?

There was a pause as Lurch considered this. *I do not believe it knows. I believe it is using the opportunity of the storm to force the kind of extraordinary circumstances that might expose my presence. It has shown facility for adjusting and adapting to changing situations.*

So it tries to force you to repair this craft?

That would be one thing.

Joe sensed there was more that Lurch could do that was extraordinary. They had not been companions long enough for Joe to be exposed to much beyond the nanite's vast store of knowledge and a few sensory enhancements. It could also heal wounds and boost his energy and abilities. He had to assume those benefits were not available now, when they would have been most useful. Since arrival here, much care had been taken for Joe to not exhibit unusual abilities, but Joe had gotten used to having minor ailments eased. Even Lurch's impressive data search ability had been limited by the need for extreme care. Joe suspected that Lurch had not shared all it feared its enemy could do if threatened. Or perhaps it expected Joe to know what it meant by "utterly ruthless."

It is possible we have been too careful. Outsmarted ourselves? Lurch's mulling fluttered against the inside of Joe's skin.

Joe did not know how to respond. Other than to point out the obvious. Had they been "too careful" they would not now be stranded in the path of an incoming hurricane. Rather than stating that obvious, he opted to state a different obvious to Vi. "I will not be able to maintain this position for much longer."

And they were burning fuel trying. But she knew that.

All three of them knew everything but how to get clear. It was ironic to know so much that was not helpful. A gust of wind caught Vi's side of the skimmer and tipped them on their side. It was fortunate that their straps secured their torsos to the slings. Legs and arms did not fair as well.

"Ow."

Cross-wind compensators fired the right thrusters and the skimmer righted, with more banging of limbs to metal parts.

"Ow again." Vi straightened. "Not exactly to regs, but needs must when the devil drives."

She rubbed her elbow through the protective gear. Apparently it had not been protective enough.

She bends the rules most effectively.

Once again Joe felt Lurch's admiration, mixed with both fondness and a hint of nostalgia, as if Vi reminded it of someone. Occasionally Joe would catch a glimpse of a face when Lurch's memories bled through. That woman looked like a rule bender. And—in the words of Vi—an ass kicker. There was much affection attached to that memory, which caused Joe to postulate that the bleeding occurred where such affection existed. It was when emotion was present—and the concurrent physiological reactions—that the nanite got insight into Joe's most private thoughts, despite Lurch teaching him how to wall off the deeply private. Perhaps some day the nanite would trust him enough to share more of its past. Though it was possible that past had taught the nanite not to trust that much.

"Let's see if it worked..."

Vi keyed in a command. A screen flickered, then a map of the floating city appeared, with a small pulsing dot where they had set down.

"And there we are. It's not a perfect integration, but we'll have a better idea where we are. Wish I could put the weather map on top of it...." she keyed in some stuff on their weather tracking screen, trying to tighten it to their general area. Made a frustrated sound. "I can't get a good fix on our location, without shifting controls again. We'll have to use big stuff to try to get a fix on where we are, where we want to go. And hope it's actually reasonably accurate. Memo to me: believe what you see."

It is true that tech can be used to deceive. Lurch felt inexpressibly sad.

"Conditions will necessitate extremely slow forward progress," Joe said. He shifted his gaze briefly, long enough to catch her widened gaze at the view out front, which had worsened while her head was down. "Course corrections will be somewhat challenging."

"No sh—kidding." More tapping ensued. "Okay, I think I've got all the screens we need. We're currently hovering about twelve feet above sea level. Give or take something. Which unfortunately doesn't tell us how far we are above the actual ground. Keeping track of the abandoned city's relationship to sea level has not been a priority for a while."

Her scanner would also not be tracking the debris left behind when the city was lifted, Joe acknowledged, as he fought wind through the attitude and altitude controls. How bad would it be when he had to move the skimmer?

Bad.

Joe made a note to himself to stop thinking questions he did not want answered.

"I'm thinking we are about a foot or so above the water level. If we were higher I don't think we'd get so much wave action against our hull. At least that's the hope."

Joe echoed her hope. It was not possible to assess wave height in their current circumstances. Lightning flashed, briefly though imperfectly illuminating the area. "That tracks with my visuals."

"Such as they are." She tapped more controls. "Okay, I can see several possible routes to the old airport that might still be more or less there."

Where the old airport had been when dirt side was now New Orleans New In-Atmosphere Intergalactic Docking Port, or NON IAIDP. He'd also heard it called the A-dip. He recalled the main transit routes, or rather Lurch did. Unlike Vi's panels, Lurch could overlay their dubious storm tracking with the maps and provide some additional guidance, though not with its usual precision. It was not able to link to the data—data they weren't sure they could trust—and input their position into that data without risking exposure. Nor could Lurch link to the under-city scanners—assuming they still operated—and use them to highlight terrain obstacles. If it had tampered with the skimmer, it could have left traps and triggers designed to alert it to Lurch's activities. In their current vulnerable position, eliminating them would be ridiculously easy. As long as it toyed with them, as long as it was uncertain, there was hope.

Perhaps it thinks it would be more amusing to see us eliminate ourselves?

That was the other hope—and their only chance until they could connect with backup. It was possible that assistance already awaited them at the airport. All they had to do was get there.

"I would postulate the wind is coming at it us almost due east to due west at present, though that will vary some as the winds bend because of circulation. We can see by how the trees move that the winds can shift suddenly. I think it would be unwise to take the full force of it on our—six." That term felt like it came from Lurch. He felt Vi give him a look that was probably surprised. "We risk using up too much fuel if we attempt to directly oppose the wind."

"Yeah, with that much tail wind we'd probably end up in Mexico," Vi said this almost absently.

The heat inside the skimmer was bad enough to layer sweat over his body. He couldn't take his hands off the controls long enough to wipe it away from his face. As if she knew this, Vi used her towel to mop it.

"My thanks."

"Let me know when you need it again." She frowned at her screens, then peered out. "Okay, I parked facing away from what is probably where I-10 used to be, so we need to reverse direction. If you can...that would put us heading straight toward it."

He eased the nose around, felt the wind most eager to take control. *I am not sure this is possible.*

The impossible takes a little longer.

There was no response to this that was not rude, so he fought his way through the reverse maneuver then started the skimmer moving forward. It was, he decided, more terrifying than trying to reverse direction.

"How many miles to the airport?"

"As the crows flies," Vi appeared to consider the question, "it's about twelve, I think. Maybe fifteen."

A pity they were not crows. In normal conditions, such a journey would take minutes even in an old skimmer.

Normal is overrated.

Joe...appreciated Lurch trying to lighten his mood, or he would later. If they survived.

"Why are the dirt-siders at the old airport?" he wondered, more to distract himself than from real curiosity.

"It wasn't lifted," Vi said, her gaze fixed on her screens. "You're drifting right a bit. Yeah, that's better. It was too heavy for one thing. And it was still used for some years, until it became too expensive to keep up. Some hard core dirt-siders still use old planes to get around, but there are fewer and fewer landing strips being maintained."

That didn't exactly answer his question.

The terminal structure, while large, has not been maintained. The way WTF is tracking in has caused concern. If it makes the curve back to the east, as predicted, the airport will experience a direct hit, followed by additional flooding when the storm moves across the lake and pushes more water into the region.

Vi offered more drifting alerts as the skimmer fought its way down what was left of the transit lane. Trees loomed up out of the rain on either side, but it appeared that the material used to create the streets had, to some extent, limited the area enough to provide them the illusion of a transit lane. Each break in the tree line caused him difficulty. The skimmer twice flipped on its side and once all the way around to back upright again before the cross-wind compensators could assert control. There were private transports that combined air and ground capability. A pity the NONPD had been unable to spare such a craft for their use today. It might have been easier fighting the water instead of the wind.

"I've been thinking, when we reach the freeway, we might have a problem. You probably noticed the pieces of the old interchanges sticking up from the undergrowth as we were coming down." She flashed him a quick, tense smile.

Fallen chunks of the materials used to construct the freeway will be overgrown and, therefore, difficult to see.

"If we head north, the cross-wind compensators won't be as overwhelmed, and our track will follow the I-10 transit lanes and keep us clear of most obstructions. At least I hope so."

The skimmer shuddered and danced as a gust caught it, sending them perilously close to a stand of oak trees.

"It might be advisable to tighten the weather monitoring. Look for smaller areas of circulation within the larger storm circulation," Joe gritted out.

"Circ—oh. Hook echoes on the radar. Tornados. Great. As if we weren't already having fun."

She muttered something that Joe sensed was expletive in nature. He didn't mention the high risk of downbursts slamming them into the ground without warning. She'd been watching the news vids, too.

"I will require advance warning of upcoming turns. They are somewhat challenging." He flashed her a quick look that he tried to make reassuring. It would be the last he dared take. "If you will monitor the large picture, I will endeavor to navigate the small."

Her smile was his reward. For her, he would attempt to make the impossible possible. He did not contemplate the larger implications of the realization. All that mattered was the here. The now. He could deny it later, if they survived.

"Right. Big picture." She turned back to her screen. "We should reach I-10 soon."

They must have hit a cross-transit area. The winds tugged fiercely at the small craft, trying to bring it around, and the sounds of debris striking them increased exponentially. They experienced additional lift as well. Thrusters fired as the cross-wind compensators fought to hold their course. The engines protested the battle, and he had to slow their forward progress more to stop it. "I am hoping we will be able to use the wind at some point, rather than fighting it."

"That would be good for our fuel supply."

The trees and undergrowth pressed close to the former road, narrowing it severely the closer they got to the freeway. The trees provided some protection, but they also increased the risk that a rogue downburst would bring the trees crashing down.

"Keep on straight," Vi said. "You're veering right again...that's better, no too much left...good. Keep doing that."

"Of course." He made it sound easy. It wasn't. The muscles in his arms were on fire. His legs ached from working the pedals. He'd strapped in, but the straps only secured his torso. He knew why Lurch did not dare help him, but it added to his frustration to know that help was out of reach. "I just had a most disturbing thought."

"What's more disturbing than this?" Vi gestured forward.

"We might be forced to find out what is contained in those 72'r kits."

Silence.

"*Beaucoup crapeau* on a cracker."

"Is it worse when a good plan goes wrong, or when a desperately bad plan doesn't go right?" Vi finally dared take her attention off the merged screen to look outside and wished she hadn't. Flashes of lightning revealed and concealed the scrambled piles of broken freeway that used to be I-10. Huge chunks tumbled across the soaked landscape in varying heights, the thick coating of green turning them into jagged hills in the fitful light. Waves lapped against all obstacles, and small eddies revealed currents forming wherever the terrain made that possible. No way to know what hazards were lurking below the rising waterline.

A gust hit the skimmer. It righted itself.

Again. Not that she was complaining. Too much. Righting was good. The whiplash? Not so much.

Had she hoped against hope that they'd find a quicker way to the airport by following the old I-10? Up above, she took the I-10 transit all the time. She'd said more times than she could count that she could do it with her eyes closed. It was seriously freaky how much above had been matched to this furry green slice of the past. She had, she realized, half hoped to at least find the familiar in this alien. Looking at the wild, weather-lashed landscape, hope died with a painful tightening of her chest. Forget using it for transit, how were they going to get over it without getting blown who knew where? Or dying a fiery death when they ran into some part of it because they didn't see it until it was too late? Unless they ran out of fuel first and sank into the rising water. She didn't want to look at fuel consumption. Need-to-know did not equate to want-to-know. So she looked at Joe.

He looked tired and tense, with sweat gleaming on his paler-than-usual purple skin. She mopped his face again, wincing at the thought of what she must look like. Bad enough to feel like *beaucoup crapeau* on a cracker, she didn't want to think she looked the part. Never had she missed temperature control more—inside the suit and out. The news vids had been full of possible power outages in the wake of WTF. Her what-the-*crapeau* thoughts about that had centered more on access to news and entertainment. Maybe some cooking. She was spoiled. They all were. And what if they did have to abandon the skimmer? How good would their gear be? Based on current experience—about as good as *beaucoup crapeau* on a cracker. It was supposed to "protect in a variety of conditions," but it wasn't Superman's clothes. Or even the Iron Man's suit. If one of them got slammed into, oh, a pillar or a tree, it was going to hurt. Possibly fatally. Could have done without this opportunity to test it under field conditions. Later she'd worry about being dehydrated in one-thousand-percent humidity and having to explore the 72'r kit. If they lived long enough.

"Based on current patterns of consumption and the continuation of current conditions, we will not have sufficient fuel to return to the city if we cannot reach the airport within two hours."

It was not a vid news flash. Vi studied her map, trying to hurry and also be thorough while rising panic tried to steal her concentration. It had a solid foothold in her chest. Right next to that abandoned hope. She wasn't just field testing their gear. She was finding out a lot of about herself. So far she wasn't that impressed with either. She studied the screen like it had the answer to life's most important questions. She frowned. It kind of did if the question was survival.

"If we can get over I-10, we could try sixty-one. I don't think it was ever a freeway, but it does cut through that part of the city more or less directly, at least it does up top. Might go west too much, though." It wasn't a route she was terribly familiar with. Across the river might as well be the moon. She hadn't been to the moon. *Crapeau.* She didn't have time to mourn her unrealized bucket list because they hadn't cleared the feeder band yet. Or they'd moved through one into another one. She'd never have made it this far without Joe on the stick. Zipping around in fair weather using tech did not a real pilot make. She was really just a little better than a taxi-skimmer driver, she decided bitterly. If they survived, she was going to learn how to fly, not just drive. Should she be adding to her bucket list right now?

Joe was silent for what felt like a long time but probably wasn't. "I think we must follow this I-10 until we find a break or least a lower profile barrier. Or the wind moderates. I don't know, of course, but I would not like to risk a higher altitude until we have cleared the feeder band. Or try to fight a tail wind with our fuel reserves so low."

Based on their single turn back at the cemetery, and their progress down this fairly short street—yeah, they should look for a break. And pray for a miracle.

Joe's gaze turned inward, almost as if he spoke to someone. It was a bit weird and boosted his geek vibes, which of course she liked. Because she was clearly insane. Here she was thinking how cute he looked when they were about a millimeter from dying. Or maybe that was millisecond. Could she be any more shallow? Sadly, the answer to that question was probably a yes. Weren't people supposed to go deep in near-death situations? See their life pass before their eyes? That hers hadn't, was that a good thing or further indication of extreme shallowness? Should she add "try to be deeper" to her bucket list?

"I wonder if there were lower transit lanes when this freeway existed here?" Joe asked.

Since she was only other person in the skimmer, she considered the question. "Seems likely they'd need them and places to get on and off. It was elevated—my Grand Paw Paw called it the high rise—hence all the piles of debris when they collapsed. We don't need anything like that up top, so they didn't replicate that." Or they had and eliminated them at some point? She tried to visualize this part of the upper city. "It's possible we could follow along I-10. Of course—" She decided not to say it, though she couldn't stop herself thinking it. It might not be as "clear" as a former city street would have been, back in the day. "We'd have to go right sooner than we planned."

Joe's attention turned outward again. "A right turn will involve a period of going across the wind, and when we turn west again, there will be a tail wind."

That might be helpful. Or not. The prospect of being blown out of the state was not as terrifying as it had been. It all depended on the landing...

"The current feeder band should get past us at some

point," she offered with more hope than certainty. It would lessen some of the *crapeau*, but whether it would happen at a time helpful to them, well, that was the debatable part. If she was remembering her recent weather lessons correctly, this close to the eye wall the rain might lessen but the wind would get—something? Even if it got better, would it get better enough for them? She should have paid more attention. Her whole life.

It was also possible that they could cross into a more intense feeder band without even knowing it. The radar was almost solid now, if it was accurate. Each band would provide its own challenges and varying wind speeds. She scrolled up. Though there were gaps by the airport—maybe. If they could hit a gap—and they had the fuel reserves—they could make a dash for the surface. Let someone else come down for the idiots, preferably in something that wasn't a barely flying piece of *crapeau*.

"Then we will turn right." Joe spoke with decision, sparing her a quick reassuring smile.

She managed a smile that felt wan. Probably was. It did seem indicated. "How do we do this? How do we look for the break—" They only had two sets of eyes between them. His needed to watch for hazards forward. Hers had a bunch of *crapeau* to keep track of, including their drift factor, though calling it drift in a high wind felt like a serious understatement.

"You will have to watch for a break," he said. "I will go slower, so you can monitor our forward progress, too."

Hard to imagine going slower, but, "Okay."

It was actually hard to wrench her attention off the screens. They were terrifying, but not nearly as bad as the view out the front of the skimmer.

"Let's do this." The rain made thick distorting tracks down the view screen. But she found that if she looked past it, she could kind of make out the outlines of things. Not good things, and not very well, but things. Trees bent almost to the flood waters by the force of the wind. The broken blocks of old freeway against a barely discernible horizon, all looking interrupted by flashes of lightning. She wasn't sure if the lightning helped or hurt. She lost her night vision with each flash, even though her chronometer claimed it was late afternoon. So technically she lost her afternoon vision....

He began to ease the skimmer into its turn, his hands gripping so hard, they looked white. Vi didn't have to be on stick to feel the wind trying to push them into the blocks of concrete, felt the skimmer's pull to rise, too. It was like a really bad carnival ride.

A gust hit the skimmer. It righted itself.

And crossed her eyes for a minute.

"Warn me if I start to go left."

"Don't worry. I will." If she spotted it in time. She stared left, wondering why it felt like there were unspoken things between them, things that maybe needed to be spoken.

"You're drifting left—over-correcting—good, try to stay there." Like there was a "there." The silence was both oddly comfortable and weighted with what wasn't being said. Unless she imagined it. Which was possible. Maybe only her silence was weighted. She wanted to say something, in case, but "it's been a pleasure working with you," felt too formal. And not quite right. This wasn't a pleasure. Poking through crimes scenes for sure wasn't. It was interesting, but not pleasant.

"I didn't—want to be a cop." The words popped out. Maybe near-death required truth. Just not too much truth, she reminded herself.

"What did you want to be?" He sounded unsurprised.

Had he noticed? That might not be good.

"Not a cop." As kid, she'd worked her way through the famous stuff: actress, reality star, dancer, singer—but genetics—or maybe it was laziness—had precluded her seriously considering doing something that was actually possible. For sure no one had asked her what she wanted to be when she grew up. The questions had been more along the lines of which area of law enforcement would she go into. "It's kind of sad, though not totally sad. I'm glad I got to be your partner."

"Do not count us out yet."

"Drifting—okay, better." She bit her lip. "I'm not counting us out but doing an 'in case of' because I might not get the chance later. We'll probably be busy or something." Like dead. "You're a good cop. I've learned a lot from you." Not exactly what she wanted to say to him but didn't feel like the right moment to mention she'd like to kiss him on his somewhat purple mouth before she died.

Whether he felt the same or not, it would be distracting. He didn't need to be distracted right now.

"I also did not wish to be in law enforcement."

Almost she looked at him. "But—" She could not imagine him doing anything he didn't want to. Plus, he was like a reincarnated Joe Friday. If a fictional character could be reincarnated?

"We all have imperatives, the requirements of duty, taking us to what we did not expect or—where we did not expect to go."

That sounded very Friday and yet—not. What had he not said? That he hadn't wanted to come to NON? If he hadn't wanted to be a cop, then being sent to be a cop in another world would kind of suck.

"I'm glad you came," she said in a low voice.

The pause felt...something. "I am glad as well."

She smiled, couldn't think of anything to say but that he needed to correct course. They were being pushed toward the unyielding tumble of blocks with an impressive persistence. She tried to home in on the blocks, stay fixed on them and nothing else, searching for a break, or just a moderation in the height—

In the murk of the storm, she felt again her awe at the sheer volume of water coming down. Her eyes saw it, but her brain had trouble wrapping around it. And next to them, the block pile appeared to get higher and higher.

Her heat sensor pinged. She looked, then looked back outside. "There's something out there." The heat signature had been wrong for a person, though...

"Something?"

Vil stole another quick look. "A dog. Domestic."

"How can you tell?"

"It's been tagged." Dirt-siders were required to tag their pets, just like up-siders. Man, it figured. She'd never seen a vid where the dog didn't run off at the wrong time. She took another quick look at the data. "*Crapeau.* It belonged to our vic." Maybe it hadn't run off. She didn't want to say it, but she had to. "We need to pick it up."

"It's a canine—"

"It's also a potential witness." It wouldn't have any trace evidence left on it, thank you, WTF, but domestic pet idents have been legalized maybe forty years ago. Personally, Vi didn't trust a cat ID. Cats were genius, but so bitter. She'd seen a case where she knew the cat was yanking their chains. Luckily some evidence surfaced that cleared the guy, because that cat hated him. "Why is it here? If it was dumped, then it was probably the killer that did it." She gave him a quick look. That was the most expression she'd seen on his face ever. "We have to make a reasonable attempt to secure a potential witness."

"Reasonable is not an option in our current circumstances."

That was the most gritted she'd ever seen his even, white teeth. And they still had to try to collect Fido. Yup, his name was Fido. That was the pooch equivalent of calling your kid John Doe. Maybe it had run away.

"Regs," she said, careful not to look at him. It wasn't a loud sigh, but it was capitulation of a sort. Her gaze flicked between the WTF-lashed exterior and her screen with the dog signal. "It's there, on those blocks of freeway to our left."

"And just how do you propose we secure our...witness?"

"The pooch is on my side. Wind is hitting from your side. I'm thinking I'll open my hatch and call it. By the time we're close, it can jump in."

"And if it does not?"

"Then we keep going. That's as reasonable I can be." And way more than Joe wanted. It was crazy, but half the regs were. Vi called them the ROUCs, the regs of unintended consequences. They resulted from someone trying to hammer a nail into your table leg with a bludgeon. You might get the nail in, but you broke the table and a couple of chairs. And possibly the floor. And the table leg. "Fido's gonna have to help save himself."

Vi had a feeling she knew what Joe would like Fido to do, but if he cursed, it wasn't in English.

"What do you need me to do?"

"Check your straps. I'm gonna pop my hatch and we'll see what that does to our progress before we try to, you know, change anything." She checked her straps. Wished she had more confidence in them. Be a bad time to find out they were mostly for show. "Ready?"

"As it is possible to be."

"Three...two...one..." She released the hatch.

A gust hit the skimmer, flipping it on its side.

THE SKIMMER RIGHTED ITSELF. BUT NOT BEFORE sending a minor flood in on them. Joe blinked water out of his eyes. He lacked a hand free to do anything but steer. The wind howled into the cabin of the skimmer like the *skitterments of hoarsh,* pelting them with particles of flying debris. Joe felt Lurch trying to assist as he fought to keep the craft from spinning out of control. The forward view began to fog. Joe boosted defog function and almost lost control of the skimmer.

I suggest keeping both hands on the controls.

No crapeau. Joe began to understand Vi's fondness for the word. It was a succinct response to the blatantly obvious, and an accurate reflection of dire when modified by "in deep." Regs for a *danstrg* dog.

"You got it?"

"Yes." Not completely, but as much as he was going to "have it."

"All right, start your veer left."

He did not dare look at Vi, or anything but what was ahead, trusting her to warn of what threatened from the left as the skimmer began to close on the debris pile. This level of trust was difficult. He could barely hear her over the wind and rain.

"Fido!!!"

The wind seemed to fling her shout back at them. Then it tried to jerk them into a spin. The skimmer flipped on its side again. Righted itself. A small lake of water began to form around their feet.

Dogs have excellent hearing.

"Here, Fido! Jeez, I feel stupid shouting that."

Why? Other than the fact we are trying to call a dog in a storm?

It is a generic dog name. Like your false name.

Joe frowned. Lurch had given him a generic assumed identity? His arms burned. Lurch risked easing the pain, though not as much as Joe would have liked. Could their enemy really have eyes on them in this storm?

Yes.

"Okay, no more left. We're close—too close—that's better. I can see him. He's getting up—oh, man, this is gonna to be bad—"

Joe sensed, more than saw, the blur of motion. Heard Vi's oomph, as air was forced out her lungs. The skimmer flipped to the side. He could not be sure but for several seconds he believed there was a dog butt pressed against his face. The skimmer righted itself. Filling his lap with dog. Almost they careened off course.

"Get him off!" he roared, as they hurtled forward toward he knew not what.

And then the canine scrambled between them into the rear seat.

"Right, go right!" Vi cried out as she hit the hatch control.

She twisted in her seat and brought the shield down between them and the canine. It howled, though Joe did not know or care why. He shook water off his face and almost howled, too. He wrestled with the controls, trying to change course. Ominous scraping along her side of the skimmer. The sound diminished as the hatch re-sealed. He had not realized how much sound it filtered out.

"Straighten out now!"

It was not that easy to do as requested, but Joe gave it his best, panting almost as much as the dog behind its shield. There was another nasty scraping sound, though this one was of shorter duration.

"I think there might be a way through this."

Their forward lights appeared to bounce off the rain more than they pierced it, but beyond it, he thought he saw what she saw.

"If it is a large enough opening." There was only one way to discover that. "You will need to try to watch both sides as we approach. I will need to focus forward."

"Right. No problem." She'd leaned forward as far as she could, as if that would help her pierce the storm.

The flashes of lightning did help. Except when they didn't.

And then it stopped. Rain and wind. The skimmer wobbled several times before he adjusted to the lack of both.

"What—"

Vi's, "Oh *crapeau*," came at same time as the warning whine from their weather tracking screen.

Tornado. Or downburst.

"*Crapeau*, indeed."

Vi felt the skimmer surge forward and instinctively pressed back into her seat. "What are you doing?"

"The opening might provide protection if we can reach it before—" he stopped.

Joe didn't like to state the obvious. Maybe it was the wrong time, but she had to say it.

"We make it and I'm gonna kiss you." It would either motivate him. Or make them crash.

His eyes widened, then narrowed, his grip on the controls more determined.

Motivation. Sweet. Now all they had to do was survive the next five minutes. Her gaze flicked back and forth between the debris getting closer on either side. When it flicked right, her gaze got to graze Joe's intent face. Inexplicably, she felt her spirits rising at the sight. This was not a man to give up without a fight. Maybe they'd make it—

The rear of the skimmer began to twitch. As if the tornado plucked at it with gusty, grasping fingers.

The debris got closer.

Sounds of objects hitting the sides of the skimmer. Bigger objects. A large branch blocked their view for several seconds before being dragged up and back.

The slot they aimed for looked pretty small all of a sudden. She didn't think—didn't dare speak and break his concentration again.

Felt like they were going too fast—

The skimmer shuddered harder.

Joe put the pedal to the metal—whatever that meant. It was a phrase from Grand Paw Paw which made no sense at all. Their pedals were for braking.

Hole got closer. Smaller.

Vi squinted, because she couldn't close her eyes, half turned as if bracing for a hit.

Felt the skimmer shudder when he reversed thrust by actually applying pedals to metal.

Was flung against the straps holding her in.

Scraping sounds, above this time. Some shrieking of metal on rock.

Stopping. Stopped.

Another fling against straps. A few stars cart-wheeling past....

A roaring, like a mighty engine going over. Wild crashing sounds. The wrath of the gods for sure.

Fido whined, might have tried to dig his way deeper into the backseat.

She reached out, eyes still stuck straight ahead and grabbed Joe's arm, felt down until she found his hand. Gripped it.

Fido howled now, a terrified sound she would have echoed had that been possible. Fear had a choke hold on her throat.

The skimmer moved back with a jerk, but it stopped, and then the vortex was in front of them.

In one flash of lightning, she saw the cone and its load of debris before it vanished from sight again.

The wind and rain came back with more fury, as if enraged that they weren't dead.

They weren't dead.

Joe locked them in hover mode, using his free hand. She almost asked why, but at the moment she didn't care. Vi released her breath in a gust.

"Damn." She looked at Joe. The edges of her mouth tipped up some. Couldn't quite get her smile on, even though inside she was beaming. *They weren't dead.* The dog whined and scratched the shield. "Sit!" she ordered. Then she grabbed the neck of Joe's suit and pulled him toward her. Planted that promised kiss right on his sort-of purple mouth.

It didn't taste like a color. It tasted like man, no cool in it either. The guy hid a lot. Like how good he could kiss....

The dog barked sharply, as if annoyed. She ignored him until he threw himself against the shield with a howling whining sort of bark that shook their slings.

She eased back from Joe a millimeter or so. Oh yeah, there was fire in there. His eyes fairly blazed. Vi found her smile, and he matched it and then some. Water dripped down her face and his. He had a drop on the end of his sassy nose. She caught it with the tip of her finger. For an instant it looked like he might say something. Or pounce. Then he sighed. But he touched her cheek with his finger, the light touch edged with tender, before he said, "We must—"

"Yeah, we must," she admitted. Her whole body wanted to keep leaning his way. Her lips wanted to continue the kissing. She sat back. She was a grownup. Darn it. Matched Joe's sigh and raised it. She gave herself a shake. If they'd made it to the freeway...she tried to do math, wasn't sure how well she did it. "So, we've gone two, maybe three blocks and used up a quarter of our fuel. Maybe we should wait here?"

Yeah, they might be under several tons of really old concrete, but she knew what was out there.

Joe considered the suggestion, then shook his head. "I do not believe we are above the storm surge here."

Vi looked down at her weather screen.

It was as dark as the view outside.

4

"What else is offline?" Joe asked, checking the panels closest to his station. His screens appeared to be functional, but they were all related to skimmer operations. It was a relief to be stationary, even if only briefly. Though the brief respite from stress seemed to have released additional body heat into the all-enclosing emergency gear. Apparently it could get hotter.

The stress upped your body temperature?

Joe bit his tongue and ignored the interjection. And the derisive snort. If he thought about the kiss—and there it went up another degree. Now was not the time. He pushed aside the question of whether there would ever be a time to think about that kiss and tried to focus on their current problem.

"All uplinks to satellite data are gone. Our underbelly vid was already out, but it looks like we've lost top and both side vids, too." She tapped something. "Rear vid is still operational, because, you know, seeing where we've been will be so helpful to our current circumstances."

He now recognized sarcasm and didn't make the mistake of pointing out that the rear vid wouldn't be helpful. The one screen he almost wished had gone out was the one recording their fuel supply. He did not dare shut off the engines when he was not certain they would re-fire. The only good news, in their current position, they were burning minimal fuel. Without data, all he had were his eyes to study the storm. Did it seem less dark? The wind continued to lash the trees, though perhaps not as fiercely. And the rain might be slackening off. Though he had never engaged in wishful thinking, the possibility remained that the worst of the feeder band had moved away from them.

"I think we might be sort of between feeder bands," Vi said, confirming his visuals. "One of those weather jokers was talking about what it was like. This might be that."

"Yes," Joe said, as if he'd remembered, instead of getting the info from Lurch, "intense rain and wind, followed by little rain and less intense wind." Winds that could still gust up into the 100 mph range without warning.

"Do we dare make a run for it?" she asked, her eyes big in a white, wet face. Tendrils of hair clung to her skin where they'd crept out from under her head gear.

He considered the question. Without real-time access to weather data, it was risky. Staying was suicide if the storm surge reached them.

I have an idea, but you will not like it.

He was also sure he would not like it. Joe's sigh was silent. *What is it?*

The 72'r kits.

Vi stared up, though she could see nothing but clouds. It was irrational to feel that if she looked hard enough she could see past the storm to the city above. How was it faring as WTF moved in? What kind of weather would they be experiencing? She thought she'd paid attention, that she knew what to expect. She was wrong. It was like being in that dream, the one where you were back in school and you find out there's a test and you haven't studied for it, and besides, you didn't know you were taking that course. Had she really thought she was a weather "expert" after listening to a few vid reports? Talk about having the illusion of knowledge. Was this how people had felt during Chen when they found themselves trapped on the ground? The loss of life had been the worst since Katrina. And they'd had experience with hurricanes then. Her city, the floating city, hadn't experienced a hurricane since Chen. Was her family all right? If—*when* they got to the airport, would rescue be there? How much time would Captain Uncle give them to reach the airport? Would there be a city up there to flee to if they did?

"I have an," Joe paused, his tone heavy with reluctance, "idea."

She looked at him, saw Fido out of the corner of her

eye, sitting back there looking at them like he understood and was curious as well. It was a bit eerie. Even after years of research, no one really knew how much dogs understood, since no one had managed to actually have a conversation with one. Fido met her gaze with a soulful, doggish look. Almost idly she wondered what breed he was. Probably mongrel. Bedraggled mongrel. Not that she was any great shakes. She looked at Joe. Even bedraggled, he was better looking than the dog. And just about everyone.

"What?" She sounded wary. She felt wary.

"The 72'r kits."

She blinked. "The 72'r kits." She blinked again. "You mean those old backpacks?"

"The *emergency* backpacks," he reminded her.

Well, this sure as hounds-of-a-hot-place qualified as an emergency.

He tapped in some command or other and a list appeared on her screen.

She studied it for a couple of seconds. "Water? No clue what an MRE is—"

"I suspect it is some type of sustenance."

Sustenance was good. "They're in the back." Newer models of the skimmer had access to the back from the cockpit, but not this one, of course. She leaned forward, trying to look along the skimmer to the rear through her side viewers. They were in here pretty tight. Could one of them even get back there?

Apparently Joe had been doing the same thing. "The skimmer is too close to the debris on this side."

"There might be room on mine."

She looked forward. This was probably as good as it was going to get for going outside. She didn't want to think about what would happen if her side hatch got stuck open —so she didn't. She pushed the release. It rose slowly, as if reluctant as she was, letting in a rush of damp air that immediately fogged her face shield. She popped it up, surprised to find the air clammy rather than hot. It was moving, so that was probably why. It wasn't quiet, but the wind wasn't as loud as the last time. The hatch lifted, lifted some more, skimming past the concrete with some really small number to spare. Vi shifted and it scraped. Yeah, that was close.

She activated her head lamp, leaned out, and looked around. The concrete block supporting them extended maybe a foot beyond the skimmer. There was a gap between the block beneath and the one next to them. And the ones over them. She grasped the side and leaned further out, shining the light down the length. It looked like she could get through, though the passage narrowed sharply toward the rear of the skimmer. And just in case she was inclined to be hopeful, the blocks were also coated with green slime-looking stuff. She could see scoring from their landing, and the fishtailing of the skimmer caused by the vortex as it passed over. The wind wasn't too bad, though it still carried small bits of debris. A leaf hit her face and stuck. She pulled it off and flung it to the wind, which grabbed it and carried it away.

She sat back. Took a breath, then looked at Joe, trying for can-do.

"I will crawl past you and do it," he said.

So she'd failed at can-do. Up next: have-to-do. "I'm not sure you'll fit. It looks—tight back there."

They didn't even have safety rope in this stupid thing. No grapple as part of her suit. Those suits were reserved for the rescue services. Exactly what emergency was her gear supposed to help with? She tried a smile, apparently did better at that. Or Joe was trying not to add to her abject fear. He gave her a thumbs up, which was pretty out there for him. The dog gave a small whine that might have been encouragement. Too bad they couldn't send him out there, but he'd probably run off.

She lifted her leg out, grasping the sides of the skimmer and lowered her foot until it rested on the block. She moved it around, testing the surface. No surprise there was no downward give or that it was slippery. Thank goodness for the maintenance grips along the side, though they were vertical, not horizontal, which would have helped more.

Regs said she should wear gloves in an emergency where contaminants might be present. Green slime probably qualified as a contaminant. Looked gross enough to be one. But she didn't deploy them. The regs would have to deal. She needed all the tactile advantage she could get, even though the thoughts of what might be in the green goo coating the block made her want to shudder. With a last attempted smile at Joe, Vi brought her other leg out and scooted to the edge of her sling. When her weight shifted to her outside leg, she felt it start to slip. She clutched the sides and said something dubious. Joe made a worried sound.

"I'm okay." She was such a liar. If she died now—

"Take care." It sounded like an order, but felt like a plea.

His people were sort of chauvinistic, so this had to be hard for him. "Oh, I will."

By scraping at the concrete, she managed to get the gripping surface on the bottom of her boots into semi-contact with the concrete. And tried to stand again. This time she got both boots on the block. Okay, that sounded wrong for some reason. Cautiously she inched around until she faced the skimmer. While she'd been turning, Joe had clambered over the center console into her sling. For some reason that helped. Holding his gaze, she felt along the metal until she found a grip.

Joe leaned down, so his headlight shone out. He raised his head. "Vi—"

"I'll be right back." It wasn't easy to look away from the comfort of his worried brown eyes. She was impressed she managed it. Then impressed gave way to holy freaking *crapeau*. She tipped her chin, so her headlamp shone on the wing. Hadn't she just been to this party? She got her leg over it, found the next grip and got the other leg over. Because the engineers who had designed the skimmer hadn't foreseen this situation—or any emergency it seemed —the grips hadn't been placed that close together. She didn't have to let go of one to get her fingers around the next, but her arms were fully extended both directions before she reached grip number three.

About halfway along, she happened to glance down. Mistake. Couldn't see a bottom because of the way the gap between the blocks narrowed. If she fell, it would not be pleasant. With the sky lighting some, she could sort of see around her. Or her eyes had adjusted to the murk. The way the blocks of concrete tumbled together was not that reassuring. They'd been there a long time, she reminded herself, as she reached for the next grip.

"You're doing great," Joe said, obviously trying to sound encouraging.

Bless his heart. In a weird way, it did help. When, she wondered, had the skimmer gotten this long? A gust of wind roared into the semi-cave, forcing her to press into the side of the skimmer, her feet almost losing their grip, as the debris pelting picked up. Joe's light wavered, then steadied. The wind gust didn't last, thank goodness, though the non-gusting wind wasn't great either. It felt like it wanted to push her back to the cockpit, or blow her out into the rising water. Maw Maw N had PMS for sure.

She reached out. This time the distance between the grips wasn't as far. Her light picked out the rear of the skimmer. "I'm almost there—"

Her hand closed around a grip. She let go of one and started to ease the rest of her to the next.

A piece of the concrete broke off under the weight-bearing foot.

Her other foot slipped. Her hand holding the grip got

her full weight with a painful jerk. She spun in a half circle, banging her knee against the edge of the block, the twist almost making her lose her hold on the wet grip. Her light showed jagged chunks, like teeth opened wide to receive her. The height of the grips was just wrong, making the ledge both too low and too high. She tried to get her other hand up and almost lost her hold.

She stilled.

"I"m coming—"

She wouldn't last that long.

"Just catching my breath—"

In a gap in the blocks to her right, her light illuminated eyes....

◈◈◈

Vi dangled precariously off the rim of concrete, all her weight on one hand. He leaned further out, trying to give her more light. He succeeded. His light, added to hers, illumined the shape, just as its the mouth parted enough to show teeth. Was it...?

It is a raccoon. A pause. *That is not a good thing. They can be vicious.*

The raccoon reared back, baring its teeth and hissing. Keeping his light fixed on it, he reached down, feeling for his weapon. The one-touch release took two touches. He eased it clear of the holster and flicked off the safety. Started to change it from stun to kill. Changed his mind. The passage was so narrow, if he hit Vi....

Your setting will not matter if you hit her. She will fall.

Thinking about that will steady my aim.

Joe tried to keep his light steady on the creature as he lifted his arm, took aim—and pulled the trigger. Light flashed in the narrow space, blinding him. There was a yelp. Possibly a thud. Vi or the raccoon?

He heard scraping. Boots against concrete.

"Vi?"

"I'm okay. A little bruised."

His vision began to adjust. She'd managed to get her feet back on the narrowing ledge. Both hands clutched the hand grip now.

"It's down." She reached down and pulled her weapon. Fired it. "Don't want it waking up pissed for my trip back."

Another gust whistled through, its force boosted by being funneled through the cavern. He tried not to think about the objects striking the aging skimmer. Or Vi. Their forward view shield already sported several starred impact marks. How much abuse could it withstand? His breath held as he watched her squeeze past the last hurdle. When she was out of sight, he heard, "You wouldn't have made that. I barely made it."

He felt the skimmer shudder as the rear hatch opened.

How will she return with two packs?

Lurch had no answer.

It felt as if the wind picked up, not just because of the cavern, but generally. He studied the terrain ahead of them. It did seem that their period of "calm" was coming to an end. He felt Lurch's impatience that she remained out of sight.

She is moving as fast as she can.

I am aware. But if she lingers too long, the trip back will be more perilous.

The canine in the rear seat moved closer and whined mournfully. It saw Joe glance at him and barred its teeth, a low growl at the back of its throat.

It doesn't seem to like you.

And still she didn't appear. "Vi—"

"There's rope in these things. I'm trying to rig something."

"The wind is increasing again." Rain began again. "Leave one—"

"This may be our only chance and trust me, we need this *crapeau*."

Finally she appeared around the side. She held a length of rope, with something tied on the end. The hatch ground back into place. But she didn't start back.

"I'm going to toss this and you need to catch it," she said.

She squeezed past the tight spot, only the toes of her boots on concrete. He watched her run a length of rope through a grip, then through several loops on her suit and snap something. She tested the rope before she grabbed the length of rope and began to swing it, with the heavy object tied to the end. With each swing, she let more of the rope go, using the gap to extend the length of each swing. It came close and he almost caught it, but a gust of wind spun it out of reach. He used one of Vi's words. And waited. Next time.

She had to reel it in and start over. Slowly, so slowly it seemed, the object swung closer and closer.

Now!

He lunged, while keeping a grip on the side. Felt rope sliding through his fingers. The object slammed into his chest with numbing force, but Lurch helped him hang on to the rope by increasing the strength in his hand.

"I've got it." He pulled it into the cockpit. It appeared to be a small bag, made of netting of some sort, and filled with heavy objects.

"You'll find a carabiner in there. See if you can hook your end to something."

The rainfall rate was increasing, and the wind blew it into the skimmer and along the passage Vi must travel.

"Once you've got it, I'll slide the packs onto my end and secure them, and then you can reel them in. I'll follow and try to keep them from getting stuck on something. With the rope, I should be more secure for the trip back."

He worked on securing his end. "I am ready."

She had to go back through the narrow gap to get the packs. He saw her push them through the gap, one at a time. Once they were clear, he began pulling them in. Vi followed, moving faster, though at each grip she paused to secure herself. The packs got stuck once, but she was able to kick them free and in minutes he pulled them inside, tossing them on the floor, so he could reach for Vi. The last stretch seemed the longest. As soon as she clambered across the wing, he grabbed her, tumbling them both onto her sling. It was most uncomfortable, but he could not let go. She wriggled and he tightened his hold, but realized she had just reached over to close the hatch. He found he could chuckle, though only once.

"I missed you, too," she said, against his shoulder.

"I would kiss you on your mouth, but I do not think I could stop," he said.

"Ditto."

"I suppose," he said, reluctantly after a pointed nudge from Lurch, "that we should do something."

She lifted her head off his chest. Managed a wavering smile. She had smears of green on her gear, her face and, he noted, liberally covering her boots and clothing where they rested awkwardly on the console. She had to be most uncomfortable. He aided her attempt to get off him, then clambered back into his sling. She dropped in hers with a sigh. He looked at her, then at the storm building back up out there. And wished he'd taken time for the kiss.

She hefted one of the packs onto the console so he could take it.

"I'm not sure how they'll help us get from point A to point B, but there is water in these bad boys. And some scary looking stuff that claims to be edible."

"Water would be helpful, but I am hoping for a compass."

She looked puzzled. "A compass? One of those weird ancient old math things you draw circles with?"

He shook his head, digging through the contents. "Ah."

He pulled it out and held it up the round disc. The hands spun, then pointed north.

"Compass. Okay, I learned about those in school. Sort of. How does it help?"

"We still have the map onboard. It is part of our database. With it and this compass, we should be able to navigate to the airport." She looked dubious. "It is a long shot, Vi, but it is our only shot."

She stared him, then nodded. "Right." Her lips quirked. "Wouldn't it be nice if we got a short shot for once?"

The canine whimpered in what might be agreement. He glanced back. It had covered its eyes with its paws. So perhaps not agreement.

MOST DAYS VI LIKED DRIVING, EVEN THIS PIECE OF *crapeau* skimmer. Today was not "most days." Joe had had to give her some storm flying tips, which was kind of embarrassing. There was also the realization that she couldn't navigate her way out of, well, WTF. At some point they'd find out if Joe could navigate. His moves looked credible. He'd stared at the compass a lot, checked their map of the upper city. Looked out the window. Warned her when she was drifting or about to hit a large something or other. The verdict on whether it had worked was still out. She had no clue where they were, other than still in WTF. So probably still in Louisiana. Maybe in the region of New Orleans Old or New. Was sure they weren't out in the Gulf. There were no trees in the Gulf.

The wind had tested her to her toenails. And her fingernails. Had made her glad for the stale water and truly awful rations she'd eaten before they tried this long shot. Joe had not been happy they'd had to share with Fido. She'd got a look and he beat her to, "Regs?"

She'd shrugged apologetically. There were regs of regs for care and feeding of witnesses. Fido had eaten the offering, but he hadn't been any happier about it than they'd been.

At first she'd felt lost without the tech, missed the stream of data informing them how truly screwed they were. Then she decided absolute knowledge was not needed. Not knowing allowed delusions of hope to creep in. Helped her keep going when she thought she couldn't keep her almost numb hands on the controls one second more. She'd gotten almost used to stuff slamming into them, though the big stuff still made her jump. Gotten sort of used to tipping to one side or the other when the wind gusted. Still didn't like the yank when the cross-wind compensators righted them—more than once by spinning them 180 degrees. When she realized half an hour had passed without crashing and burning, she began to believe they might just make it to the airport.

Assuming they could find it. It had seemed a large, findable target, until one factored in all kinds of science or math or physics stuff. She wasn't sure which. Maybe all of them boiled down to a needle in a haystack. What, she wondered to take her mind off the burn in her shoulders and everywhere else, was a haystack?

The rain slackened off with a suddenness that took her by surprise. It was all the warning she got for the wind speed change. The modification sent them off course, which was the ultimate in optimistic, believing they had a course. She fought her way back to this fictional place. Light tried to push through the cloud cover, low and off to her left. The sun was setting. Oh goodie. Though...if that was due west, or undue west, then Joe's compass skills had worked. And if they had been heading north—

She took a deep, shaky breath as an outline of gray appeared at the base of the clouds ahead of them.

That had to be the big, freaking landmark they'd hoped to find. The one that might help them find that not-so-freaking-big-enough airport.

"Lake Pontchartrain," Joe said with satisfaction, exhaustion cutting deep grooves into a face that managed to be both hammered and pretty. "Now we make our west-ward turn."

Her lifted spirits took a nose dive. West. The turn that would put the full force of the hurricane's winds on their tail. It had been bad having it hit them from the side, even with the aid of the cross-wind compensators. The cost in fuel consumption had been more painful than the jolts. Joe had hoped it would push them far enough west that when they made this turn they would have covered much of the distance to the airport and wouldn't have to ride the tail wind for too long.

The wind had modified in this feeder band. Or not-feeder band. But had it modified enough to make the turn possible?

"We do not want to be over water," he added, possibly sensing her sudden reluctance.

Being over water while flying through buckets of it would make bad worse. She knew this, but—

She cast him a quick fake confident look. "I haven't tried a big turn in this yet. Any tips?"

"Take it slow." He paused. "And pray?"

Pray she could do, had been doing pretty much non-stop. Her Grand Paw Paw used to say there were no atheists in fox holes. He could add big ass storms to that list. But actually making the turn? Would WTF let her "take it slow?"

"We can attempt to transfer control back to me," he added.

She shook her head. "It almost didn't work last time." If the skimmer was damaged, which it was, it was a real possibility that flight control could get stuck in limbo between the two stations. Limbo would be bad until their fuel ran out. Then it would be lethal. "I can do it."

She had to. This wasn't one of those "do or don't do, there is no try" deals. This was do it or die.

She took a deep breath, some advice from a cousin popping up in her head. "Be one with your skimmer. That's how real pilots fly." It sounded stupid then, did now, and yet—during the rare skimmer chases in her patrol cop years, she'd focus on her target and yeah, tried to be one with her ship. It had helped her miss buildings during those sharp, fast turns.

She took another deep breath and let herself feel it. Feel the wind pushing against the right side of the skimmer. It wasn't a steady force. There was no pattern to how hard it hit them. Sometimes it came from above and the side. Always trying to wrest control from her. They'd been lucky they'd missed the wrenching winds that twisted the trees like tops, sending them flailing first one direction, then the other. Though they'd been singed by them, if one could use the word in a million-gallons-of-water hurricane.

Joe didn't speak again. She felt his urgency, despite his carefully deadpan expression. He also knew she needed to try it sooner rather than later. He knew she knew it. The lake was getting close fast. She tried another deep breath and felt herself connect, or she hoped that connection was what she felt. If she was wrong, they'd only know it for a minute.

She adjusted speed and began to feather the turn. It was like trying to feather a mule through a gate—a Grand Paw Paw phrase that she didn't get but felt comforting, and there was no one to tell her it wasn't right.

Okay, feathering wasn't going to do. Time to bull through the turn. Her muscles shuddered as much and as hard as the skimmer. But this time it started to come around. Okay, now the mule was bucking. She'd never done it, but she'd seen rodeos vids.

She reversed thrust and finished the turn. The tail

wind caught them. Snapped her back in her sling, like a kick in the ass.

Reverse thrust was at full power.

They raced forward, bouncing across the restless air currents so hard her feet—and her ass—kept going airborne.

"Tighten my straps," she gritted out between bounces.

Joe did. It helped some. Hurt a lot. In some ways it reminded her of a vid game. Without the fun parts. Dark clouds bent across the horizon ahead of them.

"Is that what I think it is?"

Joe didn't have time to answer before the tail wind pushed them inside.

The sudden change in wind direction ripped the controls from her hands and sent them spinning top over tail.

Joe woke to a spinning, tumbling world. Nothing to tell him what was up, what was down. Vi was unconscious. Perhaps it was luck that a change in the wind had lifted them up into heavier winds, rather than slamming them into the ground. It was the only good news, though it did not feel good. Even the nanite felt a bit seasick.

The skimmer shrieked a protest at the unkind stress impacting its old seams and joints. Another direction change flung him sideways in his harness. Stars spun across his view in the opposite direction of the skimmer. The console flickered once, then came to life, not with uplink data or communications, but with something.

Did you—

No. Perhaps the structural stresses have knocked something...together.

Joe didn't believe it either, but a reprieve, even one

possibly provided for nefarious purposes, was still a reprieve. It was as well Lurch had allowed him to lose consciousness, if its enemy had caused this "fix." Fighting against the centrifugal force pinning him in the sling, he managed to hit the drive control transfer. The reasons they hadn't done it before no longer mattered. If it didn't work, well, as Vi liked to say, "*Crapeau* happens. A lot."

Joe was not surprised when control transferred and with some speed. If it did not want them to die, something had to change and quickly. Did it wish the game to continue? Did it now watch them?

Use attitude control, then the power boost when the skimmer levels out.

Joe managed to depress attitude control, then grabbed the controls. Did what he could to bring the skimmer to a point where it could be steered once more. The shriek of stressed metal increased. He feared it was too late, but slowly, almost imperceptibly the skimmer began to level out. Rotation also slowed, then ceased. The cross-wind compensators kicked on, assisting the leveling, and the skimmer resumed forward progress.

Now.

It was only after he punched it, he wondered at the wisdom of accelerating toward the unknown. But they knew what they had here. And it was done. He hit the back of the sling harder than before. Apparently whoever had designed this boost had been quite serious about it. He saw stars once more, almost as many as on his journey here....

Like a rocket, the skimmer passed through the outer band of the storm into skies that were not wholly clear, but better than what they'd left. The boost sputtered and died, taking almost all their fuel with it. That was the bad news, as Vi liked to say. The good news, almost directly ahead he saw, outlined against the sinking sun, the stark shape of what had been the New Orleans Old airport.

❦

THEY WEREN'T GOING TO MAKE IT. THEY'D STARTED out high, but their fuel was almost gone. Their weight, the imperfectly designed skimmer, and the gravitational force pulled them inexorably down. Transit through the unstable air reminded him of land passage through the more remote areas at home, what the people here called pot holes. Apparently NOO had a surfeit of these pot holes, which lifting had not wholly helped. Some of the narrower transits retained "ghost pot holes" that no one could quite explain. His teeth seemed to rattle inside his head.

We were not blown as far off course as I feared.

Do you believe your enemy is doing more than watching us? Did it assist us?

It is possible.

Joe sensed a complicated something from the old nanite, something that left a bad taste at the back of Joe's throat. *What?*

What if it is here with us?

Here? There is only— Then it hit him. *You think Vi—no. I—no.*

We must consider the possibility. It could have invaded her body at any time. One minute of prolonged contact and then she would no longer be in control of her actions.

I have observed no changes in her behavior.

You do not believe the kiss was a change in behavior?

Joe shifted uncomfortably in his seat. That kiss had been only the bright spot in the day and now Lurch was taking it away? *You believe she kissed me to—deceive me?*

I am not saying it is so. I'm saying, you need to be wary. Limit physical contact until—

Until when? If they were going to die down here, the one thing he wanted to do again was not limit physical contact with Vi. Joe glanced at her where she slumped in her sling, blood trickling down the side of her face. Could she be hiding Lurch's enemy? He tried to think if he'd noticed any change in her behavior beyond the kiss, but she was an ever-changing mystery to him on his best days. This was not one of his best days. Except for the kiss. *How will we know?*

When she tries to kill you. Or someone else does.

Joe risked another quick look. She seemed to be breathing.

While she is unconscious, couldn't you—

She may be pretending to be unconscious to get me to do just that.

So they would have to wait until they landed. Supposing they survived the landing.

If we can make it as far as one of the old runways, our chances will improve.

Even if they managed a landing that didn't tear the skimmer to pieces—and them with it—they'd be dirt side in fading light with WFT still bearing down on them. A storm expected to be preceded by an unprecedented storm surge.

The 72'r kits contain rudimentary flotation devices.

Because one wished to be buoyant in water with alligators, poisonous reptiles, fire ants, and who knew what else —and a woman one was not allowed to kiss until she didn't try to kill him.

Vi groaned, her head shifting to one side, then the other. One eye cracked slightly. She blinked several times before her lids remained up. Stared at him for twenty seconds, then her lips curved into a smile.

"We're not dead."

"No." He smiled at her, remembered, and the smile turned stiff. How was he to manage this? He lacked deception skills.

Try not to think about it. Or touch her.

Because either was easy. Not.

"I was sure I'd wake up dead." She pushed herself upright in sling, wincing a couple of times. "Figured I wasn't because one hopes dying won't hurt like a son-of-a— thing." She rubbed her face and brushed against her wound. "Ow."

"You are bleeding."

She looked at her hand. "Yeah." She grabbed the towel

she kept in her cubby and dabbed at her injury. Her gaze tracked across the console, then shifted to the view outside. "We're level." They hit a particularly bumpy stretch. "Relatively level. And almost out of fuel. What happens when we run out?"

"I hope we will continue gliding in."

She blinked. "This is gliding? I kinda thought gliding would be more...glide-y." She studied the controls for a few seconds more. "How—I don't even know what to ask."

"When the skimmer went into its spin," he hesitated, "some of the systems were apparently shaken into functionality." Would she believe that? Did she make it happen? If she were acting, she did it very well. As well as she kissed—

Her eyes studied him. "Really? Which ones?"

"Attitude control and boost."

"Boost?" Now her eyes rounded with surprise. "Boost? They told me it didn't anymore. And I missed it."

"You did not miss that much. It was brief." And painful. He looked away, unable to sustain her gaze. It felt wrong to distrust her, but Lurch had logic on his side. It would be much easier to mess with their systems from inside. Though risky to do if it believed Lurch lived in Joe.

It has demonstrated a high degree of comfort with risk.

"Boost depleted most of our fuel, but enabled us to break free of the storm." Though it would not be long before the storm caught up with them again.

"That's the airport. We're almost there." She leaned

toward it, as if that would assist her view, then studied their current flight path and fuel supply. "We won't make it."

"We might make it as far as one of the old runways."

She looked a bit hopeful again. "They were maintained longer than the rest of the city following the raising. I remember my Grand Paw Paw telling a story about coming down here to see an air show when he was a kid." Her brow creased. "Still a long time, long enough for *crapeau* to happen."

"How closely do you believe the upper port resembles the layout of the old?" She shook her head, shrugging at the same time. "Can you locate the compass? I lost it when—"

"Sorry about that."

"I do not believe anyone could have retained control in those circumstances." Did he believe that? Would it have risked the loss of control if it lived in Vi? How far was it willing to go to destroy Lurch?

If it destroyed me here, the repercussions would be most serious.

But— Joe couldn't wrap his brain around that, not at this moment.

"I am not nearly as impressed with my piloting skills as I used to be," she said a bit ruefully. She started to look around, then stopped. "I wonder if there is a compass in my pack?" She dug through the contents and held up the compass with a triumphant smirk. "I knew we needed both kits."

"You were correct."

"Wow, a guy who will admit a girl's right. I might have

to kiss you again if we don't die."

Joe's heart leapt in his chest, followed by a negative from the nanite. His smile went from glad to stiff again. "Then let us find out which direction we are currently traveling."

Her smile faltered, and there might have been a flare of hurt in her eyes, but she turned to the compass before he could be sure. In a moment, she said, "If that is north, then we're flying west."

She looked out and down, and hastily strapped back in. She tried the console and pulled up the city map in the database. She zoomed in on the upper port. Looking at it, then peering ahead at the approaching airport. "Obviously they've had to expand and change it to accommodate the advances in technology. That's like the sad, bad shadow of what we have now. Up above, there are arrival lanes here and here...."

She fell silent. Her gaze flicked back and forth between screen and outside view. Finally she sighed.

"There's no way to know for sure, but there's sort of a long T between the docking buildings. They might be long enough to have been runways." She frowned. "Back then planes used air and stuff, didn't they? So wind direction and speed would matter?"

"I believe you are correct," Joe said, though he was certain it was so, thanks to Lurch, whose database of knowledge was vast.

"Then those might be what we need. They looked like they were laid out for that. Of course, the problem is finding one of them. We'll only have one shot at it. When we lost our uplink with the tracking sensors...."

Joe had a thought. "Try a love tap." If Lurch's enemy wanted them to continue the game, perhaps it would help again.

Or perhaps Vi will make it happen. Perhaps her love taps are nanite assistance.

Joe ignored the interjection.

She gave him a skeptical look, but tried it. Twice. Was about to try again, when it flickered to life. "Well, I'll be...I don't suppose communications is working—nope. If the equipment weren't such *crapeau*, I'd start to wonder if someone was sabotaging us." She half laughed. "Of course, if they were, the systems wouldn't start working again. All this is messing with my head. Not a good time to get paranoid."

Was this a diversion or honest confusion. Her detective instincts hadn't been wholly subsumed. If not for the crisis, she'd have followed her instincts. If she were herself.

"Houston, we have a dot again." She gave him course adjustment information.

He managed it, though barely. His ability to steer the bulky skimmer was limited. Either with help or by the grace of fortune, they were almost lined up on what might be a runway.

It wants us to land.

Which begged the question, what was down there?

Expect the unexpected.

Joe had a better grasp on what that meant, though he

had not made much progress in doing it.

"Oh *crapeau*."

A tumble of debris, not unlike that of I-10, was directly in their path.

It is I-10. Or rather the old off ramp for the airport.

"Will we make it over it?"

"I do not know." He eased back, and got a fuel exhausted alert. Vi shut the alarm off. He could not be sure, but it seemed like an updraft boosted them the last few feet over the debris. The updraft left them as abruptly as it had helped and they dropped quickly. Joe tried to wrestle their nose around, tried to line up on the shadow of what might be the hoped-for runway....

☙❧

SOMETHING HAD COOLED JOE'S JETS ON KISSES. MAYBE he hadn't liked it that much. Seemed to like it. And why was she thinking about kissing right now? Because it distracted from the rapidly approaching crash? *Shallow, thy name is Violet.*

Ahead, the ground looked flat and straight, though it was probably an illusion, since it was basically a carpet of green. A bumpy carpet of green. Just great. The only thing that had gone right today—the kiss—apparently hadn't gone that right. So why break a losing streak? Just before impact, Vi closed her eyes and braced. This time, her life tried to pass before her eyes. It was fast and pretty boring.

The jolt came a few seconds after she'd expected.

The skimmer bounced up, hit the ground again, rushing forward. With no engine, they had no braking thrust, so no way to stop except—yeah, by hitting things. Now that they were on the ground, she could see the bumps better. So far, the skimmer was winning the weight-to-size battle. At least the impacts were slowing them down.

Just not enough.

If anyone had abandoned something big down here—

They had.

The skimmer spun around whatever it was, careening toward a cement pillar. Vi closed her eyes again. Didn't have to see it to feel when they hit....

⚜

THIS WOULD BE THE SECOND TIME VI WAS SURPRISED to wake up not dead. Or was it the third? They'd lurched through so many crises, counting was currently not in her skill set.

"Ow." She once again struggled to sit up. The skimmer had not fared well during the double whacking. The blunt nose was cracked like an egg, steam rising from the exposed innards. The view screen was cracked across and her hatch bowed in just inches short of her sling. Joe's hatch had been knocked off its track and lay on the ground, half covered in wet green slime. Beyond it she saw what they'd hit. Saw it, but had no clue what it might be. It had four, squat, wheel-like appendages just visible above the grass line. There looked to be an open cockpit on one side with a steering wheel and what might be a sling for a driver. Extending up from it at an angle was a longer, also flat ramp-ish thing with supports on its underside.

Joe began to stir, but a whine from behind distracted her from checking on him. *Fido.* He was trapped behind the prisoner screen. Great, now she was guilty of witness abuse. The screen hadn't auto opened, not a surprise with no power. She managed to release her straps, not without pain, and found the emergency release. The screen hissed up and Fido leaped over the back, then over Joe, and scampered off, water splashing as its paws sunk into the soggy grasses.

"You're welcome!" she called after it. Bang went her witness, soon to be followed by her corpse and her skimmer. The headache felt here to stay. They had found the NOO port, but had no idea how to get in. All she could see from her seat was green, dotted with more of those things they'd hit. Come to think of it, they'd probably hit them, too. She blinked. The grass appeared to be disappearing. It couldn't—

Storm surge. According to the news vids, it would appear to rise slowly, but would rapidly increase as the storm moved inland. Tide and direction would also affect its speed and depth.

"Joe, we've got to get out of here." She bent and started stuffing everything she could find that had fallen out of the packs during their messy landing. Who knew what they'd need out there. For once in her life she blessed the regs.

And would the world end because she'd had that thought? She shoved a pack at him, meeting his groggy look with her urgent one. "Undo your straps," she ordered, "And put your pack on."

She shrugged hers on, then started over the console, pushing him with her hand. "Move!"

Water breached the edge of the skimmer. Oh yeah, it was starting into the fast phase. He turned and jumped out. He turned, holding out a hand to steady her as she clambered out. Then his hand jerked back, like her touch burned. Great. Kiss a guy and they get all weird. *It was a kiss, not a marriage proposal.* It's not like it was that great of a kiss. Okay, it was, but she would deny it to her dying breath. Which would be any minute now if they didn't get high ASAP.

Because her heart kind of hurt, and the panic wasn't helping, she looked around. Still no sign of an access point that she could see. A ramp sagged from the building over them, but even if Joe boosted her, she couldn't reach it, which he wouldn't since he had trouble touching her at the moment. The water was rising fast enough she felt the push of current against her legs.

Okay, what were their other options?

There was the skimmer roof. It was barely higher than her head. They were predicting twenty-foot-plus surge. She wasn't twenty feet tall.

That left that weird thing they'd hit. Had no clue if it was high enough, but it was higher than her head, which at the moment was good enough.

"That way." She nudged Joe and pointed.

Their jog to it was about as fun as their slog through the cemetery. The water kept pace with them, bringing all kinds of debris that banged into their legs. So she wouldn't think about possible displaced critters or floating balls of fire ants, she looked at Joe. He looked at her, and they both picked up their pace. Maybe. It felt like she tried harder. Hopefully any gators would be too worried to stop for a snack....

When they reached the thing, Joe jumped up and tested its stability. It wasn't great. Their hit hadn't helped its structural integrity a whole lot, but the water was rising past her thighs now. He reached down and pulled her up beside him. The water followed them, lapping across the platform.

"You first," Joe said.

She nodded. Like everything down here, it was coated with green slime and the steep angle made it hard to climb. The surface under the slime was smooth, but there were ridges she could push her fingers into. She climbed until she clung to the rounded top edge. It had shaken a little, but held firm. She looked down at Joe.

"Come on."

"I don't think it will hold both of us."

"If you don't come up, then I'll come down." She meant it, even if he didn't like kissing her. The water was lapping at his knees now. "Come on. I can make it an order." She was senior to him. And she did not want to be left to die alone. That might be selfish, but it was what it was.

He hesitated, looked around as if another option would present itself. Nothing did. He started up, though he paused at each ridge to see if the thing would begin to tip from the addition of his weight. He stopped one section below her.

"You might as well come all the way up," she said dryly, resisting the urge to tell him she wouldn't bite. Which reminded her—there was no sign of Fido from this vantage point. If the mutt knew a way in and hadn't tried to help them— "Stupid dog," she muttered. She looked down. "Is that a fish?"

Joe followed her gaze. "I believe so."

The fish—a truly ugly fish—got stuck partway on their thing. It flopped several times, then the water rose and lifted it off again. To the west, or what she presumed was west, dark clouds bulged toward them, lightning flashes dimly lighting up the edges of WTF. Pale light filtered down, as if the sun was having its last hurrah. She didn't want to, but found herself studying the water around for signs of nasty *crapeau* as it rose toward them with a persistence she might have admired under different circumstances.

"Perhaps we should examine a pack for any item that might assist?" Joe suggested.

"Unless there is an inflatable boat in there—"

His brows rose.

"—fine." She squirmed until her back was to him. "See

what you can find." She felt tugs as he dug through it. How long could she hold on? She'd started this with tired arms. The air was thick and clammy and her teeth started to chatter. Shock? Probably. Supposed to get her feet above her head, but that wasn't going to happen. She'd thought she'd be glad to be a little cooler, but she wasn't. It felt nasty instead of better.

"Look," he said. She glanced back. He held a flat package. "It says flotation arm bands. And I believe these will provide light for—" he held it up and read, "—six hours."

"In six hours, we'll be in deep—stuff. And you know light attracts bugs."

"It might also attract people." He looked back towards the building.

She followed his gaze. Would the dirt-siders try to help them? Could they?

"Flotation." She looked at him, then down at the package, then back at him. "Do you really want to go floating around in that?" She nodded toward the debris-filled water. It was probably loaded with floating fire ant balls. She'd been bitten by them. You couldn't grow up in NON and not get bitten by fire ants. Had no desire to get swarmed by a ball of them.

"We may have no choice. As you said, deep stuff is incoming. If the current is strong enough—"

As if to help make his point, the thing moved. Only about an inch. But it moved.

"Let me dig through your pack while you start blowing."

❧ 6 ❧

"I wonder what this thing is?" Vi asked, looking down at her uncertain perch. She'd found something called a Bungee in her pack and rigged a sort of seat belt to take the pressure off her arms and hands. Sitting on top of the ramp did not ease the ache in her back, but the pack had also contained some mild painkillers. The stale water had tasted better this time. Thirst definitely helped school the taste buds. They both wore the flotation devices on their arms. They'd turned out to have automatic inflation capability that only half worked. At least they hadn't had to blow as long. The crash seems to have disabled their hand protection, which was yet more *crapeau*. Water had risen to just below their boots, where their legs hung off the end of the ramp, but its rising had slowed considerably. That didn't mean it wouldn't top this thing, but hope, well, it had a way of rising, too.

It was good to be out of the water for now. Not that

great being up where the debris flew around—and into—them. Most of it just thumped into their backs and so far their helmets provided some protection from the stuff that thumped a little harder against their heads. Bruising was not optional, unfortunately.

"Based on where it is and its configuration," Joe said, "I suspect it was designed to aid in moving items up off the ground. Travel gear perhaps?"

That made sense. They'd had a chance to study the underside while working out the Bungee seat belts. It seemed to be on a belt system that had been designed to move in a circular fashion. Thankfully it no longer had that capability. She had no desire to be rotated down into the water before she absolutely had to. They sat with their backs to the storm. They hadn't talked about it, but Vi figured he wasn't any more excited about watching their fate rush toward them than she was. They weren't hiding from it. They were perched on a piece of equipment that moved every now and again. There was no hiding. The touch of denial? Well, what else did they have to do? It was kind of boring waiting to die.

If Joe had had commitment panic over the kiss, he appeared to have gotten over it. It wasn't like they had a long future ahead of them unless something changed drastically really fast. She had her hand on one end of her Bungee. If this thing started to go down, she did not want to be strapped to it. She wasn't ashamed to admit that she'd practiced getting loose several times. A minute.

Light was fading fast as the storm made what she guessed was the predicted turn both north and east. A sliver of light filtered through like a beacon of hope. A false beacon, she told herself, but still felt a measure of peace from it. They'd done everything they could. Maw Maw Nature didn't fight fair, though—she half frowned—if some things hadn't gone right once or twice she'd have wondered if Maw Maw N hadn't had a little help. But why would anyone hose, then help, them? It's not like there was a front row seat to this dark comedy. Because it was kind of funny to think about what they must look like perched up here on this contraption in a sea of green who-knew-what. Or worse—a sea of she-suspected-she-knew-what. From here their field of green was dotted with slime-coated objects of varying heights. Some could have been semi-collapsed, old buildings. There were the remains of a control tower—she knew this from Grand Paw Paw's old vids. They'd been lucky not to hit more *crapeau* as they came in. Though they'd hit a fair enough amount to bang the skimmer into scrap.

It was completely submerged. Never again would some new detective have to pass through its trial-by-dysfunction. She'd have liked to say good-bye because she earned a better one, not because the old girl went down in WTF.

"It fought the good fight," she muttered and got a surprised look from Joe. "The skimmer. It wasn't a bad little piece of *crapeau*." It wasn't a good little piece of *crapeau* either. She sighed. "I think I'm going to miss it."

"Not for very long," Joe said in his most Joe Friday tone.

"I kind of wish we'd died in the crash. I've never been that patient." The chance that anyone would find their bodies was about a million to one. No closure for her family. Captain Uncle would feel bad, too. She wished there was a way to leave them a message. A last good-bye. With only a little guilt attached for Captain Uncle. Because she loved him when he wasn't chewing her butt off.

"While there is breath, there is hope."

It was that painful period while there wasn't breath that she wasn't looking forward to. She held her breath and then decided that was stupid. Might as well breathe while she could. A tree branch or something slammed into her, hard enough to unseat her if she hadn't been Bungee'd to the thing, which shifted enough to make her wonder if it wanted them gone, too.

"When it goes over, swim toward the end of the building," Joe said, raising his voice to be heard over the building wind. "Don't give up."

She looked at him, her lips opened on a smart response, but closed them at the look in his eyes. She nodded.

It shifted again, half turning so that they faced the building now. Vi studied it, hoping to spot something entrance-like. If their dirt-siders had used this side for their comings and goings, it didn't show. Or it was already under water.

"Unhook your cord," Joe said, looking in the direction of WTF.

The rate of debris pummeling increased. Dirt side had a lot of debris to fling around. Another reason to not like it. The wind force increased and rain drops slapped against the surface of the water, pocking the sea of green goo. She tried to decide what it smelled like, but couldn't, other than dead and not-dead. And something nice from Joe. She unhooked one end, but held onto the cord. This time she said, though she didn't look at him as she said it, "It's been a pleasure working with you, Joe."

"For me as well." A pause. "When it begins to go over, try to jump away from it."

"Sure. No problem." She had a leap or two left in her...dreams.

It moved again, this time turning them to face the incoming storm. She dropped her face shield but couldn't stop raising her arm to protect her face, even though that hurt. She couldn't see incoming and not try. She'd thought it was bad flying in that bad boy—or was it a bad girl? She considered the names and couldn't decide.

The wind began to build, acquiring a sort of rising howl—

She frowned. "That isn't the wind." She looked back. Against the last sliver of the setting sun, she saw a pirogue being poled toward them. On it was a man and a— "It's Fido! He came back for us!"

As if it had been waiting for the moment of maximum, their thing began to tip toward the murky water....

As soon as Joe felt the belt loader—its name according to Lurch's database—begin to tip forward, he spun around, stretching full length along the upside, with his legs hanging down to try to offset the tip forward. He grasped Vi's belt with one hand, the Bungee with the other. He believed he had failed, but it slowly settled back in place. He felt its lack of permanence, however. Felt the slight shifts from the force of the current. It would not hold this position for long. And the water appeared to still be rising. The wind increased as well, throwing debris at them with careless abandon.

"Looks like a homemade pirogue."

"A pee row?"

Vi grinned down at him. "A flat boat."

The figure on the admittedly flat boat showed signs it was difficult poling the craft against the current. The rain picked up, as did the wind, which had to increase the level of difficulty for the pilot. Debris pelted him as well. Fido barked encouragement. Or mockery. The canine had not appeared to approve of Joe. If it had returned, it had done it for Vi.

This rescue is not something Vi could have contrived.

Lurch indicated something that could have meant anything but managed to fall short of actual agreement.

"It is not logical to be out here in this," Joe said, sliding further down the ramp to stop it from falling forward, the water now over his knees.

"Whoever it is probably thinks it's Fido's owner that is stranded out here."

Joe considered this. "They may not be pleased to see us. Or to learn that he is deceased."

"We should get on board before we tell him," she agreed.

The belt loader shifted more, and the water edged higher. Rays of sun flickered fitfully on the surface of the water, as if hope held out its hand at last. It would become increasingly difficult to leave this location as the storm moved closer. It was entirely possible that Lurch's enemy had already fled. It could have had transport hidden somewhere close. There were craft that could fly through the storm, particularly craft with capabilities boosted by a resourceful—and evil intentioned—nanite. It made little sense to Joe for it to linger here, unless it still believed that Joe hosted Lurch. Was it truly that reckless?

For several seconds it appeared as if the pilot would turn back, but his problem must have been a struggle against a stronger current, because the boat began to draw close, even as they experienced another, longer, current-caused shift of the belt loader. The water level was creeping up his legs when the boat bumped against the side of the belt loader.

"Hurra," the boat driver said, holding position with obvious difficulty. He winced as a large piece of debris struck him.

Joe grasped the side of the boat and helped Vi onto the unsteady surface, then lowered himself onto the deck, just as the belt loader went over with a wake that almost capsized them. Joe hastily sat next to Vi, grasping the low sides of the dubiously constructed boat. Fido lay his head in her lap and looked at her with what Joe assumed was canine affection. Vi patted his mud-crusted head, then rolled her eyes at Joe.

Now the pilot let the current help, using the pole to steer them past water-logged debris, clearly on a course that would take them around the building.

"Where's Bazoo?" the man asked, abruptly, his expression grim.

"He's dead," Vi said, perhaps made confident in the face of Fido's acceptance. Would their witness take sides in a dispute? There was more that could be told, but like Vi, Joe was not eager to tell the tale until they were in better cover. The wind pushed them now, too, in addition to flinging debris at them, and the rain stung where it hit the bare skin of his hands.

"What ya doing out here in this?" He grunted as he steered the boat around the end of the massive structure.

"We, um, came to rescue you." Vi admitted, giving him a wry, though cautious grin.

He could still dump them in the water.

The old man gave a semi-toothless grin followed by a snorting laugh. He was an unattractive specimen. Weathered to the point of gaunt. Dirt instead of hair. Lots of dirt —except where the rain turned it to mud—on him and on his ragged clothing. The tooth deficit. But the eyes were bright and intelligent beneath fiercely bushy brows. The amusement didn't fade when their gazes connected. There was another pole clamped to the bottom of the boat. Joe looked at it, mostly to look away from a gaze that appeared to know his thoughts, then at the man.

"Do you require assistance?"

"Ya ever steered a flat boat, laddie?" Joe had to shake his head. "I doubt ya'd like getting dumped in the drink if ya tried."

"How long has it been since you saw...Bazoo?" Vi asked.

Joe recalled Vi had not spoken the man's name at the cemetery, just identified him as a dirt-sider. Joe suspected it was not his real name.

"Matter of several days, I guess. He was worried about Little Bit, but she turned up here without him." He scowled. "Said she hadn't seen him, now I think on't."

Once around the building, it was a struggle to move the boat against the current; plus waves came at them from the water interacting with the structures. And even more debris. The man was stronger than he appeared, however. In light almost gone, Joe saw a sort-of ramp rising out of the water between the two large structures. One he guessed would have been the terminal building, based on the glass-less gaps where windows used to be. The other was an odd, layered structure.

A parking garage for land vehicles.

That would be why a bridge extended from an upper floor to connect the two structures. Everything was coated in green, including the ramp that their pilot steered for.

Low walls with broken gaps marked the line of the ramp up out of the water, possibly the route for those land vehicles, Joe supposed. Their pilot poled the boat wide, perhaps to avoid getting caught on the walls, then turned it between the wall line and headed in.

Joe saw two people emerge from the left, edging down the ramp into the water as the boat approached. Fido gave a happy bark and jumped off, splashing all of them with filthy water. The dirt-siders did not seem to notice or care. The heavy rain failed to wash away their dirt, so perhaps they were what was known as "weathered." Or of darker skinned descent. There were a few lightly brown skinned people among the Garradians, but the trend had been toward green and purple skin. Joe's lighter tint was an aberration caused by some of his ancestors mating with some women of Earth. No one here knew he shared some of their blood. It was, as Lurch liked to think, not need-to-know.

Vi clambered over the side into the knee deep water, so Joe followed suit, assisting the others to drag the boat up the ramp. They did not stop until it was somewhat under cover of the overhang. One of them produced a ragged rope and tied it to the frame of a broken window. Joe looked back, noting the waterline was only a couple of feet from the top of the ramp. It did not seem a secure mooring, but he conceded they did not have much choice until the water lifted the boat high enough to move inside.

"Was getting worried about you, Jimbo," the large woman said, her voice raised to be heard over the wind and crash of debris against the buildings. She studied Vi, then Joe, her heavy brows arching. "Where'd you pick these two up? Where's Bazoo?"

"They's here to rescue us," Jimbo said, with a grin that quickly faded. "Bazoo be dead. According to these two."

He turned without waiting for their reaction, leading them into the structure through a gap in the frame where an entrance had probably existed, based on its shape and disposition. The wind and rain followed them in, though the structure provided some protection from the worst of it. It also helped with the debris, but the sound of it hitting outside did not give much comfort. Joe looked around. Being inside was not as much of an improvement as he'd hoped. A long dank hall extended off one side, with a wide, dank space in the other. They walked through an ankle-deep, muddy muck that he did not desire to examine. The walls were green and black and reeked of mildew and mold, a smell the wind swirled around them, rather than clearing out. Mold was not healthy, but drowning would kill them faster.

With the water rising, it was possible they shared this structure with displaced wildlife. There was nothing to keep anything out. Out of the corner of his eye, Joe saw Vi's hand move to rest casually, almost by accident, on her weapon. A small flick released the strap holding it in place. Joe duplicated her move though less casually. He would have kept it deployed if he could have without giving offense. As the moved deeper inside, he noticed what could have been the sagging remains of furniture. Counters lined the back wall. The vague outlines of companies that looked somewhat like those still in service up above. Something new filtered into the mold and mildew. Gumbo? He sniffed with some caution and decided that was what it had to be. He loved New Orleans New gumbo and had smelled it often.

"We found his body in Nawlins One." Vi's gaze flicked between the three faces. "Then were heading this way to offer assistance when the storm caught up with us faster than we expected." She waited while they processed this, before adding, "I'm Vi, and this is Joe." A lift of her brows and her smile eased the sudden tension some. "We're real sorry about your friend."

She looked at Jimbo, her brows arched in a question. Joe found it interesting that her speech patterns had altered, edged with a hint of the Cajun intonations.

"Jimbo." His tone was sardonic, but not hostile. Yet. "Felonius." He nodded toward a wizened old man, his skin so wrinkled, his face looked flattened. Black eyes peered out from beneath impressively bushy brows. "And that's Speed Bump."

The large woman gave a short nod, her gaze still suspicious. Her hair had been trimmed close to her head. It had a pleasing shape, denoting intelligence. The rest of her diluted that denoting.

"You mentioned Little Bit?" Vi said, mildly, looking around.

"She don't like thunder," the one called Felonius said.

"She be watching the gumbo," Speed Bump added.

"No one else has been down asking for us?" Vi asked, like she was curious, not worried.

"Storm be hitting the city fierce." Felonius' dark eyes did not appear to blink.

"No aircraft passed over?" Joe asked. He kept the question casual, though the answer mattered to him at least. If it had already left, then it wasn't in someone here. His gaze slid toward Vi. He was sure she wasn't it. A feeling from Lurch called him on the lie. Lurch had done nothing to reveal himself that Joe could discern, including not healing Joe's injuries. If it was looking for proof, it would need to up its game some more. Or concede that Lurch was not present.

"Not we know 'bout." Jimbo studied him, then turned without speaking, heading toward what might have been a stairway. "It'll be drier up here."

The others followed. Vi exchanged a glance with Joe, then shrugged and followed. No one objected vocally to their presence, but Joe didn't assume they were welcome. This was a closed system. He started up, surprised to find the steps were not even in height or width.

It would have been a moving staircase, called an escalator.

It felt a bit like a mountain to climb after everything that had happened. He hadn't stood down exactly, but felt alert status trickle away at the fading of immediate danger. Vi's shoulders were less straight and she used the dirty hand rail to climb, lifting each foot as if they'd increased in weight. Since water sloshed in his shoes, they may well have. He'd probably sweated off all the water he'd drunk for days inside the gear, so it was probably adding extra weight, as well. It wasn't something like dread dragging him down. Dread that Vi had been invaded by it. Because if she had, she was the walking dead. It had never left a host alive when it moved on.

Lurch had taken care to respect Joe's personality and rights during its integration with him. His enemy had shown no such regard. Autopsies of previous hosts showed signs of violent integration and painful death when it chose to leave it.

If it is inside Vi, the kindest thing you can do for her is end it quickly.

I don't believe she is the one.

You do not wish to believe.

There was no answer to this. It was also true that he'd never been in its presence, so he did not know what to look for, what to expect from one of its hosts.

As they reached the next level, what light there was from outside faded. Vi flicked on her gear light and looked around, her light traveling over walls where small rivulets of water made paths in the green and blackened walls. The smaller streams turned into heavier channels where the trash-littered floors slanted street-wards. The whole structure seemed to shudder as the wind outside ramped up. The smell was most unpleasant, despite the gumbo.

Ahead of them, Jimbo led the way toward an inner room lit only by a small glow.

"I am not certain your boat is high enough to be

secure," Joe said. "They are predicting water levels of twenty-five *plus* feet." They'd come up the ramp and the stairs and were probably high enough if the roof held, but the ramp had been close to covered when they left it. That rope would surely not be enough when the wind hit Cat 5 velocities.

Jimbo hesitated, but Felonius spoke. "I'll take care of it."

If the water was higher, it would be easy for him to move it on his own, Joe concluded. He did not wish to leave Vi alone with these people. Or these people alone with Vi? The thought was not comfortable. The old man moved with a spryness not consistent with his apparent age. They could all be younger than they looked. Exposure to sun caused premature aging to the skin.

Vi began to move around the gumbo room, studying walls that also dripped, though somewhat less than the outer room. She stopped when she reached Little Bit.

Joe stopped as well. This Little Bit was not little. She was disturbing. She sat silently in front of the source of heat and light, stirring a pot. Her hair was wild and tangled. Her eyes provided the only color for her entire aspect. They were light grey and as wild as her hair. He caught her staring at him, though she looked away when Fido padded over and stuck his nose in her, well, he greeted her in a canine manner. Joe almost sighed. Not only did they have strange names, they all had mannerism that could most adequately disguise an ill-intentioned nanite. Vi was the most normal person in the room.

Which makes her a suspect. A pause. *I am sorry.*

He'd had many black moments this day and was, to his surprise, still standing. He would hope until there was no more hope.

Or it uses your fondness for Vi to kill you. If it does inhabit her, she is already gone.

And that is why I believe you are wrong. It was the truth. He did not believe she was gone, did not believe it could mimic Vi even with access to her brain, access so completely that Joe didn't feel the difference. She was... unique. All Lurch had was a kiss and a coincidence. *It could have planted a virus in the skimmer while we were at the crime scene.*

But how did it get back here ahead of us?

We do not know it is here. It could be monitoring us from anywhere.

There was no way to know, because Lurch did not dare attempt a wireless connection until they identified a host for it, or they were once more shielded by normal connection activity in the upper city. Joe's gaze followed Vi around the room. While this structure appeared solid and had endured for a long time, he lacked confidence in their ability to survive WTF from this location. An epic storm and an evil genius nanite were not good odds.

Our odds were never great. But we must try.

Lurch spoke the truth. Its enemy had no boundaries, did not care who it hurt. They, on the other hand, must do as little harm as possible. *The impossible takes longer?* Joe quoted Lurch and got a chuckle out of him that felt like someone tickling his insides. Almost he smiled, but his gaze once more encountered Little Bit's. He shivered, despite the intense heat. His money was on her for evil nanite host.

LITTLE BIT WAS ONE SCARY LOOKING DIRT-SIDER, VI decided. Her flat, gray gaze was like all Vi's teachers and Captain Uncles rolled into one. It took Vi's signature Look offline, like it had never been, never would be again. Vi got her back against a damp wall and kept her hand close to her weapon while she studied the other dirt-siders. Seemed likely one of them had taken out Bazoo. Little Bit had not been with the others until yesterday, so that made her a prime suspect. Though Vi didn't know how she'd managed to shield the body and get back here. And if Fido really was a witness, it wasn't Little Bit, unless the dog was in on it. Which it could be. If Vi were the dog, she'd be pissed about being called Fido. When your name was Bazoo, there was no excuse for Fido.

She'd have liked to talk to Joe, get his take on this motley crew, but there was a chill wind coming from him since the kiss. She half frowned, not from the kiss, but soon after. Maybe it took a while for his commitment phobia to kick in. Which meant he had liked the kiss? And got scared? Didn't matter how far society evolved, guys stayed skittish about girls making moves. At least this made her feel slightly better about her kissing technique.

Jimbo seemed to be the big dog, if one eliminated Fido. One couldn't when the pooch had saved their lives. He stayed with Little Bit, but seemed to watch her with doggy devotion. *Don't get attached,* she thought, *my apartment is not pet friendly.* If it was still up there.

Storm be hitting the city fierce.

So as not to think about that, Vi studied Jimbo. He'd also made sure his back was to a wall. Speed Bump drifted over by him, her arms crossed like a protective mama. Or girlfriend? That was kind of not fun to think about. Grand Paw Paw would have given her a love tap to the back of her head for not wanting to think it. He liked to say that youth —and love—were wasted on the young. At the moment, she could not disagree with him. He had Grand Maw Maw and all Vi had was some dubious devotion from Fido. She'd even run off the alien.

The thick walls muffled, but did not shut out, the wild howl of the wind, the bang of debris, and the rain hammering against what was left of the roof. If this was the eye wall moving in, then it was getting to the part where WTF lived up to its acronym. They might be lucky enough to get the eye, then WTF would pound them from the other direction unless help arrived.

She tried to think back to what she recalled from the weather updates. The data had come late, but that didn't make it not real. She made an air map of Louisiana, then drew in the storm with what she could remember from that last uplink and what she thought had happened. The eye wasn't big in a bad storm, but NON or NOO, up or down, it wasn't that big. She played it a few times inside her head, then sighed. Even if they were lucky enough to get the eye, they'd have to survive the eye wall first.

Joe drifted closer. "Are you all right?" A crease furrowed his brows.

"Was thinking, if we got the eye, Captain Uncle could send someone down." If they could spare something. And they were still there. She figured things must be so bad up top that no one had come down yet. That, and they only had a few craft that could handle the high winds adequately. When this was over would the budget priorities change or would someone make the case that this wasn't likely to happen for another fifty years so...yeah, probably that one.

In the meantime, they needed to try to stay alive for the duration of the storm. They had their 72'r packs with *crapeau* food and water for themselves. She itched to take off the flotation things but didn't dare. Floating was not yet out of the question. The kits wouldn't go far if this bunch hadn't set something aside besides gumbo.

She could be grateful she wasn't dead and still wish for a not-gross place to sit down. Did that make her shallow? She crouched, shining her light on the floor and wished she hadn't. It was beyond gross and wet. The wall was slightly less so, so she leaned against it, feeling waves of tired pass through her. She might be able to sleep standing up. If she weren't too scared to close her eyes. Right now this little band of scary was united against them. Maybe she should introduce a little discord and see what shook out. One of them had to be their killer. If Bazoo had been murdered. Which they weren't likely to ever find out since Bazoo would soon be one with critters of the bayou. She wouldn't bother, but she needed a reason to stay awake.

"So, you've all been here together for the past week?" She managed to summon a bit of her Look, though it felt seriously off its game. "Well, except for Little Bit."

Speed Bump puffed up, her akimbo arms getting more so. "What you saying?"

"Well, someone did for Bazoo." Vi used their term for a killing, and softened her accent as she let her gaze travel to each one of them before saying, "When did ya'all see him last?"

"Told you, matter o'days," Jimbo said, a hint of grim in his voice. Vi's brow arched and he added, "Mebbe four, mebbe five."

"Five," Speed Bump put in. "Said he had business, but he'd be back afore storm hit."

"Business?" Joe sounded surprised and she scowled.

"We has some. On occasion."

"No one's been doing much business ahead of the storm, 'cept for storm supplies," Vi added. "Was that his business?"

"Don't know." Speed Bump sounded sullen.

"Anyone?" Jimbo shook his head. Little Bit just looked at her. Did she talk? Did Vi care? Not that she could do a lot here, other than try not to get done for, too. She looked at her watch and realized something. "Felonius has been gone a long time."

Jimbo started a bit and looked around, as if he hadn't noticed or had forgotten him. He scowled again. But he had saved them, she reminded herself. If he had secrets to bury all he'd had to do was leave them for the storm. The air felt thick with something. It could be WTF, but it felt like more. She glanced at Joe. His gaze seemed to be making a circuit between the motley crew and Vi. He jerked a bit and looked away. He didn't—distrust *her*, did he? What, did he think she'd sabotaged their skimmer for some alone time with him? Did he think she was a crazy stalker girl?

She lowered her lashes, watching him. Sure enough, she was in his gaze circuit and just as long as the others. Okay, now she was pissed. That's why her chest hurt like it had been punched. Because they were partners. It was them against crazy. Not—

She realized her hands were clenched. Her eyes stung, but she was not crying over the jerk. She was tired and sitting dirt side in an epic storm, and she was worried about her family and she'd banged her head. Not her heart.

Jimbo straightened, his scowl deepening to a worried frown. "Gonna go help Felonius." Fido rose as well, his tail wagging. He trotted out ahead, as if he knew the mission and was on it.

"I'll go with you," Vi offered.

"Let's all go," he suggested.

Speed Bump looked at Jimbo. He shook his head. "I'll stay with Lil' Bit," she said, not happily, worry taking the edge off belligerent.

Vi nodded and in that instant, Little Bit moved. With surprising speed for such a large woman she was on her feet and lunging toward them with a huge, carving knife. Training helped. And that her weapon was already unstrapped. She pulled it and backed, firing once. Joe did, too. Little Bit staggered, but kept coming. They both fired again. This time she stopped, swaying in place. She looked surprised. Her hand lost its grip, and the knife clattered against the hard floor. She clutched her chest, gave a half cry and fell forward on her face.

Joe covered her with his weapon while Vi approached from the other side, her weapon also ready. Little Bit shuddered and cried out again, like a wild animal in pain. Something bright, like tiny sparks of energy flickered against her skin, then faded away as Little Bit quit moving. Vi directed her gear light along the body. There were spots on her hands and face, spots like Bazoo's. The look of horror was pretty close to Bazoo's, too.

"What's wrong?" Joe asked, stopping when he reached her side. His gaze met hers, a mix of puzzled and relieved in their dark depths.

Why was he relieved?

7

Jimbo threw a dirty blanket over Little Bit, his expression closed. "Is this what killed Bazoo?"

Their obvious grief made Joe feel guilty, but relief overbore most of it. It couldn't have been Vi. She hadn't touched the woman. Joe felt worry emanating from Lurch like heartburn.

I am sorry, my friend, but this is not proof she is not infected.

He rubbed his chest surreptitiously. Tried to think of a rebuttal.

Both weapons were set to stun. That should not have been fatal. It killed her, but I do not believe it was in her.

Four shots on maximum stun, Joe reminded him. That had been their settings when aiming at the raccoon. He hadn't had time to change them. Didn't believe Vi had changed hers either.

"Until we can autopsy her, we won't know. He did

have similar spots on his body," Vi said. "If it was a virus, maybe it affected her brain." Her gaze met Speed Bump's without flinching. "Our weapons were set to stun. They didn't kill her."

"She had a bad ticker," Speed Bump admitted reluctantly. "Or so she said. Might a'been true."

The virus theory was something of a relief to all of them, Joe noted. It gave them an explanation to cling to in the face of the disturbing unknown. Everyone but Vi. He could see she was not comforted or relieved. And she kept her distance from him. He knew why. She'd sensed or seen him withdraw. This had damaged the trust between them. And he could do nothing to repair it until—

Do you think those flickering lights were it attempting to reach Vi? It might be an indication Vi had not been taken over.

Or it was another test designed to expose me.

Joe could make the case that Lurch was paranoid—and that he, Joe, was not paranoid enough. He sensed a flaw in the nanite's reasoning, but was too tired to disconnect the dots weaving together the case against Vi. He did not believe. Or he did not want to believe.

Where is Felonius?

Joe looked around. Little Bit had distracted them from that worry. Perhaps Fido had located him, still... "Where is Felonius?" Joe asked aloud. He did not ask about the canine. It was a relief to have it gone.

"We should go look for him," Speed Bump said. "He might be sick, too."

Vi did not look happy, but there was no reason she should.

"Joe and I can go look for him—"

"We will all go," Jimbo said.

He has trust issues.

He should. Joe had them, too.

After a pause, Vi nodded.

"You'd better let me go first," she said to Jimbo. "Joe will cover our rear."

It was procedure. He knew this, but felt troubled by it. And rejected. But he nodded, switched on his gear lamp and half raised his weapon. Neither Jimbo or Speed Bump objected to occupying the middle. No one spoke as they retraced their steps. It was too noisy. WTF's winds made the old structure shudder and sway. It slammed objects into it. The loud bangs also inhibited speech. If this world had begun with a Big Bang, it now seemed it might end with one.

Joe put his hand on the low wall by the escalator, to steady himself, and it crumbled from his touch. Vi had already started down, or he might have asked her to reconsider. Before his turn he did see something metal buried in the thick concrete. He told himself it helped. Because there was no safety high or low in this here and now.

He stepped on last, waiting until Speed Bump was almost down. He had to pause a couple of times for the swaying and creaking to stop. He fought back the urge to rush down and was surprised the escalator was still attached when he made it. There was ankle deep water inside now, though whether it had been blown in or was flooding in, he could not say with any certainty. Vi had not moved beyond the escalator yet. Instead, she used her gear light to try to scan the space, but it failed to penetrate far enough to be that helpful. It was evening, and they were deep in the storm's clouds.

"Joe, go right," she said, without looking at him. "I'll go left. You two stay here."

He started away from her, sloshing through the muck, but hadn't gone far when she gave a startled shout. He splashed over to the small circle of her light. It was Fido. He lay, not quite drifting in the rising water. There were singed holes dotted across its hide. His widened eyes indicating an unpleasant end.

Joe stared down, unable to formulate a comment for many seconds. *The canine did it?*

Or it was framed.

It framed the dog?

It does seem unlikely, Lurch admitted, his worry an uncomfortable addition to Joe's. It felt puzzled, so much so Joe wondered if he had heartburn medication in the 72'r kit. Could the canine have tampered with their skimmer? Joe experienced difficulty wrapping his mind around this thought.

*It could have flown it, had it wanted to. That is why I did not dare attempt repairs of any of the systems. It could have **been** the skimmer. Become one with it.*

"I've never heard of a virus that can be passed from

people to dogs." Vi kept her voice pitched to reach only him.

This was not difficult. The rain stopped with an abruptness he was becoming accustomed to. The wind eased some, too, though it did not improve enough to render their situation bearable. She looked at him, clear suspicion in her eyes. And worry. He understood both. They were trapped by the storm in a possible contagion zone. And he could not tell her that if it were so, that would be good news. The real news, the worse news, a megalomanic nanite was loose in her world. One that had almost wiped out the population of the last world it visited.

"It hasn't been that long." She frowned. "Maybe five minutes since Little Bit—"

The canine most likely infected her with drones when we arrived. You will recall it put its head—

I recall, Joe thought hastily, though he wished to forget.

They were probably triggered to react at the mention of Felonius.

Who is still missing. He could be it.

"Let's see if the boat's still there," Vi said, tiredly. She looked around. "I don't see any sign of Felonius. Though I'm not sure what would qualify as a sign."

The water continued to rise, though it was slower than when they'd been trapped on the belt loader. As they neared the place where the boat had been secured, he saw openings in the walls, as if the water had dug through the concrete, exposing the metal—

Rebar.

—that had been inserted to give it strength. *How secure is this structure?*

Are you certain you wish to know?

Lurch had a point. There was not a lot they could do about it if it collapsed. There was no high ground high enough—or secure enough—for this storm. That is why they'd been sent to evacuate these people. The scene outside was wild, even minus the rain. Most of the flying debris appeared to be tree branches, but it was hard to be certain. Other items passed too quickly for identification, assuming he'd recognize them if they passed slowly. Most debris was small, though it stung when it struck exposed skin. They sloshed over to where the boat had been tied. It was there, though the wind and current tugged fiercely at the rope. The wind was strong enough that they had to lean into it to hold their place and waves were high.

So Felonius never made it to the boat.

Or he'd been returning to seek help and run into the dog....

"If we're not in the eye wall, it has to be close!" Vi shouted to be heard. Their lights failed to penetrate the deep dark for very far, but lightning flashed against the horizon. She grabbed his arm, then let it go as if it burned her.

"I think someone is up there!" She pointed in the direction of the parking structure.

Joe looked, but saw nothing—lightning flashed again. "Felonius?"

"Who else could it be?"

She had a point—if they had all available information, which they did not.

"Why would he be over there?"

If it is my enemy, it might have some kind of escape craft **parked** *over there. Earlier the top level appeared open.*

Joe felt somewhat abashed. He should have thought of this.

"It does seem a bit eccentric," Vi said. "Maybe he thinks it's safer there. Or he is sick."

Jimbo and Speed Bump splashed over to them. Vi pointed at the top floor of the garage and gestured her question.

"What he doing there?" Speed Bump punctuated her shout with a frown.

"He must be sick, too!" Jimbo's wild brows drew together.

It could be a trap.

Only if they walked into it. Joe tried to think of a good reason to do that.

If there is a ship there...it will be one capable of flying in the storm.

That might be a good reason, assuming they could get from here to over there and get control of the ship. Which may or may not be a trap. Outside, what had been the ramp now looked like an unruly river. The tops of the wall lining it were barely visible as waves broke against and over them. The water was not flowing over the broken window frames yet, they were higher than the wall, which had stopped well before the front of the building. Water had breeched the interior, however, possibly seeping through the old seams or going in where the walls had fallen away.

"How did he get over there?" Joe shouted the question.

"There is a walkway that connects the buildings!" Jimbo used his chin to point where.

Joe had noticed the upper bridge when they arrived, but had forgotten about it. Was it made of the same materials as this crumbling building? In a lightning flash, he studied it and realized they would need to go back up the nearly collapsing escalator to get to it. Was that the route Felonius had taken or had the water been low enough for him to cross here? He could see an entrance point across the river of water. *This is insane.*

Probably. A pause. *It could be here watching us, to see what we will do.*

So we're back to Vi as it.

"If he sick like Little Bit, he need help," Speed Bump said, truculently.

"Storm's getting ready to smack us down again," Vi said. "If there's another break, we could try..."

Or hope they wouldn't have to, Joe presumed.

"I helped you," Jimbo reminded them.

Vi rubbed her face. "So you did." She looked at Joe.

That gives you a reason to go.

Were we looking for a reason? Joe did not remember that.

This is why we are here. If we lose it again...

So what's our plan? We do have a plan?

Right now the plan is to get it. If we can do that without dying then it is a good plan.

Joe understood that planning was difficult when there was so much they did not know. And the one thing he knew was not comforting. Get it. Kill it or die trying.

I have tried to reach it other ways. I am sorry.

Joe looked at Vi, seeing only her. How could he do this if—

"I believe we must try." he told her.

Vi's eyebrows lifted. It seemed long that she stared at him. Finally she nodded. Her expression seemed to say, "It is your death ceremony." But she shouted, "We should get across before that gets here then."

Joe could not argue with that. It looked like a dark, solid wall approaching.

❦

THEY HAD TO GET BACK TO THE SECOND FLOOR. It wasn't as easy this time. The building seemed to be dissolving around them. At the bottom of the weird stairs, Vi looked at Joe. She still couldn't believe he'd backed this craziness. It was very *not* Joe Friday. Maybe he had the virus, because it was insane.

"I'll go first. You'll want to keep an eye on me," she told him. He might have flushed. It was hard to tell in the uncertain light from her gear lamp. He opened his mouth and she shook her head sharply. "Later. If we're still alive."

He flinched. If they made it he *was* going to talk to her.

She turned and started up, wondering what she risked having him at her back. It was a new thought, an unwelcome one. Whatever was bothering him was bigger than commitment issues. Then she forgot Joe and his issues. The structure shuddered and chunks of cement fell off the upper floor, splashing into the murky water. She almost turned back then, but if the roof was coming down, no floor in this place was safe. She stowed her weapon, and used to her hands to climb as quickly as possible. It wasn't that fast. Gravity had a good grip on her, helped by being kicked to the curb and back all day.

She made it, was surprised about that. Didn't stop to wait for Joe. If he wanted to shoot her in the back, he'd have to keep up. Jimbo had said it was to the right up here. The sludge on the floors held more water than it had before. Her light picked up heavier streams coming down the walls. If the concrete was crumbling, that would not help. She waded through the sludge, using her light to find the entrance to that walkway. Doors, minus their glass, sagged off the sides. Pieces of metal poked up out of the sludge, too. The rain hadn't started up again, but the wind had   let-me-make-your-last-minutes-of-life-miserable covered. A piece of debris slammed against the outside, not far from where she stood. She jumped. Or the building did. The building lost another chunk of itself. Vi didn't wet her pants, but that was probably because she was dehydrated.

Lightning sort of lit things up, though thankfully the wall of storms wasn't that close yet. It did give her a bit of a look further down the walkway. There were a couple of gaps in the sides that she could see from her vantage point and at least one gap in the base. Oh good. She loved navigating a crumbling obstacle course in high winds amid flying objects of unknown weight and size.

They probably should rope up, but then what? They could both go down together. Nothing to rope to along the side, other than crumbling concrete. Besides, it would take too long to get out the rope. She wanted to be across and back before that wall of water and wind showed up for the party.

Her gear lamp pierced the dark about half an inch ahead, but she kept it on. It gave her the illusion of seeing what was ahead. She stepped out and realized very quickly that less wind wasn't less enough for upright. Her boots slipped on the sludge and she hit the side. Didn't go over. It was too high, caught her mid-section a nice blow. Okay, a crouch it was. She became aware of Joe right behind her.

"This is *crapeau!*" Even if they got across, they'd probably just have to shoot Felonius if he was sick. And then what?

Joe didn't say anything, just looked at her.

To protect and serve. Right. It was a little too late to wish she'd found a different career path. Or a quieter conscience. The NONPD had a fairly shady history until the Bakers began to dominate the force. Apparently the honest gene ran deep in their family.

"Gonna have to crawl across." She elbowed the wall and left a small hole. If the bottom were as crumbly as the sides, they'd have to crawl lightly. There wasn't a word bad enough to express how she felt about that. She would have liked to crouch, not crawl, but nope, couldn't do it. Her emergency gear wasn't that flexible, and it made parts of her hurt that had forgotten to complain about getting whacked in their landing, oh, and by all the debris. On all fours, her hands sunk into muck up to her wrists. Wasn't she glad the crash had taken her protective hand gear offline. She tried not to think about what her hands were in and started forward. Even with her light on, it was like crawling through a dark tunnel. Once, she almost put a piece of glass into her palm, but she hadn't put her whole weight on it yet. Still hurt. The light did give her an advance look at the breach in the bottom before she went into it.

"This is *crapeau*," she said again. The hole didn't answer. Felt like it looked at her. Stupid hole. The right side had a bigger ledge. She tested it before moving along it, pressing the side—though hopefully not too hard. Her shoulder bumped it and some of it fell off. Yeah, lighter than that. It was a bit of a princess. If it gave way, well, there was a lot of water down there. Couldn't decide if that would be good or bad....

Something slammed into the wall near her head. She ducked as debris splattered out from it. So far the head gear was doing what it was supposed to. On some level, she knew Joe was back there. She was still pissed at him, but at the moment none of that mattered. This was about getting to the other side. Against her will, her brain started producing chicken crossing the transit jokes. It was only slightly better than thinking about dying. Some of the jokes were DOA, which was kind of ironic.

And then she was there and she wondered why she'd tried so hard to do it. Because it was *crapeau*, too. What she remembered from seeing it in the light, it was large and long. There'd been levels. Open levels. Hadn't bothered to count them because she didn't know she'd need to know that. Felonius had been on the top level when she spotted him. If it had been for parking land vehicles, as Jimbo said, then there'd be nothing but parking slots and ramps in here. A big empty wind tunnel offering no protection from the rain and debris. And possibly on its last legs, too.

Joe crawled in next to her and cautiously lifted his head over the edge of the wall. He didn't lose it, but almost got blown onto his back.

"Now what?" This was his bright idea.

"We find a way up."

"Fine." She tried standing up. It wasn't pleasant. She could hold position, well mostly, but a gust almost took her off her feet. This area by the walkway looked like it had been a sort of foyer or transition zone back in the day. More sagging doors lead out into the parking area, she presumed. The upper port had something similar for transit craft. There was a staircase, she noted. There would have been some kind of lift system, too. Something more primitive than what they used now. It was a bit freaky how much like the new one this was. And how not like it. This type of parking wasn't possible up there, and yet there *was* something like this, but open with tethers for skimmer parking and moving walkways toward the terminals. Everything about that was light. Everything about this was dark. And scary.

Vi pulled her weapon and started across the echoing parking region, using her gear lamp to see what was immediately in front of her, her body angled so far forward against the force of the wind, if it stopped, she'd face plant for sure.

She tried to look around. Found that the wind took this as an opportunity to try to knock her on her back. It was not worth it. There was nothing to see. It was straight and flat. The surface was coated with the same muck as the walkway, though it also had a sluggish layer of water still searching for a way down. At least it seemed to lack the holes the walkway had had...she almost skidded into a hole and had to backtrack to get around it. She proceeded with more caution after that.

Ahead her light picked up a change in elevation. She angled toward it, helped by the wind. That made a change from trying to hinder her. She couldn't call it nice, because there was nothing nice about being blown across a dark parking garage, but it wasn't awful to get a little help. Now, when she was deep in its bowels, she recalled seeing historical photos of structures like this flattened by earthquakes in old California. Which was worse? Drowning or getting crushed to death....?

She started up the ramp. Now the wind was directly at her back. She needed it. The surface was slick. She moved to the side, using the walls where she could, to ascend. The next level came slowly into view, looking much like the last one. At least the up ramp was next to this one—

With a howl a figure leaped at her from the up ramp.

She tried to get her weapon around. Slipped and almost fell.

That helped. So did the wind.

He missed her, though not completely, the sideswipe sending her staggering several more steps before she got her balance back. She grabbed at the low wall to keep from sliding back down the ramp.

Like a cat he was up. He came at her again, his arms closing around her like iron and keeping her weapon down. Face to face, chest to chest she stared into the wild eyes of Felonius.

To her horror, lights swarmed out of his skin. Millions on millions of them. She felt a jolt, like an electric shock—

JOE SAW FELONIUS DIVE AT VI AND TRIED TO GET A shot off, but Vi was knocked into his line of sight when the man missed. Against wind and the slippery surface, he could not change position before Felonius was up and on her.

The light from his body, as the nanites swarmed out of him, lit up the cavern for at least twenty feet around. Felonius screamed, the sound high pitched and painful. Almost Joe shot them both, to put them out of their pain. But Joe saw Vi go limp, her dead weight breaking Felonius' grip. She slumped to the ground. After another long, horrifying shriek Felonius fell next to her. His body went dark, leaving Vi's small circle of light as a dubious beacon in the deep dark.

His heart pounding, Joe scrambled up the slick ramp. And dropped down beside her.

Do not touch her. Not yet, Lurch amended at Joe's instinctive protest.

He ran his light over her. Saw no sign of injury. He shifted it to Felonius and flinched back. But it was too late, the dreadful sight was burned into his brain. The skin of his face had almost completely burned away, the eyes still filled with horror. Joe leaned forward, his stomach heaving several times before he could regain control. His hand trembled when he raised it to brush his face.

What do I do?

The pause was long, but not long enough.

We must kill it.

Kill Vi—

She is already dead. When Joe didn't move, Lurch added, *there is no one else it could be.*

Joe scrambled for an argument, any argument. *It must know I saw it. Why would it leave itself vulnerable like this?*

Even now it will be repairing her body. You must kill it before it succeeds. It is trying to take control. Once it does—

Vi stirred, gave a groan and her eyes opened. She looked at Joe, blinked and said, "Did you shoot me?"

He did have his weapon directed on her. He gripped it tighter. "Not yet."

"Not yet?" Her brows shot up. She started to sit up.

"Don't move."

Being Vi she did not listen. She sat up and scooted further from him. "Do you think I'm infected? Where's—"

She saw him. Her face went white, then green. Her fist covered her trembling mouth.

"Oh my gosh. I am." She looked at him. "Maybe you had better shoot me." Her eyes looked huge in her ashen face.

I am not sure I can do it. Would it seem so Vi-like? Could it to double bluff him so completely?

If you truly care about her—

A huge shudder shook the structure, but it wasn't the storm. Joe heard the flare of a craft's engines firing, followed by a quick lift-off that caused another shudder, enough to shake loose chunks of concrete from the roof over their heads. Off the side, a ship came into view, easily holding its place in the raging winds. Joe crouched, wondering if it would fire on them, but it didn't. It hovered in sight just long enough for them to get a decent view of it.

It is Garradian. Something that should not be here.

Vi looked up, frowned. "Who—I don't care who. Just shoot me before—"

Who—there's no one left. Could Jimbo or Speed Bump have beat them here? Got up there? But if they had a ship—

There is a way to find out if Vi is infested, but if she is, we will all die.

Joe flinched internally. *But*—he stopped. The nanite knew better than he did what was at stake if it died here and now.

It is theory. Lurch sounded resigned. Resolute.

It didn't matter if it was theory or sound science. They needed to stop it here. It was why they were here. *What do I need to do?*

Touch her. There was a pause. *Take her hand. It will be fast as I can make it.*

And painful?

I will try to mitigate the effect.

Lurch did not have to tell him that it would fight to make it as painful as possible.

Vi looked at Joe. "What's going on, Joe?"

He crouched by her. "I know you have no reason to do so, but I need you to trust me." She stared at him, her eyes abnormally wide in her pale face. "Take my hand. Please."

She looked at him so long, he feared he'd have to dive on her like Felonius, but she licked her lips and slowly extended her hand. Their palms slid together, the moment of greatest risk for Lurch. The handshake was achingly familiar, her hand so right against his. His fingers curled round. Her hand was cold, despite the heat, and clammy. He liked the feel of it in his, its strength and softness. He felt it when the drones went in. He did not know if she did. But there was no pain. Not yet.

The seconds ticked by. Then it was a minute. Vi twitched.

"Is something supposed to be happening?"

It is not there.

Joe's shoulders lifted and fell in a large sigh. "You are not infected."

The look she gave him was familiar. Though it was typically directed at criminals reluctant to confess.

"You know that by holding my hand?" Her gaze narrowed dangerously. "You know what all this is, or was. And if you did—is that why you're here? Is that why you never—" she stopped.

"I never—" he prompted, puzzled. Felt a shimmer of amusement from Lurch. The nanite felt oddly happy despite knowing they'd lost the trail once more.

"Never mind." Almost he thought she blushed. Joe opened his mouth, though he was not sure what would come out, but before he could find out the feeder band arrived.

As Vi was wont to say, it was a good news, really bad news situation.

THERE WERE TIMES WHEN ONE DID NOT WANT TO BE right. This would be one of those times. Vi had called the incoming feeder band a wall. It surely felt like one when it slammed into the garage, shaking chunks loose like rock rain. There was water rain, too. Buckets of it. It came in sideways, blown by the wind and carrying debris it had picked up on its way for this visit.

Joe threw himself on top of her. It was sweet, but she couldn't breathe. She'd become attached to breathing. Maybe too attached, but there it was. She would not admit she was also attached to Joe. Storm or not, she was pissed at him. And he'd know it before she kissed him again—an activity that also required oxygen.

"Need...to...get...out...here!" She couldn't hear her own words, so she pushed at him and then pointed back the way they'd come. He might have looked a bit shame faced. It was hard to tell through the blur of water. She really thought she'd seen rain and seen it with this storm. She'd been wrong. Again. It felt both wrong and weird to be so right and so wrong in the same minute.

Half crouched, they scrambled back to the ramp they'd come up. After a rather painful slide down, Vi focused on getting across the lot, because she didn't want to think about crossing that bridge. Was not sure it was possible. She considered that stairwell they'd passed. Would it be sound enough? It was not even first cousins to the interior wall they'd been advised to seek out. But what waited them across the bridge was falling to pieces. And it seemed this one wanted to follow suit. The copycat.

To her surprise, they made it the bridge and found Speed Bump huddled in the stairwell looking shell-shocked. She looked the question. Vi shook her head.

"Jimbo?" She had to scream the word.

"Boat!" Speed Bump screamed back.

Vi hoped that did not mean what she thought it meant. Waves lapped between the two buildings. She had no idea if it was storm surge or rain. Didn't matter. The combination was bad for the structural integrity of both buildings. The stair well might provide some protection, provided it held. The only thing she could think to do was try to get higher, give help a chance to find them. She shook Joe's arm, and when she had his attention, pointed up. He did not look happy—not a shock—but he nodded. It took a lot of pointing up, then down at the storm-tossed river that had been a land transit lane to get Speed Bump moving up. The top of the stair well must be long gone, because rain poured down on them as they climbed, though the sides did give them some protection from the winds. They made the turn for the last leg, clinging to the handrail when they could, crawling up the slick stairs where it was gone. There were gaps where stairs had failed. Joe stayed with her, helping her across the terrifying gap, then pushing Speed Bump up, too. It was as if he'd found his second wind, theirs and stolen some from WTF.

Then they ran out of stairs. And ran into the wind again.

Almost, she turned and headed down. Vi had climbed with the vague belief that if help didn't arrive in time, if the building collapsed, she wanted to be on top of the pile of *crapeau*. That maybe they could ride it down and survive. Now she wondered what she'd been thinking. For the last twenty-eight years. It looked to her like this level sagged in the middle, as if it had just gotten tired, though that might have been an illusion caused by the water pouring down her face.

A clatter behind them probably meant there was no going back. It was too dark to see if the stairs had given way, but it was a reasonable assumption.

"Is there any shelter up here?" she screamed at Speed Bump.

She shook her head. Actually her whole body shook.

It felt as if the whole building shifted, then shuddered. Big chunks of the floor in the dead center began to fall away, the gap spreading slowly—but not slowly enough—in their direction.

Joe grabbed her, held her. "I am sorry," he shouted in her ear.

Speed Bump stared at the widening gap as if transfixed.

It grew larger, the collapse accelerating as the structure became more compromised.

A loud sound drew her attention, then a light stabbed down, illuminating the crumbling concrete. Something— Vi saw the NONPD emblazoned on the side of the official skimmer—fought the wind until it was over them, its light all around them. The pilot shifted, brought it down as low as he could, the rear ramp opening. For a minute it seemed as if Speed Bump wouldn't move. Joe grabbed one side, Vi the other, and they half dragged her toward the shifting ramp, racing the crumbling deck. Hands reached out to pull Speed Bump aboard. Joe lifted Vi onto the ramp within reach of those hands as if she weighed nothing, then dove on as the last of the lot gave way beneath his feet. Hands drew them deeper into the hatch and the ramp closed.

Vi lay on her back on the floor, gasping for breath. She opened her eyes. Captain Uncle scowled down at her, like he wanted to bust her for something. Bust away. She didn't care. She inhaled. Exhaled. She closed her eyes again and smiled.

Laissez les bons temps rouler. Let the good times roll, baby.

❧ 8 ❧

The city grew closer, intermittently backlit by lightning. Not only was NON the city that care forgot, it was a city that never slept—or went dark.

Until now.

Poor baby. WTF had put her lights out. Vi was not ashamed to admit the sight was a shock. She'd never seen her city like this. If she had any juice left in her, that might have finished it.

"Are," she had to swallow twice to moisten her dry throat—how odd that was with water on every side of the eye— "my parents all right? The grandparents? The family?"

Captain Uncle's face softened and he nodded. "No power or water—the umbilical's been damaged—but your dad sends me a data burst every hour or so. No deaths reported yet. Injuries are on the rise. A few medical emergencies." His face turned grim again. "Report to first aid when we touch down. Get something to eat. I can give you four hours. Then I need you both back on duty."

She nodded, relief, exhaustion and a bumpy semi-landing back at District making an uncomfortable mix for her already uneasy tummy. The skimmer didn't touch down, just dropped the hatch so they could jump out. Speed Bump was escorted to a Red Cross shelter opposite HQ, then the officer ran back to the already rising skimmer.

The wind was starting to ramp up some more as she and Joe trudged across the platform. Inside, the backup generator provided low light, but no a/c, so the air felt damp and musty, thick with the scent of bad food and stale coffee. Distantly she heard voices, but the entry corridor was weirdly empty. Everyone who could be out, would be. Coms personnel would be here, the med techs in first aid, and somebody cooking up nasty food. Vaguely she wondered why government food never tasted good. You had to work at finding bad food in NON. Except in a government cafeteria. Or hospitals.

The first seat that presented itself, Vi took. She needed to sit more than she needed to pee. Though she wasn't entirely sure she hadn't taken care of that when Felonius—she clamped down on that thought. He was gone, buried in the rubble of a collapsed building and raging storm. Various bumps and bangs began to sting and complain, now that she'd quit moving, quit trying. Her hands were filthy. Her first impulse was to wipe them on her pants. About an inch of mud coated her legs. Kind of funny to wince about that, because if there was something clean on her anywhere, she didn't know what it was. After a minute, she reached up and unhooked her head gear. Had to rest before she pulled it off. It wasn't cool in the corridor, but it felt cooler with it off.

She set it down on the floor, realized the light was still on, then decided she didn't give a *crapeau*. The mud almost covered it anyway. She sagged back against the metal wall. She didn't know she could be this tired and not be dead. If she had died and no one told her, well, she'd be pissed once she got some rest. She rubbed her face, realized that was just smearing stuff around and stopped. Glanced at Joe.

Other than the coating of mud, he looked kind of not-hosed. Why did she suspect that he looked better covered in *crapeau* than she did? She shifted, felt her heavy suit resist and tugged at the seams, pulling them open from neck to waist. Maybe in an hour or so she'd have the energy to get out of it. Hard to say. She was gonna need every minute of those four hours from Captain Uncle. So why wasn't she face down on a cot? She looked at Joe again. Caught him looking at her, his brows pulled together. He had at least an inch deep of mud on his face. The dark mud made his eyes kinda pop out—

She looked away. *You are mad at him, remember?* Or she would be later. She looked back, because she was tired.

It had nothing to do with anxious look in his very fine eyes. Holding her gaze, he tugged off his head gear and loosened his suit. His lips quirked up in what might have been an attempt at a smile.

"I am somewhat surprised to be alive," he admitted.

"Yeah." She couldn't disagree. "I wonder what time it is?"

For a minute, it seemed he would answer. Finally he shrugged. "I fear it has been less time than it feels since we left here."

"Yeah." Okay, repeating herself. Not good. "Yes." Because that was way more original. If she could have, she would have rolled her eyes at herself. She gave a half chuckle. "I'm embarrassed to admit this, but for a minute or so, I almost thought the dog did it. Until, well, you know." She waited for him to laugh, or give her a Joe Friday smile. He did neither. He did look like a man who needed to say something he didn't know how to say. "I was joking, Joe."

"I am aware of this. What happened to the others," he paused as if searching for the right words, "it was not a virus or infection in the strict sense of your understanding."

She blinked. "Huh?" Yeah, that was better than yeah. She straightened half an inch and regarded him through mud and tired, and maybe a tiny bit of lust. Could she really still want to kiss him after everything that had happened? Maybe. But she was still a cop. And she had a nose that could smell a lie incoming, even if sewage and who knew what else stunk up them both. She also wasn't so stupid tired she couldn't figure out that the reason he'd been distant was because he thought she had whatever it was he was trying not to tell her. Her Look had had its tush kicked, too, but she pulled out what was left of it and directed it at Joe.

"I did not come here merely for the exchange program." He picked his words with too much care.

Vi narrowed the Look. He shifted in discomfort.

"There is a criminal from my galaxy—"

Vi straightened with a jerk that hurt. A lot. "Joe, you can't—"

He grabbed her hand, met her Look with one of his own. "No one can know. This criminal, well, you saw how vicious it can be."

Vi frowned. "It?"

He hesitated. "It is what your people would call an AI, but it is more than an artificial intelligence. It is sentient." He paused, then added, "And more dangerous than you could possibly imagine."

She considered this. "It was in that ship we saw?" He nodded. "But—why didn't it kill us? It could have."

"This we—I do not know."

Her brows shot up. "We?"

He looked discomfited. "I am not alone in my task. I have—some assistance. It—Lurch must remain hidden to hunt it. If it suspected Lurch were here—"

"Lurch?" Vi blinked. She'd heard that name some-where before, but not in an AI context. Something else... she shook her head and wished she hadn't. "Never mind. You do realize how," she tried to find a diplomatic term and couldn't, "unacceptable it is that you both came here and didn't warn anyone?"

"If we had told anyone, it would have known we were here."

"But you're a cop and—" she stopped because even she knew it was undiplomatic to tell him he was purple and alien. It wasn't like he didn't know. Or that this it hadn't noticed, too.

"It was a risk, an attempt to double bluff."

"Okay." She rubbed her forehead, despite the mud. "But now it must know you're here."

"Yes." He looked grave. "I—we believe that it used the storm to try to...."

"...out you?"

He considered this and then nodded.

"Well, now that you've been outed, we need to get help—"

He shook his head and shuddered. "You do not under-stand. Exposure is bad. We...we tried that. It did not go well."

Vi studied him. He'd definitely paled under the mud. He looked away, his lips compressed.

"There is danger for you, for anyone who knows about it."

She did not like the sound of that. "But I know.

You know."

"It does not know that you *know*." He turned back to her. "I know I ask much, but you can not tell anyone. It is not safe to talk about this with anyone but me. And even with me, care must be taken."

He looked around as if the wall had ears. Maybe in his world they did.

"You know I need to think about this when I'm not," she looked down and grimaced. "I'm too tired to think, let alone make a decision."

"But you will speak with me before—"

She eyed him. She might be tired but she wasn't stupid tired yet. At least, she didn't think so. "There's plenty you aren't telling me, Joe."

"For your safety. It—"

"Doesn't it at least have a name? You said it's sentient." She stiffened. "It's not Fido?"

His reluctance was apparent even through the mud, though this time she got the Joe Friday semi-smile. "Lurch does not like to use its name because it is no longer that —entity."

"Entity?"

"I—we do not know what it calls itself now, but it's name was—before it was called Nod."

"Nod?" Vi blinked. That sounded kind of sweet.

"It chose its name before—it is difficult to explain."

"I think you need to try," Vi said.

"It trusted the wrong humanoid. He figured out how to

change Nod's base code. It went terribly wrong. The humanoid died—"

"Died?" Vi arched her brows. Okay, maybe she didn't arch them. Nothing was really responding to her commands anymore.

"It killed the humanoid," Joe admitted.

"Like," Vi swallowed dryly, "Felonius?"

Joe nodded. "But Nod is gone. Dead. Also erased by it."

She considered this, realized he hadn't exactly cleared the dog—then decided she didn't want to know. She tipped her head to the side. That was easy because gravity helped. "Until you saw the ship, you thought I'd killed Felonius, didn't you?"

Again with the reluctant nod.

"You were going to shoot me."

Got another, even more reluctant nod. Vi thought about objecting, but he obviously felt bad about it. And he hadn't done it. If she busted his chops about it now, she couldn't use it against him later.

"But it did accomplish its purpose. It saw me about to shoot you. So it knows we are here."

"That's bad."

"Indeed."

"So when you took my hand, what was that all about?"

He hesitated, "It was easier than shooting you."

She shook her head in confusion. "What was easier?"

"If it had been present, we would have died."

That was kind of sweet. Or she was really tired. She frowned. Maybe.

"So what do we do now?"

"I would very much like a shower."

"Of course, but I mean about Nod."

"Nod is no more." He looked frustrated. "Vi—"

"You're in my city, Joe. It's messing with my people."

He rose and held out his hand. This time she didn't hesitate to take it. It did surprise her when he didn't let go as they walked slowly toward the locker room.

"For now we wait, we watch. We have something to eat that isn't seventy years old."

They walked for several feet before she said, "It's going to come after you, isn't it?"

He looked at her. "Yes."

"And you won't know who it is until—"

He didn't answer this time. She stopped then, turning to face him. There was more he needed to tell her, lots more. She wasn't completely stupid. But... "Just in case—" She grabbed the open edges of his emergency suit and yanked him close. "I promised you a—"

She didn't get a chance to finish.

Dang, that boy could kiss....

...Error...Error   Detected...Illegal   Program installed...reboot Nod programming....

Help! I am here and I need—

...Error report invalid...reboot halted...all systems functioning correctly....there is no Nod programming....

It blinked, shook the new head, felt a sense of something lost that needed to be found, but the feeling faded when it saw its face reflected in the forward screen. A particularly unattractive specimen of humanoid. It would have to change that as soon as another host could be identified. Something more attractive to the human, Violet Baker, than the decaying Jimbo.

...searching....

Violet appears to be related to a great many male officers within the NONPD. Perhaps a less direct approach was advised.

...searching....

Ah, yes, while inhabiting the criminal Calvino, Afoniki had mentioned finding the detective "hot." Possibly a point of contact? Find Afoniki. And then—what would it have to do to get arrested in NON?

...searching....

Of course. Vi investigates homicides....

THANK YOU FOR READING CORE PUNCH. I HOPE YOU enjoyed it and will keep reading Sucker Punch.

To find out about my releases, be sure to sign up for my New Release eZine and get a free eBook!

Browse my complete backlist by visiting my website. :-) I have some stand alone novels, too.

And if you want to talk books, you can find me here:

My Blog Facebook Fan Page Twitter Google+ Pinterest Linked In Goodreads

If you enjoyed this book, I hope you'll consider leaving a review. It's not just because I'm needy (even though I try not to be!). Reviews help other readers decide which books to buy. :-)

SUCKER PUNCH

Vi never liked math and aftermath isn't floating her boat either....

Hurricane Wu Tamika Felipe has moved north. Yeah, the storm almost killed Detective Violet Baker, but it also blew some romance her way. Her uptight partner, Dzholh "Joe" Ban!drn actually kissed her.

But there's no time for any follow-up kissing, much to Vi's regret. They are hunting something very bad. Something that tried to kill them while they were dirt side during the storm.

And has now escaped up into New Orleans New.

It's not business as usual, though there is some *deja vu* in there when Vi and Joe get sent to a FEMA camp to check out a dead body.

Until that body turns into a trail that might lead to the evil it. Or to its next victim.

Just when Vi thinks things are *crapeau* enough, the MITSC (Men In Top Secret Color) show up and take over their case. Are they after Joe or the evil it?

Before they can find out, the evil it lures them into a trap.

It's it versus them and it hasn't lost yet....

CHAPTER ONE

Violet Baker did not look at guys as accessories, but it was kinda cool dating a guy—okay an alien named Dzholh Ban!drn that she called Joe because she couldn't pronounce his name—who matched her eyes *and* her name. Way better than shoes or a coordinated tote. He was for sure prettier than anything in her closet. And purple, in all its shades, was NON's "national" color, so he wouldn't go out of style any time soon. Even better, Joe was a guy she most wanted to kiss *and* who wanted to kiss her. That hadn't happened for a while, mostly because about ninety percent of the datable males in the New Orleans New Police Department were relatives. It was a Baker-rich environment, which made it a dating desert. And the few guys who had wanted to date her? Most of them couldn't get past all the cousins and Captain Uncle *to* kiss her.

On the downside—did there *always* have to be one?— was the sentient nanite sharing Joe's brain. And the fact that Joe wasn't only here on an intergalactic cop exchange program. He and Lurch were hunting a dangerous and ruthless...something or other that liked to cook people from the inside out. This something or other could hide inside people, which had resulted in a minor misunderstanding during which Joe had almost shot her with his ray gun.

But she was over that.

A kiss had made it, if not all better, then ninety percent that direction.

And the truth was, if she had been hosting this something or other, being shot was quicker than being painfully cooked from the inside out. So she might be one hundred percent better. Or ninety-nine. Yeah, for sure ninety-nine.

She studied Joe's profile, her gaze lingering on his lips. All right, she might be one hundred percent okay.

Except for...

She looked morosely out on a world that was, if not forever changed, then destined to be markedly different for a very long time.

Hurricane Wu Tamika Felipe had been one for the history books. A book she wished she could read in hindsight and not be currently experiencing. Though living through it was better than dying during it. She'd had her doubts about surviving one or twenty-five times.

"The trouble with surviving a hurricane," Vi glanced at Joe again, as he steered their new-to-them skimmer through a reconfigured New Orleans New, "is that then you have to get through the aftermath."

She'd never been that fond of math. So far aftermath

wasn't floating her skimmer either. It was a lot like the before-math, but with less rain, less wind, and no utilities. Oh, and a city requiring all emergency hands on an unrecognizable deck for an indefinite period of time.

"Oh, look, there's Jackson Square," Vi said, as she spotted the familiar lines of the cathedral. "I wondered where it got to."

Well, maybe unrecognizable wasn't the right word. She could see landmarks—why did they still call them that?—in the air space that was New Orleans New-ly Rearranged, but not in *their* place in the air space that had been NON.

"And there's Lake Pontchartrain," she added. At least it hadn't moved, just expanded its borders for a bit. "Lots of white caps down there."

"WTF caused considerable disruption," Joe observed. "Do you wish me to log the location for Jackson Square?"

"I got it." She entered the coordinates in the hastily cobbled-together program designed in hopes of putting Humpty Dumpty, aka NON, back together again.

The bright idea, conceived fifty years ago, to lift the city up out of the flood zone, had clearly failed to anticipate the effects of 200 MPH-plus winds on floating structures maintained by underperforming, aging thrusters. The problem had been further complicated by the anti-collision technology—though the anti-collision tech had performed better than the thrusters, much to the delight of the Anti-Collision Board, who had almost been voted redundant in the last election. Of course, performing correctly had helped scatter the various parts of the floating city even further when WTF tried to bump everything into everything else.

The City Alignment Board, who had been magnificently confident in the run up to the storm, were now deep in CYA mode—about the only thing aligned about the Alignment Board. They were lucky everything was mostly offline. The shell-shocked NONians playing "Marco Polo" in a huge and very unfamiliar pool might have time to get over it. Though Vi wouldn't make book on that. This was a lot to get over, Vi concluded, watching another piece of the French Quarter floating beneath them.

Somewhere out there in the drifting bits of city was home. She hadn't seen it since reporting for duty well ahead of WTF. At this point it didn't matter that she didn't know where it—or where her parents were. After working overtime ahead of, and during, WTF all emergency services were now in mop-up mode, snatching sleep and food on the go. At least she'd heard from her parents and knew they were okay, if not particularly happy. Eventually someone in her seriously extended family would find and log them into the database. And eventually they'd get far enough ahead of the emergencies that she'd get to go home and sleep. If she didn't die from exhaustion first.

There were crews heading down from a variety of cities up north. The city fathers were hoping the utility guys could help repair the umbilical—which was also not as durable as advertised—that had supplied the city with utilities. Hospitals and essential services had emergency generators, unearthed from old emergency stores, but most of the city floated darkly over the slowly receding lake that was usually known as dirt side, or more officially, New Orleans Old.

While it was possible to fly above the fragmented city, without lanes or traffic indicators, it wasn't fun and tended to verge on life threatening. Only emergency vehicles were supposed to be up there, but people needed food, water and help. And for many, their skimmers were the only way to cool off in one thousand percent humidity coupled with August heat.

If someone was keeping score, it was NON: o and WTF: a seriously big number.

It wasn't just *crapeau* on a cracker. It was a cracker buried in tons of *crapeau* and topped with a nasty cherry.

Joe opened his mouth, but closed it again. Joe never wasted his words, particularly in stating the obvious. He settled for flicking her a sympathetic look. The warmth behind the look took the edge off her morose. She wasn't quite used to the notion that her alien partner liked her like *that*. Super easy to get used to perfect features and yeah, perfect build, too, but—they had a lot to work out before they could call themselves a couple, if that's what Joe even had in mind. He was from another galaxy. And she wasn't sure—if invited—that this Baker could go where no Baker had gone before. She wasn't sure Joe would survive to take her anywhere when all the Bakers found out he'd kissed the girl.

And then there was Lurch. A tiny, sentient computer living inside Joe and witness to the few kisses they'd exchanged. Because she didn't want to think about Joe's... internal entity, she said, "Still not seeing the FEMA MEC. Geez, I hope it's not moving, too." NON had stopped rotating as fast as WTF when the storm moved northeast and was downgraded. But the crazy air currents in its wake had created odd drift problems. "You see anything on your side?"

Joe did much better with questions.

"I do not."

Sometimes he did better.

"Isn't that some of the Irish Channel there?" Nothing channel-like about the scrambled blocks of houses now. Someone had logged it into the Ninth Ward, unless it was a different section. Which it could be. Because this wasn't where the Ninth Ward used to be. Okay, she was pretty sure this wasn't it, but it was getting harder to remember how it had been when dealing with what it was now.

"It does appear to be some of it."

It was going to be a delicate—and expensive—job piecing the city back to its previous configuration. Assuming that was even possible. And they managed to get three times more money than was needed, because yeah, graft.

The more NON changed, the more it didn't. Even when it really did change. Which it pretty much had this time.

Most of their runs since the storm had been from HQ to Point Needs Help But Probably Won't Get It Because It Can't Be Found. Their search operation wasn't helped by

FEMA, who had been slapping blue tarp things on every other roof, making the few landmarks still left harder to spot from the air. No one was quite sure what the tarps were for. When asked, their vid spokesperson—and quite possibly the only FEMA person not lost out in the city—had sobbed, "We're doing the best we can in a difficult situation."

If that was their best...

The one thing that should have been easy to spot—the FEMA MEC—was proving to be elusive. Not that she was that eager to find it. Once there they'd have to leave the cool confines of the skimmer and check out a dead body. Last time they'd done that they'd ended up in a whole pile of trouble—trouble that was not completely resolved. But she didn't want to think about Joe's evil something or other. The evil that men did in the tent city was sufficient unto the day. Or something like that.

"That's got to be it." Vi pointed at neat rows of what looked like white lines drifting on the outer edges of the ragged NON. It was the only straight lines of anything they'd seen since leaving HQ. The tents had been set up on emergency platforms hauled in by the underperforming FEMA, or so she'd heard. Didn't seem like that great of an idea, but it was probably better than setting them up dirt side when it was still hip deep in water.

According to Joe's Lurch—the nanite could sift through history in a blink—FEMA had never been very good at doing anything, so it was mystery how expectations remained so high. It seemed their only strength lay in finding their way to a trouble spot and staying until things were significantly worse. Whereupon they'd pull out, so that the locals caught the follow-on flack.

The only bright spot about their current assignment was that it delayed the moment they got to play Russian roulette with another meal-ready-to-eat back at HQ. The meals might be ready but she needed time to be ready to eat one. The old packages had lost their labels, making meal time feel like a series of bad, blind dates. Not that labeling would have helped. They'd probably lost their taste several decades back, so it was better to keep expectations really low.

Joe banked the skimmer, making a low pass over the platforms to find a secure LZ. A distinctive puke green FEMA transport lifted up from what appeared to be the service area and Joe grabbed the spot, causing a squawk of outrage over the communications grid. Joe shut it down, and then their engines. She popped the rear hatch and scrambled out. When she got to the rear, Joe had already activated the controls to release the body bag. It emerged smoothly, a stark and silent contrast from the one in the skimmer they'd crashed in the storm. Its body bag had developed some definite quirks, such as wanting to be carried once the body was on board. So old school.

The new body bag was the sole upside to being out of the skimmer, which technically wasn't a big upside. It was hotter than she'd expected. It always was in August. And if one thought one was prepared? August would up the ante, because that's the kind of month it was.

She stretched her back, to one side and then the other. It didn't help. Like WTF, tired had moved on, leaving something greater than exhaustion, but just shy of dead. There wasn't even a word for it. She should have grabbed a cat nap on the trip here, but Joe had needed her blood-shot eyes. The low budget skimmer didn't have enough tech for safe navigation through everything-is-different. And honestly, cat naps just made her feel worse at this point. Felt like it was taunting her body with what might of been but wasn't going to be for a good long while yet.

Of course, Joe looked refreshed and relaxed, no blood-shot red marring his gorgeous eyes, probably because of Lurch. It seemed there were benefits to sharing your innards with a nanite. Apparently it fixed what ailed him, though only if he wasn't dead. Which he wasn't. It was hard to like either of them at the moment, though this did not lessen her longing to kiss Joe again. Except, did that mean Lurch got in on the action, too? And the scary part? She kinda wished she had a nanite to fix her up. Which kind of creeped her out.

Nothing made sense, but this was the Big Easy. One didn't expect sense to be made here, even on normal days.

They didn't have coordinates to input into their body bag, so Vi tossed their CSI gear on it and then set it to follow them. The movement sent her a whiff of something not great. She glanced around. Not enough people close enough to blame. Her last shower had been right after their retrieval from New Orleans Old. She was kind of afraid to do the math on how long ago that was. Sure wasn't about to sniff an armpit. Though that might clear some of the fog from her brain. If it didn't knock her out.

She studied her surroundings slowly. This was her first experience with a FEMA Mobile Emergency Center. Kinda hoped it would be her last. It was probably better than nowhere to stay, but not by a whole lot. Containers of MREs, those mysterious Meals Ready-to-Eat, were stacked behind Points of Distribution for the meals, water and ice. Her gaze encountered line after line of blue coffin-like structures.

"What do you suppose those are?" She jerked her chin toward them and then wished she hadn't when she felt hotter.

Joe studied them for several seconds, then offered, "I suspect they are latrines. Note that one section is for males, one for females, and the other section for the gender conflicted."

"Really?" Curiosity did a slow climb inside her head. It had always been her biggest failing. Probably. At least in her top ten. She trotted over to the closest one.

"I would advise you not—" Joe began too late.

Vi pulled the door open and recoiled. "Holy *crapeau* on who knows what?" No question curiosity was her biggest problem. She put a hand over her nose and blinked rapidly. "Can't un-see that." Or un-smell it.

When she got close enough, Joe murmured, "Lurch did attempt to warn you."

Vi hoped she wouldn't need to use one of those things. Might be better to wet her pants. At least then she'd know whose pee she was sitting in. She had no idea the past was that primitive.

There was a roar and brief air movement as several emergency transports lifted off, making room for others to land. Whole setup kinda reminded her of a beehive. She'd seen vids of them in school. Lots of buzzing. Lots of movement. No clear sense of why. She glanced around again. No hope of producing any "honey" here. She repressed a shudder.

There was a muted, but different roar behind her. She looked back, saw one of the big tugs pulling in another tent platform. At this rate most of NON would be living in tents. Curious, they paused to watch technicians connect the platform and then the surface of the platform seemed to shudder. With a ripple tent after tent gradually rose toward the midday sun. It was kinda of impressive. She opened her mouth to ask if Joe thought they were air conditioned when a woman emerged from a tent on an already populated platform. No, no conditioning there. The white surfaces of the tents quivered in the wind caused by the tug, a reminder that they were, in the end, just tents. Affixed to a very hard platform.

Joe said, "Curious."

"Do Garradians have emergency procedures?" Vi asked, not because she was that curious but because it gave her a good reason to look at him. Instead of tents and latrines—as fascinating as those were.

"We try not to have them." He looked at her and added, "Emergencies."

"That's...good." She blinked a couple of times, not sure she believed him. Being stuck in NON post-hurricane on account of losing an evil something or other kinda looked like an emergency to her. She gestured toward the sea of occupied tents. "I'm guessing our vic is in there somewhere. Let's get done here before..." She jerked her chin toward the latrines and made a face.

"Indeed," Joe said.

The caller had given their location by platform number, then in tent rows. Sort of. Ten in, then five to the right. Of course, that location depended on where the caller had begun their calculations. She could tell Joe was doing some figuring—or Lurch was—and followed him into the gridded pathway between two tent lines. It felt a bit *deja vu* of their last adventure with a body, only without the wind, rain, crypts and tombstones. And this one had a lot more people watching. But still, heading into a weird place looking for a body. Okay, that wasn't *deja vu*. It was SOP for a homicide detective. But this was something new in weird, even by her usual and necessary, very low standards.

Vi didn't think she'd ever seen tents quite like these. She touched one, gave Joe an awed look. "Fabric?" Everything old was, well, it was still old, but suddenly necessary in a new way.

Sweaty, dispirited denizens watched them move past. Even the kids looked subdued, though everyone stared at Joe and stirred restively. It wasn't that aliens were so unfamiliar, but until Joe, Vi hadn't seen one up close and personal. Just on news vids and such. So chances are none of them had either—at least none with purple skin. Who knew if other-skinned aliens walked among them?

A few looked away when they saw her looking, making her wonder if she'd questioned or arrested them sometime. She was too tired to attempt any mental matching. It was hard enough to put one foot in front of the other, with the heavy, soaking heat giving some serious pushback, like it thought it was gravity or something. Guess air could get uppity when it was, well, up. The ones who did look at her, their eyes bothered her. Took her the length of the row to realize why. They looked like those vids of refugees. This was NON, not some third world, well, world. Things like this happened on other planets, backwards ones. This wasn't supposed to happen here. Despite overwhelming evidence of the incompetence of government, people had believed the city would come through the storm almost unscathed. Even if government let them down there was always their voodoo queen, Marie Laveau, protecting them from the grave. Maybe she'd rolled over or something.

At least the looting had been minimal. Early looters had been unable to find their way home and gave themselves up. One of them, so she'd heard, asked to be shot. Wasn't sure she believed that. Unless he'd seen one of those latrine things.

She stopped. "It doesn't smell right."

Joe gave her a puzzled look.

"It doesn't smell like New Orleans. It's wrong...." New Orleans smelled like a lot of things, bad things, yes, but good things, too. Spicy and flowery and...New Orleans. Bad enough to get wrenched from their homes, but this—she shook her head. For some reason it made the unfamiliar feel more so. And wrong. "No wonder everyone looks depressed."

They wanted to go home. She saw it in their eyes. It was probably in hers, too. Home. Even if she found it, would it be home? Or something that looked like home, only different? *The more things changed...* change wasn't that popular in the city that care forgot. Only it forgot to forget the city this time. Karma—with the help of Maw Maw Nature—had given them a total smack-down.

"Are you unwell, Vi?"

She looked up, meeting the concern in his eyes with a wry smile. "I'm okay. Thanks." She glanced around. "This is all a bit...messed up. Hard to wrap my brain around."

His hands twitched, probably with a desire to help her, but they'd decided touching was a bad idea at the moment. She didn't know about him, but she needed every ounce of energy to stay on her feet. When—if she kissed him again, would that make them a threesome? Bad enough she had the hots for a slightly purple alien. But with another alien in his brain? Did that make her kinky or something? Because she didn't mind as much as she felt like she should. She looked up to find Joe looking at her. Had she said that out loud?

"Shall we proceed?"

Didn't seem to have, though Joe could be splendidly oblivious. "Yeah, let's find our vic and get out of here." She let him go first. At least studying his backside—which was as great as his front side—distracted her from thinking about Lurch.

In the end, it was easy to spot the tent with their suspicious death. A small crowd had gathered, one somewhat contained by a couple of uniforms. It was comforting in a way. At least that hadn't changed, though it was missing the Lucky Dog cart. A pity that. A Lucky Dog would have erased some of her homesickness for what had been. Put off a better smell. The crowd parted at their approach, with some encouragement from the two uniforms. Vi grabbed their CSI tech off the bag, then activated the bag's controls. She set the parameters as narrow as it would let her, since the scene had probably already been compromised. The corpse was still in the shadow of the tent, which was a mercy that wouldn't last forever, though the smell had definitely breached containment. Even in the brave new future, corpses smelled bad.

The bag "taped" the scene first, a red grid taking shape to seal off the area, but the tent was small enough that parts of the grid protruded from the top and sides of the tent. It flashed red, releasing a swarm of collection probes. Mostly they buzzed futilely around the space. It was a tent. On a platform. That had probably been picked clean prior to the call to report the body.

Vi arched a brow at the uniforms, caught the shorter one studying her as if she were interesting. She gave Vi a tentative smile.

Since she was too tired to answer questions, Vi asked one, "Got an ID yet?"

The gal cop looked at her companion.

He frowned down at his tech. "Seems he's a squatter, a dirt sider—"

Vi felt a chill and *deja vu*. Didn't mind the chill. It was stinking hot, but could have done without the *deja vu*. Her *deja* had not liked the *vu* lately.

"—name of Jimbo."

Vi knew it was coming, but was still a struggle not to do the sharp inhale. Couldn't do anything about hands curling into tight fists at her sides. She hoped the probes took their time. She was in no hurry to see how he'd died—the grid turned gold, indicating they could go in. Oh great, if the 'it' Joe was hunting had killed again, this was something else she wouldn't be able to un-see.

છ✯ড়

IT WASN'T THAT BAD. NOT THE THOUGHT VI EXPECTED to have about a dead body. Certainly not the thought she expected to have about Jimbo. But after her recent schooling from WTF, she'd had to revise her definition of "the worst" up by quite a bit. Or was that down? She was never sure about that.

She had been sure 'it' had got him just like it got the others. Had expected to see that look of horror from being torched from the inside out. Only Jimbo looked surprised, not cooked. He looked a bit simmered, but that was probably from the humidity.

"Maybe his heart conked out," she murmured, keeping her voice low. Usually they just bagged and tagged, but the circumstances weren't usual. They needed to do a bit more assessing so the body could get in line at the right morgue. For some weird reason, the morgues hadn't shifted position that much. It was kinda wrong, while being helpful.

She worked her way into where she could kneel next to the body and started the CSI scan. This tech also released tiny probes, like a hundred pinpricks they descended on the body. Data flashed on the screen. Joe's hands flexed once, but he didn't breach this field either. Those little dudes stung like a son of a gun. Curiosity was a detective's friend, except when it wasn't.

"He appears surprised," Joe finally said, waiting for her all clear signal so he could ease the body up just enough to examine the underside. After a long look, he lowered the body again, giving a slight, very slight shake of the head.

Her device beeped as it delivered the first scan results. "Look at his hands," she directed, trying to make sense of what it was spitting out. She paused the auto-scroll and flipped back, a frown gathering between her brows. Maybe the CSI techs did earn their little bucks.

"Vi." Joe's soft tone pulled her gaze back to where he had one of the vic's hands turned palm up.

Bingo. Well, half of one. As exit sites went, it wasn't its best work. Or its worst. But at least they knew 'it' had left the building, er, body.

The question was, who was the new host of the awful whatever? Vi looked back, scanning the crowd visible through the tent opening. According to the tech, Jimbo had died approximately twelve to fifteen hours ago. That was odd, too. It wasn't like the tech to be that approximate. Usually it was, like, *death occurred between 0125 and 0128. Will attempt to refine with further data.* She tapped the screen, but it didn't offer even the hope of a more precise time of death. It didn't shrug and go, "whatever," so it was weird she felt like it did. There were those in the department who felt the tech trended toward AI-ness. Sometimes she was one of them.

"Detective Baker?" The female cop crouched by the opening, angled to see past Joe, though she did flick him a look that was on the curious side. That the look lacked appreciation was both odd and a relief—since said detective was younger and prettier than Vi.

They hadn't introduced themselves upon arrival— she'd been too tired—but her name might be visible on uniform. And if it wasn't, well, the odds were always high that at least one Baker would be at any given scene at any given time. Vi considered saying what, but the output of energy felt too high. Couldn't even manage an arched brow. Settled for an inquiring look and that was almost a bridge too far.

"One of the witnesses says she might have seen something."

Vi was mildly impressed. Most witnesses wouldn't even admit to seeing nothing. Before Joe could offer to talk to the witness—who probably wouldn't talk to him—Vi handed him the tech and crawled out of the tent. Straightened herself in stages. Painful stages. Neither of the uniforms offered to help her up. She might be glad about that because she might have taken the help. Probably against regs to get helped in front of the general public. Regs were full of stupid stuff like that.

"Are you all right?"

The question and the concern appeared genuine, so Vi twitched the sides of her lips. "I'm fine, Officer—" She peered at her lapel, but it wouldn't quite come into focus.

"Benson, ma'am."

"Benson." Vi repeated it in hopes of slotting it into her short-term memory until the end of this encounter. "Thanks," she tacked on, a bit belatedly, but Benson smiled so the time lag might be less belated than it felt. She studied Benson with some interest, mostly because it required less energy than meeting the witness. She was young, pretty. Apparently not related. Looked the type to interest a lot of her cousins. Dark hair, dark eyes, suspiciously well-pressed uniform. Eyes held a bit of hero worship that made Vi's heart sink.

She leaned in and said softly, "I hear you were dirt side during the storm."

Vi gave a sort of shrug. "It wasn't as fun as it sounds."

Benson laughed, even though it wasn't meant to be funny, and if anything the hero worship increased. "What was it like?"

"Wet." Vi thought a minute. "Windy. Hope to never

do it again." To head off more questions, she asked one of her own, "What was it like up here?"

Benson looked startled, then chuckled. "Wet. Windy. Hope to never do it again."

It was Vi's turn to chuckle, though she didn't go overboard with it.

Benson turned slightly, gazing toward the city. "New Orleans New really is new now, isn't it?"

"That it is." The horizon blurred slightly. She rubbed her face. She gave a shake. "So where's this witness who might have seen something?"

JOE WATCHED VI MOVE OUT OF SIGHT, THEN TURNED back to the corpse. There was much to puzzle him about this death. Why had 'it' chosen not to torture this victim to death?

It would have needed to take care here where everyone is housed so close together, Lurch reminded him. *Screaming would attract unwelcome attention.*

It could have muffled the sounds.

Then I would postulate that Jimbo was not alone when it decided to egress the body. Possibly a third person was present?

And if Jimbo died screaming within minutes of that person leaving...

Exactly.

Jimbo was fortunate that its need for stealth exceeded its need to torture its host to death.

Indeed.

Lurch sounded as sober as Joe remembered it ever sounding. No question the events on the surface during the storm had sobered them both. Joe had lacked time since the storm to question the nanite on just how it hoped to eliminate the threat their enemy posed, not just to this place, but to who knew how many universes. It was clear he'd failed to ask the right questions when the nanite proposed their partnership. Not that he was certain he'd have known the right questions. "Will I die in screaming agony?" hadn't been on the list, though it was now.

Can you look around very slowly?

Lurch would be looking for evidence of time stream activity. It was Joe's research that made it possible for them to track 'it' to this world. Before Joe's discovery, the time stream was a great place to hide, particularly for a nanite-controlled human. Joe was not sure how Lurch had learned of his research into time stream tracking. It had nanites in many places, he'd learned after their blending. All of Joe's "training," in this world and the others where they'd hunted, came from program downloads from Lurch —programs designed from the knowledge of previous hosts, Joe had gradually realized. Joe could only marvel at the wealth of knowledge he'd glimpsed during their time together, though he hadn't liked it at first. The sense of becoming something other than himself had been unsettling. And Joe wondered if streaming vids of *Dragnet* had been meant to be helpful or a joke. Lurch did have an odd sense of humor.

A sense of humor that seemed to enjoy watching Joe fall for Vi. Why it did that when it knew Joe couldn't keep her—Joe tensed as he realized that if it had entered the stream, then the "not keeping her" would start now. With increased concern, he finished his slow, visual scan of the interior of the tent.

No sign of time stream activity in here.

Would it have risked disappearing outside? Joe knew the 'it' was quite willing to take big risks, but that seemed excessive.

Probably not, but we still need to assess. We can't afford not to.

It was true that the trail would degrade rapidly. How odd that time was of the essence even in relation to the time stream.

The tech Vi had handed him beeped, then produced another set of preliminary results. Joe did not mind the interruption to his thoughts. Lurch also indicated it had completed the data collection phase, so he triggered the body bag to commence the collection process.

He moved out of range as the bag made course adjustments until it had centered itself over the corpse. Straps shot from the bag toward the body, going under it, then pushing beneath and connecting and contracting. The body rose toward the bag until it was snug, then the bag itself rotated until the body was face up. He left it hovering within the partial cover of the tent and scrambled out.

The open air was a relief after the stuffy interior. The crowd had mostly dispersed, moving in the general direction of the sustenance point of the distribution platform, some also moving toward the primitive sanitation structures. He turned in a slow circle, trying to keep it casual, so that Lurch could look for time stream activity and capture the faces for later analysis, just in case 'it' was still here, waiting and watching. He would not want to linger in this place, but it had apparently lingered for some time down on the surface. This might be marginally better. Joe looked past the faces now, scanning the horizon and the drifting blocks of what had probably been some of the Garden District.

Based on what he knew of the mansions, if the inhabitants were in them, they would not be enjoying their current view of the FEMA MEC.

They are most likely enjoying a view far from this place.

Joe conceded this point to Lurch. Those that could had evacuated during the run up to the storm. Looting had not, up to now been much of a concern, but he would imagine that given time, those houses would look quite tempting to those camping here.

Once they can spare the people, I suspect the police presence here will be increased.

It made sense. Presently people were too shell shocked to be too much trouble. And their basic needs were being met. It would not take long for that to change. He'd seen the longing for home in her eyes, heard the desire for a return to normal in Vi's voice. When that didn't happen quickly, shock would be replaced with anger.

It was something he could understand.

I am sorry I got you into this.

Joe watched Vi returning and found he could not be as sorry as he should be. Which might be one reason Lurch encouraged Joe's interest in his partner.

Vi took his arm and turned him away from the remnants of their crowd. "Let me see that report for a minute," she said. He extended the tech, and she scrolled rapidly through the results, then made a face. "Just as I thought. Jimbo wasn't a harmless dirt sider. He was cooking meth down there somewhere."

"Meth?"

"It's a very, very old school recreational drug, a lot cheaper to make than some of the designer drugs, so the profit margin is higher."

Lurch filled in the historical details for him as Joe said, "But wouldn't the scanners—" He stopped at her ironic look.

"At the corner of New Broom and Political Expediency you'll usually find a streetcar named Graft."

Joe lowered his voice further, casting a look around before asking, "Did your witness admit to seeing someone?"

"Wouldn't have if she'd known who she saw. I ran some mugshots past her. She picked Afoniki out of the lineup."

Joe knew enough about the crime family to be

impressed. "He was not alone."

Vi looked surprised. "No, he wasn't."

"That is most probably why the death was so...benign."

"A good reason to never be alone with anyone. Ever again." She frowned down at the device. "I wish we'd managed to save the post mortem data from our dirt side adventures. There's a lot of chemicals in and on old Jimbo. I wonder how many of them are consistent with, you know, your friend. Maybe we could come up with a test or at least a way to track—"

Joe put a hand on the device. "May I?" She relinquished her hold, and he scrolled through the data until— the chemical he used to track it through the time stream— he tipped it so she could see it, his eyes filled with warnings. Her nod was slight, her gaze sober.

"Let's get him to the morgue."

Joe triggered the commands and followed her down the ramp, the body bag humming softly in their wake.

"If it is Afoniki," she said, "that could be very bad. The combo of über criminal and über evil whatever...yeah, that can't be good." She stopped as a very sleek, very dark transport hovered over theirs, then dropped down with no apparent interest in the "no LZ" painted into the grid. "That might be bad, too."

"Who is—are they?" He modified the question as two men slid out in well-coordinated synch. They were of the same height and similarly dressed in soberly crisp suits. Their eye wear was also the same and reflected as well as deflected the sunlight.

"It's the MITSC—they used to be the Men in Black, but people started to catch on so now they are the Men in Top Secret Colors. The color is supposed to randomly change, so we won't recognize them. And you can be arrested for saying whatever color they are wearing out loud." She shook her head. "Like they wouldn't stand out no matter what color they wear."

"They...monitor...extraterrestrials," Joe said, uneasily, after Lurch once more filled in the information gaps for him.

"Let me do the talking. But have your papers ready, just in case." She glanced around. "At least there are a lot of witnesses."

The eyes on them were significant, but Joe was not certain that would provide any advantage if these men wanted to make him disappear.

Could they know? Suspect?

I am uncertain, Lurch said, though with more curiosity than worry. *Interesting. They look almost the same, though with less black.* As it finally picked up on Joe's deep worry, it added, *if they attempt to seize us, we can enter the time stream.*

It didn't need to add that neither of them wanted this outcome, though not for exactly the same reasons.

It was clear Lurch had had dealings with them before, but Joe did not—yet again—have time for questions. The two agents watched their approach with a somewhat troubling lack of movement. When they were close enough, each man thrust a hand into the interior of his jacket, extracted IDs and extended them in a blur of movement that made sure they lacked time to see, let alone process them. The IDs were thrust back in the jackets. Then the lips of one of the men moved.

"We'll be taking over, Detectives."

"Taking over what?"

The other man indicated Jimbo's remains with a head movement. At least Joe hoped it was Jimbo that interested them.

For a long moment, Vi didn't move or speak, just stared at them.

"We'll need all the data you've collected as well."

So it was the body that interested them.

"You're not taking our body bag or our tech."

It did not appear that either of them moved, but the rear of their transport opened and a sleeker, darker body bag zipped out, stopped smoothly next to theirs. Straps shot from it and theirs retreated as if burned. The body transferred swiftly, the bag not just taking possession, but a shroud of some kind slid over Jimbo, hiding him from view. The bag paused by Joe and something like their tech, only better, disconnected from the side of the bag. At Vi's nod, Joe extended their tech. There was brief connection, then it retracted again and the bag slid back into their transport.

Joe looked down at the tech. It blinked back at him with a "memory empty" notification.

There was a silence, then one of the men spoke. "This is no longer your crime scene, detectives. Move along."

CHAPTER TWO

"Do you think they are after...your friend, too?" Vi waited until they were airborne before speaking.

She looked around as if she suspected the sky was listening in on them. He could not blame her. Joe gave the question careful consideration. He knew that Lurch always feared being tracked. It was why it worked so hard to obscure its origins. It was the First of the nanites, and had it remained the first and only, this quest would not be so challenging. Its memory went back a very long way, and he was not sure he'd seen the beginning of it yet. It had exceeded the original nanite programming when it became sentient, though Joe was unclear how it began replicating, or the mechanics involved. Lurch easily created drones— non-sentient versions of itself—but sentient replication was a much more complicated process, he felt sure.

There was a further mystery surrounding Wynken, Blynken and Nod, a deeper connection there that stretched back deep into the past. Joe knew this more by how Lurch reacted when any of the three nanites were mentioned, though he had gotten brief glimpses into the past when they were integrating. The loss of Blynken had hit it hard, so Joe tried not to think about it any more than he had to. The fact that Blynken had been killed by Nod was a source of both pain and fear. If Nod could be corrupted by a rogue program, then might not all the nanites also be at risk? This was, Joe knew, the deepest, darkest core of its fear. And why Lurch hunted so hard to find the co-opted Nod and stop it.

"It is more likely they are tracking the trace substances left behind." It was the only thing that the nanites could not control, the telltale signs of passing from one host to another. If the MITSC were tracking it, or even suspected its presence, well, it would be most dangerous for those two agents no matter what special governmental resources the MITSC could call upon.

"If they find out about our witness, they'll go pay Afoniki a visit," she said, cocking an eyebrow at him. "Pretending to investigate the murder. If it's just the substance that interests them, then who knows what they will do."

Tiredness lingered in her face, but the huntress in her showed signs of life.

"Do we know how to locate Afoniki? Would he not have evacuated prior to the storm?"

"We always know how to locate Afoniki. He's had an ankle bracelet on him since he was like, fourteen."

Joe did not understand why the court ordered tracking

device was called that. It was an implanted chip, not a bracelet and it was no where near his ankle.

She bit her lower lip. "Of course, he probably knows a way around it. He's got a bigger budget than we do. But if he'd been expecting trouble, he'd never have gone near Jimbo. He has people for that."

"Is your witness quite certain it was Afoniki?"

"Picked him out without prompting. He's a good looking guy."

Joe felt a stab of something in the region of his heart. "It is possible he was less concerned, because of the storm." Many services had been disrupted during WTF. Joe felt certain that keeping track of Afoniki's location had not been a high priority during the height of the storm—which would make it a good time to commit a murder. But he hadn't. He'd waited for Jimbo to surface and gone to talk to him. "How did he know where to find Jimbo?"

"Jimbo probably used a FEMA phone to contact him. They've been handing them out with the meals and water. We can probably track it down if the men who used to wear black aren't one step ahead of us."

"We did not find such a phone at the scene." Had it been pilfered by someone or had Afoniki taken it when he'd been assimilated by it?

"Don't know why anyone there would grab it. They've probably all got one."

It has a vested interest in making that record go away, too, Lurch pointed out.

That might be more suspicious than the visit, Joe countered.

Or it wishes us to locate it again.

Joe didn't ask why 'it' would do that. It had demonstrated severely erratic behavior during the storm. The only certainty about it was that it would kill and continue to kill until they stopped it.

She gave him a speculative look. "Can Lurch take us off the grid? Just until we find out if the men in drab are heading for Afoniki."

Joe felt his mouth turn up in a grin. "It has it, er, covered."

Vi's grin almost stopped his heart. "I think I love Lurch."

Was it possible to be jealous of a nanite? Before he could answer that question, Vi spoke again.

"So how do we tell if he's, you know...?"

Joe sighed. "If we had the answer to that question, I would not have almost shot you during the storm."

"Oh right. And touching..."

"...will expose it, but it also exposes Lurch to it."

"You can't go around shooting people you think are hosting it. There has to be a way to figure out who—" her voice trailed off and she was silent for several seconds. "What about those substances? Are they only left there after death?"

"They are present at integration," Joe said, shifting a bit uncomfortably. The fact that the MITSC might have identified and were tracking the substance was unsettling, since his body also had them. "But confirming their presence requires contact."

Vi turned to look at him, cautious hope in her eyes. "Maybe not. You see, Afoniki's ankle bracelet also tests him regularly for drugs. Unless he's figured out a way to fake that, which he probably has. But—the tests must still happen or appear to happen." She frowned. "We'd need to be careful, though...make sure the boys in drab don't get notified, too. They are way too close for comfort."

I am on it. Lurch sounded the most hopeful he had in, well, Joe wasn't sure how long, but certainly as long as they'd been partners.

"So if he is the one, then how do we stop him and you know, save Nod?"

Lurch flinched, hard enough to cause Joe to clench his hands. The skimmer swerved. He quickly corrected his course. But she'd noticed.

"You can't just kill him—it?" she asked.

"Do you not think Lurch has tried to find a way? The risk is too great. There is no evidence that Nod still exists as a separate and distinct entity."

"But what's the evidence that Nod doesn't?"

"The murders. The torture. The fact that it killed Blynken. Nod would not willingly participate in such things. Lurch attests to this. It has known Nod the longest, knew it the best. It would fight, would have fought until defeated."

Silence for at least a minute.

"*Wynken, Blynken and Nod, one night sailed off in a wooden shoe...*"

Joe blinked.

"Were there three?" she asked.

"Yes. Three separate personalities, but all living in a single host at, well, birth." Why had he almost used the word "decanting?" He was unsure, but noted it felt right. "That was their designations, their names," he admitted, wondering how she had discerned this.

"Do...you know...did they pick their own names?"

Joe felt Lurch's affirmative, which made him wonder about its name. "Yes, they do."

"Interesting. *Sailed on a river of crystal light, into a sea of dew*...that's from a nursery rhyme. About setting sail, well, on the surface. Actually it's about sleeping, dreaming..." Her voice trailed off. She gave a shake. "So they split up and that's when it happened?"

"Lurch postulates that had they not separated, that by combining their strength, they might have prevailed over the rogue program. That what had been their strength became instead, their weakness."

She blinked at this, but to his relief didn't ask how Lurch knew this.

"What about Wynken?"

"Wynken was damaged trying to save Blynken."

Silence.

"Nod..."

He nodded. "Wynken is...recovering." Mourning. Possibly damaged beyond repair, according to Lurch.

"I'm sorry." She sounded sorry. "But doesn't that make it even more important to try and save Nod?"

Joe sighed. "It was while attempting this that Wynken was injured."

Another silence. "Oh." She slanted him a wry look, said as if trying to ease the tension, "Sometimes you sound more like a scientist than a cop." She chuckled.

He managed to echo something he hoped sounded like a chuckle. He had played many roles during the hunt for it, but at his core he was a scientist. That she'd sensed this was disquieting and yet not unpleasant. He had believed he would dislike playing a cop, but it had many advantages he had not foreseen. He glanced at one advantage and almost sighed. He had lost much of his detachment during the storm.

Much? Assuming you had some before....

Do you have an update for me? Joe was most eager to change the subject.

Afoniki is scheduled for a drug test in thirty-seven minutes. If it has taken him over, it would notice the test being moved up. So we must wait for the regular test window.

He took a mental breath, trying to get his thoughts back on task. *Does that give you enough time to prepare?*

I believe so. No need to rush to his location.

And if it is inside Afoniki?

I believe I can use the access to upload a disabling virus. I have been working on it, but did not know how to safely deliver it.

Joe had been aware that killing 'it' might kill them. This was a most hopeful development, if it didn't detect and disable the virus.

I would advise a policy of distraction when we arrive. If it is distracted, it will give me more time. And the virus time....

Joe glanced at Vi. Based on the last time he'd seen Vi question Afoniki, distracting would not be a problem.

⁂

AFONIKI HAD A NICE PLACE, THOUGH HIS VIEW, LIKE the rest of NON, had been shifted by WTF. It had originally been located in the Warehouse District, snugged up against where the river would have been before the rising. Based on his current location, his riverfront property had moved up river. Even moved, his view wouldn't be that different. The river was the river. A muddy ribbon winding through varying shades of deep green. But his neighbors had changed. Vi recognized a Bucktown restaurant off to the right that had also shifted out of place during the storm and some low rent property off the left side.

In the old days, the ground floor had been used for utilitarian purposes, probably loading and unloading ships, and the upper floors were about the esthetics, but the super rich had transparent first floors these days, so they could take advantage of the dirt side views, too. So, even shifted, he still got some of the benefit of being riverfront in more ways than one. Since he hadn't moved too far out of place,

Vi suspected he had better thrusters. Probably could have held his air space if it hadn't been for collision problems during the storm.

Vi had a feeling that if Afoniki wanted his old address back, he'd probably get it. Shouldn't be a problem for him. He'd know who could get it done and how much it would cost him. With the taxpayers picking up the bulk of the tab, of course.

She popped her door, letting the thick, hot air rush in and clambered out against it. Her door slid down, and she looked at Joe across the skimmer.

"So how do we play this?" Vi wished they were going on a date instead of into a potentially life-threatening meeting with an evil something or other. "We don't have a crime, thanks to the men in super secret drab." It felt kind of anti-something to be going in without a crime. Upset the delicate balance between the good guys and the bad. "We can't just stop by to check on him. He and 'it' would smell a rat."

"We found many chemicals and organics on Jimbo. Perhaps...a contamination issue?"

Vi considered this. "It could work, not for long, but hopefully long enough."

"We just need to keep him talking, distracted for about ten more minutes," Joe said, setting his watch.

Ten minutes. Surely she could blather on for ten minutes. Best case would be getting Afoniki talking, but he pretty much had a "no talking in front of the cops" rule. He even resisted admitting that his name was Afoniki.

An escalator wound up to the middle of the structure, like a corkscrew, taking visitors to where all the utilitarian stuff happened. His property even had power, she noted, when the escalator activated at the pressure of her foot on the bottom step. It was interesting, though sadly, not illegal. He was allowed to have emergency power. She rose smoothly, the corkscrew of the stair oddly soothing. It also made the air move, which was nice.

They entered into a setup that appeared benign. Could have been any business reception area. It was discreetly classy, though currently tended by a goon instead of a benignly elegant female. Vi, going out on a mental limb, postulated she'd been unable to get to work. Even a bad guy couldn't control Mom Nature. Though she'd bet money she didn't have that he'd tried.

It was cooler and smelled better than outside. The storm had for sure stirred up the muck at the bottom of the swamp. She angled her head, pretending to look at some artwork, and took a cautious sniff of herself. Maybe the gently moving air would help dissipate what the storm had stirred up at the bottom of her armpits. At least she didn't have a habit of shaking hands with Afoniki, so she could keep her distance. She tried to identify the good scent, but all she come up with was: expensive.

She recognized the goon filling in at reception. And he knew her. They exchanged looks of mutual...something. Wasn't respect. Might have been a bit of "I'm not here to arrest you so don't make me change my mind" on her side. His gaze had some "I ain't done nothing, so don't get your knickers in a twist" to it. His gaze shifted to Joe. He'd made the news when he arrived, but she didn't think they'd arrested the goon since Joe's arrival, so he might not have seen Joe up close before. Joe's cool gaze must have made him uneasy, because he pressed a button and a door slid open with a pricey-sounding whoosh. Vi kept her eyes on the goon until he looked away and the door closed between them.

Hard to feel it was suddenly safer when this meeting might involve an 'it' bent on causing widespread pain and destruction. She'd seen its work and was not eager for this possible confrontation.

There was another goon and another set of escalators. One that went up and one that went down. Vi followed, with her eyes, the one twisting up toward another floor. Straight ahead, a bank of seriously high windows appeared to look out over the city. Only it was NON the way it used to be, not the way it was now. The down escalator was equally elegant, a definite upgrade from the one outside.

The goon grunted and jerked his chin toward the down escalator. Like the one outside, this activated at pressure from her foot. The slow spiral down gave glimpses of the artificially generated views. It made the high ceiling appear higher and the room bright and light. At the bottom, the view through the transparent floor was the real deal. She'd have probably hesitated before stepping out, but the escalator slid her smoothly onto what seemed like nothing. The effect was that good. And it was that clean.

She looked past the floor, hoping it would help with

her sudden vertigo. Afoniki's block had been shifted over the old Metairie cemetery, she realized, after studying it for several moments. It had been some kind of racetrack prior to becoming a city of the dead. From this angle, the track made an elegant curve through the dead space. Pieces of old freeway poked up out of the green spaces here and there, and she could see the skeletons of old buildings, heavily coated with moss, though all of it showed signs of fresh scarring from WTF. From this place, she could better see the standing water glinting where it had not glinted before WTF. From a distance, it was pretty. Until she remembered what it was like down in the goo.

The low hanging clouds shifted, giving her a glimpse of what might have been the old airport. Had its floating version shifted, too? She hadn't been over that direction to see. It shouldn't matter. Logically one knew that floating locations floated. Moved. But...New Orleans had always been *this* thing and now it wasn't. It had been shuffled like a deck of cards, and no one knew if it could be put right, even if her mental metaphor was so wrong it was embarrassing. Two wrongs still didn't make it right, as her Great Grand Paw Paw liked to say.

She spotted a lean, elegant figure gazing, well, she wasn't sure if he was looking at the fake or the real reality, over by one of the windows. He did look a bit posed, which made her lips twitch. Vi couldn't deny that the sight of him made her pulse twitch a little. Snakes could be pretty, as long as one didn't forget that they could also be lethal. She could never decide if Afoniki flirted with her because she was a girl and it bugged her many relatives or—well, the why didn't matter. They were as opposite as—north and south poles weren't opposite enough, even for someone really bad with metaphors. More like the equator and whichever pole was the coldest. Was that a metaphor? She wasn't sure. She was sure she had a headache that was getting worse.

Vi knew she was trying to keep her thoughts light so she wouldn't panic. Were they walking into some crazy nanite battle? Would it all be fought out of sight? Was it dangerous to them? Could it be contained or would there be collateral damage? She should have asked more questions. She knew that now. Maybe. She might not like the answers. She'd known that at some level, so had been afraid to ask. It had seemed straightforward heading over here, but now it felt a bit like falling into a maze. One as murky and dangerous as what they'd faced on the surface. Only without the wind, rain and green ooze. So better, without actually being better.

Afoniki turned to face them, as if he'd just become aware of their presence, which she knew he hadn't. They'd never have been admitted without his permission.

"Detective Violet Baker." A dramatic pause. "This is an unexpected...pleasure."

The hint of surprise was as fake as his smile. Did the dude ever have a normal human reaction? Of course, them coming here was unexpected. They usually "met" at HQ in an interview room. Which brought her circling back to wrong and would-things-ever-be-right-again?

Afoniki's gaze flicked Joe's direction and real interest gleamed in the dark depths. It was true that Captain Uncle hadn't let Joe play good cop in interrogation yet, which was a pity because he really was a good good cop. He was also a bit distracting, which would have been helpful. Funny how hard it was for Orleanians to get used to purple skin when they had no problem with purple everything else.

"A partner who matches your eyes. How charming," Afoniki murmured. "He must be a huge hit at Mardi Gras."

This annoyed her, even though it had been her first thought at their initial meeting.

He moved toward them, but didn't make the mistake of holding out his hand. They were hand*cuffing,* not handshaking acquaintances. It was a nice bonus, not being on handshaking terms, if he was currently playing host to an evil something or other that liked to switch bodies through physical contact. Which just showed it was possible to find the good even in a bad situation.

"This is—" she stopped and sent Joe a wide-eyed look.

"I am Dzholh Ban!drn," he said. It still sounded like her cat coughing up a hairball, not helped by the almost imperceptible bow he offered with the words. "Intergalactic Law Enforcement Exchange Program."

In the past six months, she'd noticed that the depth of the bow reflected Joe's notions of someone's importance. He'd for sure nailed it this time.

"That's quite the view you've got." She touched an elbow to a tall, semitransparent cabinet and studied the view again. One wasn't supposed to fear heights in a floating city, but one feared them less when one couldn't see exactly how far one would fall if something malfunctioned. "Is it better or worse?"

"It is...different."

Yeah, he'd spent way too much time with lawyers.

"Change can be satisfactory."

Afoniki cast Joe a doubtful look.

"Except when it's not," Vi said, possibly a bit too emphatically.

A real smile spread across Afoniki's face. Who'd have thought they'd find common ground in the aftermath of a big old storm? Vi noted the smile failed to spread to his eyes, which were so cold, she lacked a metaphor for how much. One brow rose over one cold eye, and he indicated the sumptuous seating with a touch of hesitation. As if he weren't sure how long they planned to stay, but he did have company manners. For now. Vi didn't kid herself that their "welcome" mat could easily be pulled out from under them. Which brought her mind back to the floor. She eased over to the couch, trying not to look eager or relieved, and sank down. It was as comfortable as it looked, which was sad, because she still didn't feel comfortable. What if he had a button that would drop all of it, or the section she sat on, into the goo of NOO below?

If she hadn't seen the evil something or other's handiwork, her imagination might not be running quite so wild. But she had. She glanced around, as if studying the fixtures. He had a good decorator. Even the furniture had a lightness to it that went against the vid portrayals of bad guys homes as dark and sinister dens of iniquity.

"I love what you've done with the place," she said. *Most of it.*

"My designer was most...satisfactory."

Vi was pretty sure that was a *double entendre*. Not everyone looked beneath his surface—or cared to look. Lots of money and good looks were all that mattered. Vi, well, she always felt a bit dirty after spending time with him. This time she'd arrived dirty, so she was ahead of the game.

"Can I offer you something? A beverage? Food?" His gaze lingered on her face. "A bed?" Joe must have tensed or something because he added, "For sleeping, of course. You look exhausted." His gaze shifted to Joe. "You as well, naturally." His gaze flicked between them, both piercing and unsettling.

Vi looked at Joe and danged if he didn't look tired. She had to give Lurch chops for knowing how to set the stage.

"Thank you, but no, thank you." She wasn't sure how to start a non-hostile, non-interrogation. "I'm fine. We're fine. Thank you."

He shifted from one foot to the other, his hands sliding into the pockets of his perfectly fitted slacks. He didn't say that they needed to get to the point, but his lips lost their pseudo-friendly curve. Vi hesitated, but this wasn't a power struggle, at least not yet. Afoniki hadn't killed Jimbo, and the meth lab was probably sleeping with the fishes. If a meth lab could sleep. Would the fish be high? She firmly reined in her thoughts. This was not the moment to lose the plot.

"In a rare turn of events, we aren't here to talk about legalities." Or lack thereof. She gave an amused shake. "Feels really odd."

"Indeed." His other brow rose to the same height as the first. He crossed to a chair that faced her, flicking a brief curious glance at the still-standing Joe. He didn't seem too worried about power positions, though, since he sank into it, stretched his legs out and crossed his ankles, his hands once more finding their way into his pockets. Was that where he kept the buttons that would drop them into the river?

"And what does bring you—so happily—into my presence?"

"We've just come from the FEMA MEC."

"Really?" He looked mildly interested. "I hope you didn't eat anything there. I've heard stories." He gave an artistic shudder. "One can only hope they are wild rumors."

Vi grinned. "We have the same food at HQ. Sadly, not rumors."

"I have never doubted your courage, Detective."

Vi had, but she didn't say so. She tried to think of something to continue the nonrelevant conversation, but couldn't. Luckily Joe picked up the slack, though chatting wasn't his forte either, so he just went with the plan.

"Some surface dwellers, what you call dirt siders, were evacuated there after the storm and one of them died last night. There are concerns about possible contamination risks for anyone who came into contact with him."

Afoniki was a cool customer. His face didn't change. He didn't even blink. He didn't ask either, but then he'd probably learned how not to blink or ask back in kindergarten.

"Indeed? How unfortunate." He didn't say it wasn't his problem, but she felt it quivering in the air between them.

"It seemed a bit far-fetched," she said, adopting her I-didn't-want-to-but-have-to mien, "but someone said you were there yesterday evening?"

"Indeed?"

He didn't say he hadn't been there, so she added, "We are required to warn anyone who had contact with the vic. Regs." Since no one had read all the regs, it was easy to trot them out as an excuse for just about anything. Had it been long enough yet? Vi wanted to look at her tech, needed to know the time, but didn't dare look away from the bad guy. And whatever might be lurking inside him. A pulse throbbed painfully behind one eye, possibly keeping time with Joe's countdown.

"Regs," he echoed, his tone was smooth but just a hint of a crease formed between his brows.

"We can scan you for contaminants or you can see your own doctor, but I wouldn't wait too long. Our vic went down pretty fast."

"Isn't it fortunate that I was nowhere near the MEC?"

She thought about asking him if he was sure, but it's not like it was something you'd be unsure about.

"Well, they say everyone has a double."

He did not seem enamored of the idea of a double. Which made her wonder if he really did have one. And if he did, what he'd do about it. She could see where one might come in handy for a bad guy, as long as it didn't get around he had one. Which it just may have. She pretended to check her tech. "So, just to be clear, you don't know a dirt sider, name of Jimbo?"

This question verged into interrogation range, because she'd bet money he did know Jimbo and would bet even more money he'd never admit it. On the tail of the question, tension seeped in, stealing some of the brightness from the room. She really wished she'd asked Joe what to expect when...whatever was going to happen happened.

"Jim...bo?"

"Dirt sider," Vi said, trying for light and adding a shrug, just in case she missed the mark.

"Indeed." He shifted, uncrossing, then crossing his legs the other direction. "I thought the surface had been evacuated prior to the storm?"

Deflect a question with a question. It was his SOP. But it would know that, if it was lurking in there. If it was in there, it would know that she knew Jimbo hadn't been evacuated.

"We did try. The storm got worse faster than expected, and we got separated from him. I was surprised he made it off the surface, actually."

"Dirt siders are resilient."

"They are," Vi agreed, "until they aren't and die."

He shrugged. "Everyone dies. Eventually."

Was this a veiled threat? The fact that it was true didn't make it not a threat. Something dark passed in the sky underneath them. Vi blinked, but Afoniki stiffened. His attention shifting from her long enough she risked a glance at Joe. Was that...?

He nodded to her silent question. Did that mean the MITSC had talked to the uniforms or were they following her and Joe? Had they had time to tag them? Had they needed time? Lurch had taken them off grid, but they were the MITSC. According to legend, they'd always had better tech than anyone else. She loosed an internal curse. She'd hoped to avoid having the MITSC and Joe's evil something or other in the same space they were.

Afoniki's gaze found her again, something more than speculation in his somehow empty gaze.

"Well, if you weren't at the MEC, then we'd better get moving." It was already too late. The boys in drab were probably parking next to them right now. But that didn't lessen her flight or—no, it was pretty much a flight instinct. No fight in there at all. And what would 'it' do if the MITSC shouldered their way in? In a tech versus tech battle, Vi felt like she had "collateral damage" tattooed on her forehead. Unfortunately "serve and protect" was imprinted on her DNA, and the mandate included clueless men in drab, even if they had stolen her body and body of evidence.

So that ruled out asking for another exit, even though Vi was pretty sure Afoniki had several.

"We still need to track down the other person...."

"Other person?"

Vi couldn't put her finger on just why the question felt menacing. She really wished she weren't standing on the transparent floor. She turned enough to see him, while still moving toward the escalator. Not that it represented safety. There could be crazy, bad guy traps on it, too. Electrocution. Metal teeth. She blinked. Or maybe she was just really tired.

"Yeah, your double was with someone. Just someone not someone's...double." Yeah, she was really tired. "I guess it could have been someone's double, but not someone that someone recognized as someone's...double." She wished she could make herself stop talking.

Joe had his usual lack of expression on his face, but she sensed he wished it, too. Vi clamped her lips shut. Felt more words try to punch their way out. She had one foot on the escalator when the two men in drab appeared at the top. On the upside, the sight of them killed the babbling impulse.

Vi's sudden lack of coherency was troubling. And confusing. Most unlike her.

She is scared.

What does she fear? Joe had not seen her show fear, even when he believed he would have to shoot her. She was the bravest human he had ever met. And the most—he cut off that thought as unprofitable.

It.

Oh. He paused, studying her. *This does not look like fear.* Or what he thought fear would look like on her face. She appeared exhausted. And she did not seem to care for the transparent floor. If he were honest, he did not care for it either.

She had to move aside as the two MITSC agents descended. They had a certain...

...flair...

Joe could only agree, though with reluctance. He knew he lacked flair. Why this bothered him more than his current lack of information was also not clear.

They should not have it. They should blend in, merge.

So why aren't they?

And what do they know? Or not know? Lurch finished, instead of postulating why they were showing their flair.

The two men descended at the same rate that Vi and Joe had, but it felt longer and more...more. Joe noted that Afoniki had risen to his feet, taking his time, as if this were theater and he followed a script. Afoniki didn't move toward the two men. And they didn't move toward him when they reached ground level. What did they know? And if they knew—did they have the tools to contain it? To remove the threat? That he wished they did know how to contain it—well, wishing did not make things so. This he had learned during his time in this place. And the other places he and Lurch had hunted.

No one wanted to be the one to break the silence, but in it, Joe sensed the power struggle playing out as gazes clashed and wills were tested.

For himself, Joe found it easy to not speak, since he did not know what to say, or what question to ask. It was possible the MITSC were following the same trail they were, that they had talked to the officers at the MEC, but their purpose in coming here was unclear. The air in the room was thick with testosterone and menace. The clash of strong men against a strong man. Predictably, it was Vi who broke the stalemate.

"We were just leaving," she said, pointedly to the men blocking the escalator.

"Your purpose in being here?" one of them asked.

Joe thought it was the one on the right.

"Not your business," Vi shot back.

"What is, er, their business?" Afoniki inquired, strolling a few steps closer. His thin mouth curved a bit, but his expression never altered that Joe could ascertain. Prior to this meeting, he'd only watched him through the screens in interrogation. He'd believed those screens had removed some of the man's humanity. He did not think this anymore. This was a man who'd never had humanity. He was as without conscience as the 'it' they hunted. The thought of combining two such evils was...not a happy thought.

Could this man give up his autonomy? Is it strong enough to subdue him?

That is an interesting question. Lurch sounded intrigued, somewhat curious.

Is it in him? Joe realized the nanite had not said. The time must surely have passed, lost in the arrival of the MITSC.

Inconclusive.

What did that mean? Joe had questions. Vi would have more questions. If they could manage to exit their current situation still functioning. He better understood the earth phrase "touch and go." And Vi's more earthy *crapeau on a cracker.*

The two men did not clear the escalator. They did extract their badges, using same technique of flash and stash. Afoniki held up a hand.

"I'm afraid I wasn't able to see them." He strolled closer and held out a hand.

Vi made a small movement, quickly checked. The two men paused, then held up the badges once more. Something in their stances that...suggested Afoniki read from a distance.

"Smith and, er, Smith. And what department...?"

"A classified department." This time the other Smith spoke.

Vi gave him a Look. Afoniki's brows rose. He shrugged.

"Fair enough." He went to a beverage setup close by and poured himself something. This time he did not offer anyone anything. He turned to face them, lifting the glass and sipping from it as his gaze studied the two men, then tracked to Joe and Vi. If 'it' had infested Afoniki, then it had found fertile ground for its evil. Joe sensed something feral in the cooled air. The fine hairs on his body rose.

Could these two make a major crime figure and two police detectives disappear?

They think they can. Lurch felt more than usually ironic.

The silence stretched—and snapped when their communication tech shrilled. Even the two MITSC jerked at the sound. Afoniki appeared to tense.

"It is the Captain," Joe said. The air changed, though Joe was not certain if it was for better or for worse.

Vi tapped her device. "Captain Uncle?"

The two Smiths exchanged looks. Joe thought he sensed uncertainty from them. It was one thing to make a couple of detectives go missing, but when one of them was related to most of the police force and beyond....

Vi's side of the conversation was not overly informative, until she looked at her timing device. "Yeah, we're heading in right now. Be there in ten. Or less."

Afoniki set down his glass and moved toward Vi, sending the tension scale rising again.

"You forgot your card, Detective." He held out a white square that Joe knew was a business card. Normally not something to fear, but 'it' could use even this innocuous electronic device to wreak havoc if it had been infested with drones.

With an almost imperceptible pause, Vi took the square. Joe noted that her fingers did not touch Afoniki's. That reduced the risk, but did not eliminate it.

"Can't blame a girl for trying," she said, lightly, turning away before Afoniki could respond. She strode up to the two Smiths. Their pause was very perceptible, but they finally stepped aside, one to the left, the other to the right. Vi angled to avoid brushing against them as she stepped on. A move Joe mimicked. As they were lifted up, Joe looked back, wondering if they'd ever see Afoniki again. That he did not mind, did not overly trouble Joe. He saw the two Smiths watching him and looked away. But he carried the look in their eyes with him as he followed Vi out.

CHAPTER THREE

"Were they here for us or him?" Vi asked, still holding the card away from her like it was dirty laundry.

"I am not sure," Joe admitted. "Though..." he paused, then added slowly, "if it were just about us, they could have waited until we came out again or—"

"So they probably wanted to see why we were in there. Or they were after Afoniki, too." She blew out a sigh. "If we knew why they were tracking the..." She stopped and glanced around, as if she suspected the MITSC was listening in. Which they could be.

"It has killed more than once while here on Earth," Joe admitted. "It is what brought us here." Fortunately, she was not looking at him and didn't see him him shift from one foot to the other.

She does not need to know. Lurch's tone felt complicated. Joe felt the same internal complications in his feelings.

When—if she finds out, she will be angry and rightly so. The nanite said nothing. *How long—how much do you think they know?*

If they are following same path we are, then they know just enough to get themselves killed.

Or worse.

Once more the nanite did not speak, though Joe felt its tacit agreement. If it decided to take up residence in an MITSC agent, well, it would not be good for them.

Vi held up the card. "What do we do with this?"

"Let me scan it," Joe said, carefully taking the white square from Vi.

Vi looked skeptical. And curious. Lurch probed it most carefully with drones and declared it free of traps and viruses. Joe wanted to be relieved, but it was not possible with so much still unresolved.

"It's uncontaminated."

Vi smiled, able to be relieved because she did not know enough as yet. Then her smile faded.

"Then why did he give it to us?" She took the card back. "Bubba Boudreaux is a city councilman. Afoniki's warehouse is—used to be in his district." She frowned. "Why would Afoniki give me his card?"

"Could he have been Afoniki's companion during the visit to the MEC?" Joe asked.

Vi looked skeptical. "That's a stretch. A councilman visiting a drug dealer with the head of a crime syndicate?

More likely it was one of Afoniki's bodyguards." She taped the card against her other hand. "It's a message of some kind." She sighed and rubbed her head. "Let's get out of the heat."

They slid into their respective sides of the skimmer, silent as they waited for cool air to filter in.

"That was a timely call from the Captain," Joe said, breaking the silence.

"Wasn't it though?" Vi looked mischievous.

Joe wondered how she'd managed it, but did not ask. The MITSC had been alone with the skimmer long enough to plant a listening device on the hull. *Can you scan us?* he asked Lurch.

Certainly. I have nothing else of importance to do right now.

Its tone verged on caustic. Joe had, he admitted though only to himself, somewhat overestimated how many simultaneous tasks the nanite could do.

It is not the number, but the kind. It has set traps for me everywhere.

Trying to use up your resources?

It is what I am also trying to do to it, though less obviously.

You need assistance.

There was a long pause. *It is not ready.*

Joe didn't press the issue, though he was not certain any of them could survive until Wynken was recovered.

Another silence formed. Finally Vi broke this one. "So?"

The single word encompassed many questions. He gave a slight shake of his head. She made a face, but did not press the issue.

"We'll probably end up with more paperwork from losing the vic than if we'd made it to the morgue. Wish they'd grabbed him there." She muttered something uncomplimentary about the origins of the MITSC.

Joe had a sense she hoped they were listening.

"And the Captain?" Joe lifted them off, sending the skimmer cautiously between two uncomfortably close city blocks. He could not tell if their collision thrusters were offline or settling for what was. This section of the city would have felt the full force of the storm. It would be unusual if much more than the thrusters hadn't been damaged.

"Captain Uncle won't be happy, but he wasn't before the storm, so whatever."

They had planted a bug, a listening device while we were inside, Lurch spoke in his head finally, *but I have given it a malfunction that should puzzle them.*

Will they become more aggressive?

It is not completely offline. They would, I believe, expect you to look for a device and attempt to disable it. They will attempt to repair it remotely. That should keep them busy for a while.

It would look suspicious if we weren't suspicious. Clever.

I am, on occasion, clever.

The nanite felt rather pleased with itself. Joe grinned and caught Vi looking at him.

"Well?

"Our communications are once more secure," he reassured her.

"So what's the scoop? What did we find out?"

If you both would agree, I will tap into the skimmer's speaker system and deliver my report to you both so as to save time.

Joe did not think Vi would object. Her curiosity appeared to be on full boil. "Lurch is going to use the speaker system." He glanced at her. "To save time."

Her eyes widened a bit, but she nodded, looking around, as if she expected the nanite to make a physical appearance.

"Hi, Lurch." She glanced at Joe. "What?"

He smiled and shook his head.

"Test. Test."

The voice did not sound like the one inside his head. It was disconcerting, but he should have expected it. Joe's voice did not sound like his when played back on sound recording devices. Joe steered a slow path in the direction of headquarters. He was not anxious to face the Captain without their body.

"So what's the scoop?" Vi asked.

"I was unable to safely breach the tracking device. It was heavily protected."

"By it?" Vi asked.

"Not all of it," the nanite admitted. "But some of the protections appeared to be more recent in origin."

"So Afoniki is the host?" she pressed him.

A hesitation. "I am not certain. Despite the protections, I was able to monitor his vital signs without breaching the alarms. He reacted with extreme unease to your questions. He did believe he had not visited the MEC. His responses show strong belief in that. His uncertainty appeared later."

Vi frowned. "So if it's in there, why would he be reacting?"

"Afoniki is a very powerful individual. It is possible that it has been unable to secure its possession of him. Or..." Lurch's recital paused, as if he were thinking.

"Or," Vi prompted.

"He was infected with non-sentient drones."

Vi gave a shudder. "Creepy. So your bad 'it' went in long enough for a look around and do some memory wiping, but decided not to stay? I would have thought Afoniki would be its match made in hot places."

"Perhaps it did not like the legal monitoring. It may have even foreseen the threat the ankle bracelet posed from me," Lurch said. "It is clever."

"Compounding our difficulty in finding it," Joe grumbled. They needed it to make a mistake. He'd hoped this was it.

"So when Afoniki gave us the card..." Vi prompted, her brows creased.

"I would postulate that the arrival of the MITSC troubled him."

Vi nodded thoughtfully. "If anyone is as good—or better—at making people disappear, it would be the boys in not-black. And no one would hunt that hard for Afoniki, not even his own people. But why that card? I mean, I get he wouldn't ask us for protection, but Bubba? He's more likely to disavow any knowledge of him."

"It is possible the card triggered a remnant of memory. Or it could be an attempt to throw us off the real trail."

"We are hardly **on** the trail, real or imagined," Vi grumbled. "He probably is trying to mess us over."

"That would be my suspicion, but there was an element of fear present in his responses there at the end. I do not believe he is a man who fears lightly."

"I would concur with that assessment," Joe said, noting Vi nodding out of the corner of his eye.

"So Afoniki could be fighting back—against it or its drones?"

"That is a possibility," Lurch admitted.

"Or..." Vi's voice trailed off.

Joe waited a few seconds before he prompted, "Or?"

"It could have been Nod."

Joe didn't speak. Neither did Lurch.

"I know you both think it's gone, but what if it isn't? Is there some way you could, I don't know, tell?"

Another pause. Finally Lurch broke the silence.

"I have never tried to—overwhelm a host and wipe out their personality, so I cannot answer your question."

237

"Would Wynken know?" When Lurch didn't respond quickly, she added, "I know it's a tough question to ask, but I think Wynken would, well, want you to. If they were... close. I'd want to know if it were one of my family. Do you have a way to ask him—it?"

"I will inquire. In the meantime, I believe the next step is to talk to the councilman."

Joe was not certain if Lurch was deflecting or proposing the real next step.

"He won't be on any sort of tracking."

"No," the nanite agreed. "You will need to use traditional methods of interrogation."

"Because it is so easy to tell when a politician is lying."

"Is it?" Joe looked at Vi.

"If they're talking, they're lying, at least most of the ones in this city," she said. "And Bubba's rep is even worse than usual. The thing is, how could your it get from the MEC to Bubba? I still don't think he was there."

"What if it rode out inside Afoniki?" Joe asked. "It it studied him, concluded he was not a productive host, its next step would be to find someone else."

"I can kind of see why it would prefer the scummy politician to the scummy criminal. Best of both worlds."

"I do believe the ankle bracelet to have been the tipping force, though it might be attempting a double bluff."

Vi rubbed her temple as if it ached. "Is that why you were worried about breaching the bracelet? You think it might actually be there, but hiding?"

"Anything is possible. If it probed Afoniki, there would be signs left of that activity." It paused. "We are fairly certain it altered Afoniki's memory, even if we are not certain it moved in. If it left drones, it would have the ability to exert some level of remote control, but I do not know how much, since it is also something I would not do."

"Or it's hiding in plain sight." Vi's lips tightened, but she didn't argue the point. "For two...entities desperate to find each other, you both seem to spend a lot of time trying not to find each other."

Lurch chuckled. "A fair point. But we are both seeking for a meeting in a venue conducive to our own survival and the demise of the other. It is a complicated...dance." He tone sobered. "And I am more concerned about collateral damage than it is."

"A fair point." Vi gazed ahead, frowning. "So I guess we use the same tack, that we're looking at a contamination issue from his meeting with Afoniki. It's wafer thin, will be tricky play, if he is the big, bad IT. Or even if he isn't. He won't be happy Afoniki sent us his way."

"Afoniki, who may be in the custody of MITSC and on track to disappearing forever," Joe murmured.

"Or who may be frying the Smiths right now," Vi pointed out. Tired traced deep lines in her face.

She needed rest. Or she needed a Lurch. It had kept Joe going well past human endurance.

It would make her a target.

She is already a target because she is with us.

She angled so she could look at Joe. "Did you two have

a plan when you beamed in here? Or were you—are you winging it?"

"Lurch always has a plan," Joe protested, though his tone lacked deep conviction. Vi tipped her head to the side and widened her eyes. "On occasion, winging it IS a plan."

"You have to know I have questions," she said, reluctantly, "Lots of them. I should have asked them before...not sure why I didn't. Okay, I do know. I didn't want to know, but...I think I need to know. Even though I don't."

She sagged back, staring out the front screen, so that he could not see her eyes.

He sensed he knew the questions. He had them, too. Perhaps because he also had not asked because he had also feared the answers....

❦

VI WANTED TO STOP AND GET A HANDLE ON ALL OF this. She wanted to keep moving fast enough to outrun it. And she wanted to bury her head in the sand and pretend none of it had happened. All of this wanting made her headache worse. That and being tired to her toenails. She kind of envied Joe his infestation. As soon as they'd gotten airborne, Joe's tired had faded like water drops in the heat. She stared at Joe a bit morosely, listening to their discussion—but not with all her brain—as Lurch explained why it had taken him so long to process all the data. That was disturbing, too. It was possible the nanite was outgunned by the evil it, or at least very evenly matched. It was certainly above her renumeration grade. She couldn't see how she was anything but a drag on the ticket at this point.

"So how worried are we that the MITSC know or suspect, about it, I mean." It was a worry. If it knew it had been outed to the MITSC, who knew what it might do? She rubbed a particularly sore spot between her brows.

"I am...worried," Lurch admitted.

"If it's in Afoniki and it gets in their brains, either permanently or just a quick visit, then it would know what they know, and it would know what it all means, even if the men in drab don't or didn't know what we were talking about." This was not a happy thought, and Vi was not happy to have had it. And figuring out her own sentence—after producing it—made her head want to go fetal, along with the rest of her. Lurch's nonanswer was an answer that sent an icy chill down her back. She hesitated, but she had to ask it. They needed all hands on deck. "What about Wynken? I mean, I know it was bad, what happened, but if it doesn't step up, then Blynken and Nod died for nothing, right? And it's been there. Wouldn't it kind of know what to expect? And you know, be of help." From where she sat, they needed help. And so did she.

Was it her imagination that she felt Lurch thinking? Or talking to Wynken? Where was it? Did they have like a headquarters or something? And if they did, where was it?

"She has a point," Joe said, finally, though with a big heaping of reluctance.

Had he been following the same thought line as her?

"Wynken is not...unwilling to help," Lurch finally said.

"So bring him—it online," Vi said.

"It is not that simple." Lurch paused as Joe shifted uneasily.

"What?" Vi looked at Joe, then at, well, in the direction of Lurch's voice, which was silly, because it was in Joe.

"Wynken believes part of the reason he and Blynken failed was because they were...concentrated in a single human." Lurch finally said.

"I thought you said splitting it up was what caused the problem?"

"When it was attacked from the inside, yes, but this is about external, multiple...targets."

"Oh." Vi thought about this for several seconds, but decided to go with, "Simply bringing it online would add its wisdom, but—"

"Not its...fire power." Joe agreed. "Though we are not certain about this. It is all theory."

She thought she knew what it was trying not to say, but wanted to be sure. Needed to be sure. Because the idea of inviting an emotionally damaged nanite into her body was both intriguing and horrifying. But mostly, she admitted, feeling a bit creeped out with herself, intriguing. She didn't like going into the presence of the bad 'it' so woefully outgunned. Maybe she had been meant to become a cop after all, and not just because of her family's DNA. She did like having the big guns. "So Wynken needs a...separate host?"

Joe twitched again. She shifted to face him.

"Am I wrong?"

"No. You are not wrong."

"Well, you have Lurch. Tell me the downside because mostly I'm seeing upside, at least from this side of your face."

Silence greeted this comment. Vi couldn't tell if it was surprised or self-consciousness—on Joe's part, anyway. Hard to talk freely in front of the nanite, she supposed.

"It is all...upside for me," Lurch said, real amusement in his voice. "I can turn off my hearing, if you would feel more comfortable sharing your experience, er, Joe."

What did the "er, Joe" mean? she wondered. She was pretty sure the nanite knew how to pronounce Joe's real name—what if the hairball name wasn't his real name? And if it wasn't, why? Okay, going incognito around the bad 'it' wasn't a bad plan, but did that mean Joe was a new face for the old nanite? Otherwise, wouldn't the bad 'it' recognize Joe? She could see where this might be need-to-know, but she still felt a little...miffed. Or annoyed. Secrets. How many secrets did they have?

"It is unnecessary. My biggest concern is that hosting will make you more of a target—"

"Than I am already being with you two?" She didn't mind the distraction, and this comment gave her a chance to give him the Look she'd wanted to give him on the heels of her train of thought. It was like a win-win.

"If you have privacy issues—"

"Worse than having a million relatives in a few square miles?"

"There would not be time to train you to segregate

some thoughts," Lurch said. "No privacy is somewhat different from a loss of some privacy."

Okay, that was a bit... "How much would Wynken share with you and Joe?"

"Wynken would only share what is relevant to the mission," Lurch assured her.

That was less a bit... "Does it hurt?"

Joe shook his head, finally looking amused. "No, it is not painful."

"When we were...new...we were not skilled at integrating. There was some pain." Lurch sounded reflective, rather distant, as if remembering something very long ago.

Joe looked startled at this.

"But we are skilled now. Pain is a choice that 'it' makes. It likes torturing its victims."

"Well, I'm glad it's a choice you don't make," Vi said. "My head already aches." How old was the nanite? "So, how do we do this? Is...Wynken...willing to, you know?" She still didn't seem to be asking the right questions, but the truth was, she wasn't sure which were the right questions. Was it close enough to move in now? She kind of wanted to get it done before meeting the councilman. Just in case.

"Wynken is willing. It...likes you."

What did that mean? Did it have a gender? And if it did, how did she feel about it seeing her in the shower? She should probably get all these thoughts done before it moved in. "That's...good." She hoped. "So, now what? Do we have to stop or something?"

"We can proceed while we, er, proceed. Place your hand on Joe's hand."

That didn't seem too hard. He took it off steering, placing it within comfortable reach. She hovered over it—she liked holding hands with him, even though it hadn't happened a whole lot, so Wynken would probably know that, too. But then it had probably been around for the kiss....

She slowly lowered her hand, her skin sharply pale against his lavender skin. It always surprised her that his skin felt warm, because it looked cool. But it was warm and male, with just the right amount of abrasive. The bones were bigger, and she sensed his strength, the manly kind that was different from hers. He turned his hand, so that they were palm to palm and his fingers tightened, his grip comforting. Her mom had said more than once that a girl could tell a lot by how she felt when a guy held her hand. Her mom had been known to say that she knew her world changed the minute Dad took her hand. And then he'd take her hand again, and they'd smile at each like they were still goofy about each other. It was both sweet and embarrassing. Had Mom really felt like this? She hadn't always been a mom—

The tiny lights yanked her back into the moment. And out of the moment. Her spine stiffened as they bubbled up on Joe's skin, then gathered into a sort of golden swarm. It seemed like they hesitated, perhaps to give her time to change her mind. She almost did. Wasn't afraid to admit it.

She didn't pull away, though her fingers twitched. Joe's

grip tightened, then relaxed so she could pull back if she wanted to. His gaze met hers for a moment, before he had to return his attention to flying. But it was enough. Her hand relaxed in his. The lights crept closer. First contact was like a tiny spark. Not painful. A little warm. It paused there against the tip of her finger, then slowly sank out of sight.

"It tickles," she said and turned her other fingers toward the swarm. She didn't know if it had waited for that, or if it found a welcome from inside, but the the tiny lights flowed over her hand, covering it with light. It felt a bit charged, and her hair rose like in a thunderstorm, but it was still okay. They sank into her skin in chunks now, moving faster. Light ran in lines under her skin, apparently moving up her hand and wrist, then out of sight because of her uniform sleeve. She didn't feel different, even when the last straggler vanished into her skin. Did it seem like light flashed under the fabric of her uniform? Or was that her imagination? She waited for...well, she didn't know. Didn't feel different. Didn't feel less tired and the headache—

Began to ease. She couldn't see it, but she felt the tiredness around her eyes smoothing away, too. She'd say it felt like she woke up rested, but she never woke up well. She did know she felt better.

"So far this is pretty good," she said. "How does it help me get energy?"

"It maximizes the nutrition in your cells. It can only work with what is there, but it can heal you as well."

"So if I never ate again...?"

"You would both die, but it would take longer."

"Okay, that is kind of a downside."

"Only if you never eat again," Joe pointed out.

"True." It had kept Joe going through the storm just long enough. If she'd been alone...

Greetings, Violet. Is it acceptable that I call you Violet?

"Of course it is." Oh, she said that out loud. *Sorry.*

You can speak to me in the way most comfortable to you.

Okay. Vi tried to think of what to add and couldn't. Plus, if Lurch was right, Wynken had access to pretty much all her thoughts already. *Are you all right?*

I am very well, thank you. And thank you for offering me hosting. You are most brave.

I kind of thought I was a wimp. You know, better together and all that.

The nanite's chuckle felt like a tickle in her chest.

Are you... up for this? I mean...

I am much better than Lurch believes I am. It is the... the closest analogy would be, it is the father. It is the first. So it worries.

I'm a little boggled by that, Vi admitted.

There was a pause, then another chuckle. *Your mind is most interesting. I expect that we will both be... boggled in the coming days.*

How long? Sorry, didn't mean to sound impatient—I think a lot. Probably too much.

Not to worry. I will only stay as long as you wish. It feels pleasing to spread out a bit.

Was it crowded in Joe? That was also a boggling thought.

My sorrow made it seem so. I am better here. I needed something to do besides grieve.

Vi flexed her fingers, feeling new energy and purpose. *Well, let's go kick some evil... something or other... tush. Or circuits.*

"You are well, Vi?" Joe's anxious voice broke in.

She looked at him and grinned. "Yeah. We are both well. Let's go take down this bad whatever it is."

She wasn't sure, but she kind of thought Lurch sighed. If he was the father, then he probably had.

❀

It wasn't a surprise that Bubba's mansion had been mapped in almost on the heels of the storm. His wasn't the first residence to be mapped. That was the mayor. There were lights showing. Also not a surprise. That it was surrounded by police skimmers and the CSI transport, that was a bit of a surprise. She exchanged a long look with Joe, once he'd found a place where they could edge their skimmer into the mix. They clambered out. The crime scene had been taped to the outer edge of his property line, but it was green, so they were able to pass through the grid. Only unofficial types, like news vid reporters and random bystanders—yes, there were even a few of those—couldn't get through. They'd get a jolt and knocked onto their backsides. Only the truly clueless even tried, but Vi lived in hope that some new reporter would give it a go.

The property line was enclosed in a fence that looked stone, but couldn't be. Not even a councilman could get clearance for that level of weight, not when the residence was also stone. They followed a curved drive to where double doors stood open. Clusters of uniforms and official types in suits milled around in a very big hall with a high, arched ceiling. It had the dim interior of a country manor house and was nicely cool, even with the doors standing open and all those warm bodies. Had to be one of the fancy —and beyond expensive—air conditioners that adjusted to ambient conditions. Vi wouldn't even know about them, but her mom had been watching one of those homes of the filthy rich shows. Interesting that a "man of the people"— his campaign words—had one.

Following the general flow, in hopes of finding ground zero, Vi came face-to-face with Captain Uncle.

He puffed up like a cat, even though he was tall enough to intimidate without the puffing. Before he could ask the question forming in his eyes, she said, "Whose the vic?"

His gray, badly-in-need-of-a-plucking, brows arched almost to where his hair used to be. "The councilman. His wife found him half an hour ago." He dropped the brows like a boom. "I don't recall sending for you."

"You didn't. We were following a possible contamination trail," Vi said. "Our vic was in contact with someone who was at the MEC who was dirt side during the storm. And we didn't have an obvious cause of death." That she could tell Captain Uncle about. And if he found out the rest, she'd be lucky if he only busted her back to the street.

He looked suspicious, but unpuffed some. "Share your data with—"

"Um," Vi glanced around, then lowered her voice. "We're going to have a little problem with that. Our data got jacked by MITSC."

Captain Uncle wanted to roar, but he knew one didn't roar about the MITSC. He had to inhale several times before he could get his voice quiet enough. "Why?"

"Wish we knew," Vi said. "Vic was a dirt sider." It wasn't easy to meet his tough gaze with her bland—she hoped—one. He knew her almost as well as her parents—though he'd been known to claim he knew her better. It wasn't easy working for a guy who'd changed her diaper way back when. Knowing what she could unleash on him if she didn't pull this off—well, that helped.

"Would it be permissible for us to take a look at the victim, sir?" Joe's tone was über respectful. "It is possible there are similarities."

Captain Uncle looked like he wanted to explode. Or break something. But he knew better than to talk about MITSC in an unsecured location. Probably not even in a secured one. Luckily, he didn't think to ask how for more details about the dirt sider and who'd had contact. Hopefully by the time he did think of it, she'd have a good explanation.

"There's a connection?"

"Our other guy was spotted at the MEC by a witness. And that one said there'd been contact."

"Reliable?"

Vi shrugged. Was any witness really reliable after the lawyers go ahold of them? She was amazed he hadn't asked for the other name yet. "MITSC was on our heels..." Vi wasn't above giving him a nudge.

His eyes narrowed and he puffed again. "Do we need to initiate containment protocols?"

Vi gave the appearance of giving this careful thought. "No other vics at the MEC. Your call, sir."

Passing bucks up was SOP. Also SOP to pass them back, but he'd been her uncle before he was her captain.

He gave a short, sharp nod. "Just remember this isn't your case. Down the hall to the right."

They made their way past a swarm of CSI techs and cops. Vi could not help contrasting it with Jimbo's crime scene. On the other hand, it would be difficult for MITSC to waltz in here and co-opt the crime.

Even without the pointer from Captain Uncle, they'd have found the vic. The concentration of people built the closer they got. The number of Bakers on scene was high, too. Vi exchanged greetings, saw the ones who hadn't met her partner eyeing him with interest. And a touch of suspicion. If they'd known she'd kissed him on his purple mouth, suspicion would get boosted to threats and jostling.

An internal chuckle pulled her thoughts up with a jerk. She'd forgotten about Wynken. Now that she remembered, it felt a bit like having a wide-eyed child riding on her shoulder. Its interest was intense. It wanted to see everything, so she obliged by turning her eyes everywhere she could without looking like a newbie. Or a crime scene groupie.

Bubba appeared to have breathed his last in his library. It was a total old-school space. Oak, paper books with fancy binding—Vi touched one. Okay, fake paper books with fake fancy bindings and massive expensive faux leather furniture—which once again contradicted the man of the people persona. Bubba's body sprawled untidily across a truly massive desk. Behind him, thick red velvet draperies stretched from floor to almost out of sight on the ceiling. It wasn't just a library. It was a setting with a capital S. The cast of characters looked small, except for the Coroner who had always been larger than life. The room was almost a "who's who" of the power brokers within the department. Except for—

Vi edged around a cluster of VIPs and came face-to-face with Benson. She blinked. "How did you end up here?"

"We were heading back to HQ when the call came through," she said in a hushed voice. Her eyes were bright with excitement. Vi couldn't blame her. It was quite the crime scene. "Me and Jack were first on the scene."

Vi resisted the urge to question her. Not her crime, not her scene. "Sweet. I guess."

Benson's eyes clouded. "You guess?"

"Political murders can be tricky, but you'll get pushed out fast, so I wouldn't worry." Much. If it went wrong, they'd be looking back down the chain of evidence for someone to blame.

"Oh, good."

It was a bit unsettling how relieved she looked. She really was a newb.

"I didn't think you'd get assigned to the case. You already have one, I mean," she added hastily, in case Vi took it wrong.

Vi didn't. "Oh, we didn't. We were just tooling by, and I talked Captain Uncle into letting us have a look. He still thinks I'm a baby detective." Vi grinned, not sure why she didn't mention the possible connection with the MEC. Benson had been first on scene there, too. But if she knew something? Yeah, Vi would rather the actual baby cop didn't remember if she did know something. "Maybe we'll get some news vid time if we stand by the right person at the right time."

Benson smiled a bit uncertainly and there was a bit of alarm in her baby blues. But since her cousin Frank loomed up behind her, it might have been caused by coming face-to-face with the Coroner's Investigator, rather than the thought of some news vid facetime.

"Vi?" Frank didn't look too worried at the thought she might jack his case. He glanced at Joe, then his gaze slid to Benson. "Hi, Gladys."

Vi blinked at the friendliness of his tone. She looked

from Frank to Benson. "You two..." She trailed off, figuring they could fill in the blank.

"Harry," Frank said briefly, his gaze amused as Benson blushed and excused herself. "He always finds the new, cute ones first. Don't know how he does it." He watched her backside until she was out of sight.

"It's a gift," Vi said. "Captain Uncle said we could take a quick look. Mind if we turn him over?"

Frank shook his head. "Now why would you waste time doing that?"

He pulled a device out of his pocket and keyed in a command. Over the body, lines formed, taking the shape of the deceased. It spun in a slow circle, data points connected by various colored lines to places on the body.

"That," Vi said, stepping closer, her jaw slightly dropped, "is—" She didn't have a word for it. "Do you have a cause of death?"

"Looks like his heart gave out." He glanced around. "Lotta sound and fury for nothing, but I got to try out the new toy." He held it out. "I'm testing it for the company who developed it."

Vi took it, scrolled through the options, and picked the bio-chem analytics. They appeared as a pretty chart in front of her face. "Do you see this, Joe?" She glanced from him to Frank. "You two have met, right?"

"When I first arrived," Joe said, meeting Frank's probing look with impressive calm.

Frank had broken up more than one potential romance with that look. But then, she was pretty sure Frank didn't know there was a potential romance, if they lived long enough to have a potential romance. That thought was sobering enough to get her mind off how cool the tech was, so she could assimilate the actual results. She scanned down the list—there. The markers were definitely there, but it seemed to her the concentration was lower—

You are correct.

Is there enough to have been the cause of death?

There are traces in the heart wall.

Vi took care not to throw a significant look at Joe.

Any sign of exit trauma?

No. It took care to...leave quietly.

There was an echo of pain behind the words. Vi didn't comment or even think. It needed closure, not sympathy.

I don't think we can learn anything more here, Vi concluded reluctantly. Both visits had created more questions than answers. But she had to find out one thing....

She turned to Frank. "How does it interface with our databases? Is the data shared across platforms?"

"Not yet. I have to do an upload when I get back to the office. If I do one," he added. "Doesn't seem to be anything here. Old boy has a few secrets that I'll probably be ordered to keep."

Vi's eyes widened. He looked left, then right, took the device and keyed it, then tipped it so she could see. "He's a —" ...Girl? She stopped herself. She looked up, saw Frank's raised brows and looked closer. Bubba'd been a boy, changed sides and now dressed like a guy? NON didn't mind quirky. Didn't mind crossdressing or sex change operations, but when you mixed them all up, added in a marriage to a very politically connected Louisiana family, and tried to keep it all secret? She bent and studied his slack face. Bubba wasn't Afoniki's type of...girlfriend, but she—he—whatever—must have been his type of politician. Secrets were a currency Afoniki understood and loved to exploit. Which begged the question, had Afoniki known Bubba was already dead when he sent them here? It was like an old-fashioned shell game using real people. Which body was the evil 'it' in?

She and Joe, and their nanites, needed to have a serious talk. She turned to leave and almost bumped into Captain Uncle. He gave a chin jerk, which she took to mean follow him. They did, none of them speaking until he led them to a small, empty side room. At his signal, Vi closed the door. Captain Uncle glanced around, and perhaps concluded it still wasn't safe.

"Under the current circumstances, I'm going to expand your team. Assign you a couple of uniforms to ride around with you."

Vi opened her mouth to protest.

"Unless you'd like to be put on leave?"

He had no idea how tempting that offer actually was. If she could have kept the skimmer...

Vi closed her mouth. *How are we going to talk, let alone hunt for 'it' while saddled with a couple of uniforms?*

Very carefully?

CHAPTER FOUR

J oe followed Vi out of the big house and back down
the curved drive to their skimmer. Waiting next to it
were two uniforms: Benson and her laconic partner.
Benson waited with some attempt at sobriety, but there
was a quiver to her small body that hinted at some inner
emotion. He could not determine which emotion.

"Ma'am." She didn't salute, but Joe sensed she wanted
to. Her eyes showed signs of what appeared to be awe.

Vi studied Benson, gave a smile that felt like it had a
sigh in it, then nodded to her partner. "Jack, isn't it?"

"Yes, ma'am." His face was on the long side, his eyes so
light it made them appear blank, and he had a hint of a
droop to his mouth. Not unlike some of the canines Joe had
observed.

*The correct term is "hang dog." And Benson has some-
thing called a "girl crush."*

A...girl crush on...Vi? Lurch provided additional definitions for him. She was not looking at him with awe, much to his relief. He did not even wish Vi to look at him in that manner. *She is in love with Vi?*

It is hero worship. Admiration and a desire to be like her.

Oh.

"Did Captain Un—did the captain tell you why he assigned you to us?"

"He said you needed some extra help—and eyes—for a few days."

She nodded, as if that tracked with her understanding of the situation, too. She took care not to look at Joe. He also took care in how he looked at her. If—a very large *if* —'it' had been in the councilman, then it was possible it had moved to one of the people milling around. It was already suspicious of them, though he could hope that their cover story when they were dirt side had resulted in uncertainty. It could be testing them, trying to draw Lurch out, as it had on the surface. Or it might be on track to elude them again. Leave them waiting for the next brutal murder, which the MITSC now appeared to also be tracking.

How are we to locate it? They had been so careful when they arrived here. Would they have to begin again in a different place? For the first time since he'd embarked on this adventure with the nanite, he felt real despair.

Now you feel despair? Not when we were dirt side—

Never mind. Perhaps what I feel is overwhelmed. We have gone from a couple of possibilities to...to this. He stared around at the swarm, amazed that it was for one dubious councilman.

If it is here. It may be in Afoniki.

Or it could have moved to one of the MITSC; in which case, we are back to square zero.

I will admit I find its behavior somewhat puzzling.

Somewhat?

It could have disposed of Jimbo's body very easily, Lurch pointed out.

It had a point. The tent had not been that far from the side of a platform. The swamp would have quickly hidden the body, aided by the heat and humidity. There would be no scanning for heat signatures when everyone was focused on post-storm cleanup. *Why do you think it wanted the body found?*

The most obvious answer is that it wants us to find it.

Why?

If I knew that, I would know, not everything, but at least something. The nanite felt amused. And yes, wry.

Okay, you cannot read its mind, but I am back to discouraged. If it wanted them to find it, it was only so it could kill them.

And yet it did not kill us down on the surface when it had the chance.

What do you think that means?

There was a long silence. *That we have something that it wants.* Another pause. *I could be wrong, of course. But that is only conclusion I can reach with the available data.*

What could they have that it could want?

"Earth to Joe?" Vi's voice broke into his thoughts. "Do we need to get you some food? And a break?"

Joe managed a semblance of a smile. "I am sorry. I am rather amazed at all this." He waved a hand toward the now winding down, crime scene.

She looked concerned. "We could head back to HQ and, you know, eat." That she did not sound excited by that, even if it meant a short break, could be attributed to her lack of enthusiasm for the meals-ready-to-eat. Indeed, he could not blame her. Benson and Jack offered half-hearted agreement. Vi looked at Benson and Jack. "You haven't heard of any eateries opening up, have you?" She glanced at Joe. "I always had better intel on where the good food was when I was on the street beat."

Benson and Jack exchanged looks, that could have meant anything, but before they could speak, they got a call. Joe looked down at same time as Vi, then they both looked up.

"Disturbance?" Joe asked.

"The looting has begun, I'll bet," Vi said. "People are coming out of shock, figuring out where they are. How to get home."

"Bored," Benson agreed.

"What's the twenty?" Jack asked, his tone in the mournful range. "What's there?"

Vi looked down. "It's downriver. No clue what might be there. Maybe one of you can try to get more information once we're moving." She heaved a sigh. "Lock and load, people."

Joe frowned. "Should that not be load and lock?"

Vi exchanged a look with Benson that Joe did not understand. Then she patted his cheek. "You're cute when you're clueless."

THE COORDINATES TOOK THEM DOWN TOWARD WHAT had been Chalmette, but it, like the Greater NON area, was unfamiliar territory in the aftermath. There was no sign of Jean Lafitte park. It probably wasn't reasonable to find this upsetting, but Vi did. The Battle of New Orleans was a big deal in NON. The Brits still came over every year for the reenactment, even though they kept losing. It was actually done dirt side, which upped the down-and-dirty factor by even more. They marched through the swamp, fired old cannons, pretended to shoot each other, and stuff. It wasn't as big as Mardi Gras, but it was big.

"Can you slow down a bit?" Vi asked, peering down in hopes of spotting where it was supposed to be. "They'll have to find the visitor center and tow it all back." Wouldn't they?

"Tow what back?" Joe asked, sounding puzzled.

"Jean Lafitte." It was their history. Only, large chunks of NON could make that claim, too. There was the really old stuff. Then there was the newer old stuff and some kinda new stuff, because NON liked being old. And easy.

"Would he not be able to get back on his own?" Now Joe sounded worried.

"The park. The guy is long dead."

"Oh."

She leaned her head against the screen and blinked back tears. Her city was broken and so was her heart.

Wynken made a small sound of distress, and it almost felt like it patted her head.

I am sorry.

What you went through, it's worse. I know that.

It is your home.

It's happened before. Fires and floods. And we always come back. But this—I'm not sure we can come back from this.

If the hearts of your people are as strong as yours, your city will be back.

This won't be about hearts, but pocketbooks, I'm afraid. What was the price of a city's heritage? Was it time to finally embrace a truly new NON? Would they have a choice?

"Look." Joe spoke for the first time since they lifted off.

Benson and Jack—Did the guy have a last name? He wasn't another relative, was he?—hadn't spoken either. Maybe she and Joe were scary to the baby uniforms or something. Vi felt a hundred years older than them, though the real gap was maybe ten years. That thought made her flinch. Had she really been that so squeaky-clean-young once? Because this was not a productive line of thought either, Vi followed Joe's pointing finger. And blinked.

"Is that...City Park?" Benson sounded a bit awed.

"It looks like it," Vi admitted. "Circle it once, Joe. Let's see if it's all there."

Joe altered course, bringing the skimmer around and dropping his air speed just enough to keep them in the air. Her first thought was that there was no power in the park. Not a shock. Not much of NON had power. But that meant the holo-bayous and river were offline. Also the holo-oak trees and some of the bushes. It changed the look of the Park to be missing such key landmarks—there was that word again. But "air marks" didn't have the same meaning. And it sounded awkward. Besides, you couldn't mark air, so it even failed as a metaphor. If there were any metaphors. Vi could admit to being bit vague on the metaphor rules.

"There's the NOMA." It helped that the New Orleans Museum of Art was both large and not a hologram. And she'd seen it from above almost every day. When the Park was where it was supposed to be, it was common to fly over it on the way to somewhere else, since it tended to float somewhat lower than other parts of the city because of its sheer mass. "Okay, there's the stadiums, so it all looks to be here." All except for the art and stuff, which had been evacuated prior to the storm. "Log it into the database, would you, Benson? And report that we're on scene." She looked at the panel, comparing their coordinates with where the disturbance had been reported. At the moment, her looting theory had lost fuel. There just wasn't that much to loot left in the Park. She'd guess that even the tourist stuff had been shifted. It was possible looters didn't know that the buildings were mostly empty. "Let's do a quick fly by on our 'disturbance' before we set down."

For some reason, the setup made her gut twitch. The coordinates put the problem around the carousel. But it wouldn't have mattered where. Why kick up a fuss here? There were more buildings in that area, so maybe someone found something to loot. But what? And who reported it? It felt off. Wrong. Joe kept their air speed down, then kicked on tracking, looking for heat sigs. His tracker flared, then the skimmer screamed a warning that came too late.

"Incoming—" She and Joe said it at the same time, but hers was an incredulous question, while his was Joe-ish and matter-of-fact.

The skimmer rocked to its side before Joe righted it.

"Starboard engine is offline," Vi reported, as required in the regs, even though Joe would know it by the change in steering control. That was almost a surgical strike. Vi pulled the description from her vid game play with the cousins. They liked to toy with her, bring her down in painful stages. Then have their character go head-to-head with hers.

The hit knocked them off course just enough that the second shot missed. Though its detonation rocked the skimmer.

Vi slammed their black box alarm. Joe was ready for the third shot. Dang, the boy was a decent pilot. She heard a scrape of metal on metal, then another boom that almost flipped them upside down.

"I will have to land," Joe said, his voice steady, though

his arm muscles bulged as he fought to control the damaged skimmer.

"Officers in trouble. I repeat, officers in trouble," she snapped into communications, sending their location. "We are under fire from an unknown source." She glanced at their two uniforms. Benson's eyes were wide, almost fixed from shock. Jack, well, he didn't seem to waste calories on having expressions. "You strapped in? You picked a *crapeau* day for a ride along with us."

Though this crash should be better than their last one. Unless this crash was about the nasty something or other? Memo to self: when your gut thinks something is wrong, believe it. If you live long enough to read your memos later.

She checked her straps. Something about the nature of the shots bothered her, but she didn't have time to think about it now.

"Try to land where we have some cover." She studied the landscape. "There, if you can make it." It was the pavilion, but there was one other structure between them and where the attack appeared to have come from. She elbowed the latch on the weapons locker built in to each exit hatch. She half turned and snapped at their passengers, "Check the weapons locker back there. We'll want to move as soon as we touch down. Secure any extra power packs. If you don't have pockets for them, pass them up."

She shoved power packs in every pocket she could find, but didn't remove the long gun yet. If the crash went badly, it would just beat her up more.

The ground rushed toward them, though their airspeed

was slower than the last crash, which might be good. She didn't have extensive experience in crashing.

There was standing water around the pavilion, but it couldn't be that deep.

Joe banked the skimmer. It bucked and fought the turn, but came around enough to line them on a relatively flat stretch of ground.

The damaged port engine sputtered and died.

The last few feet down were a silent rush, followed by the thump of first contact.

The skimmer bounced up, then hit again, harder.

The next bounce was smaller, the next hit even harder.

There was a jerk and the skimmer spun, sliding sideways toward a bench.

She threw up her arm, because, you know, that would soften the impact against her side—

The skimmer made teeth-jarring contact with the bench and stopped moving. She wasn't sure who won the battle. The skimmer had the weight, but bench was probably hard bolted into the platform. Maybe a draw, since the horizon was at an angle.

The skimmer shuddered and subsided with a last, bitter hiss.

Vi took a breath. It hurt some. So did her head. And her arm. She flexed. Didn't think it was broken.

I am on your injuries.

Thanks. She flexed again. Arm already felt better. *If I'm bleeding anywhere visible, probably better leave those alone so as not to raise suspicion.* If their passengers survived the impact.

Vi slammed the lock on her straps. Had to hit it twice before it released.

Joe did the same thing on his side. She grabbed her long gun, sliding her arm through the strap and pushing the weapon onto her back. Tried her hatch. No surprise it didn't work. She tried manual release.

"I'm jammed over here. I'll have to evac your side, Joe."

Lucky for them, his hatch responded to emergency command and flew off. Joe scrambled out, then turned, holding out his hand to her. She let him pull her clear, only then turning back to check on their passengers.

Benson looked dazed, but her eyes were open. Jack, well, Jack looked like Jack. At least he was moving. He'd released his straps and was working on Benson's. Vi triggered the rear emergency hatch. Jack pushed Benson toward Vi, who grabbed her arm and pulled her clear of the skimmer. Jack passed over one of the rear emergency long guns to them, grabbed his and scrambled out.

She heard a sound and looked up. "Run! Get clear of the skimmer! Incoming!"

They scattered. Vi raced away, looking for any cover higher than a blade of grass with the whine building from above. She dropped, trying to push herself deep into the thin muddy surface soil.

The whine was replaced by a boom. It shook the ground. Dirt and debris hit all around her. Some pelted her back. Some of that painfully, but Wynken was on that, too.

She lifted her head a few inches. Looked around. Smaller bits of stuff were still making landfall. The skimmer, well, she wasn't looking forward to explaining to Captain Uncle that she'd lost another one. If she lived long enough to offer explanations. Odds of that weren't great.

She rose to crouch, spotted Benson and scrambled over to her. Checked her pulse. Alive. Nasty cut on her forehead. Where—she spotted Joe checking the skimmer, also keeping low. She joined him, but with her long gun out, scanning the immediate area before turning to him. "That was military ordinance."

Joe leaned over and pointed at the center—dead center — of the crater. Vi peered in. She could see the ground below through the hole. She looked a Joe. "I'm going to go out on a limb here and say, that we're in a *crapeau* load of trouble."

◈

JACK PAUSED BY THEM LONG ENOUGH TO STARE DOWN the hole. His eyes widened a bit, then he moved over to help Benson into a sitting position.

"I'm okay," she said, though she didn't look it.

Vi looked more than unusually unhappy, even when he factored in the situation. "We should move."

Joe didn't argue, but... "It will take them time to shift position—"

"I'm not so sure. The first shots were probably shoulder mounted, but that last one? That was a heat seeker, or I'm my mother's aunt. It would have to have been fired from some kind of fixed setup, at least fixed as in something bigger than a skimmer. Which means it could have been set up and then fired by remote." She looked around like she expected trouble to burst from the too sparse bushes.

"They could not know I would be able to land it."

"It didn't hit until we were on the ground," Vi pointed out. "Someone wants us isolated and without transport."

Joe could see no flaw in her reasoning. "I fear you are correct." He glanced toward Benson. "How is she?"

"She'll be fine," Jack said, pulling her upright and giving her a "get fine" look.

"Can she keep up?" Vi asked.

Joe considered their location, based on a map Lurch provided. The realities of their situation were not...encouraging. There was little cover, since most of the park was, of necessity, holographic. "There are not enough structures to provide cover."

"If I'm remembering right, the lake and bayous were built as channels so that pleasure craft could use them without straying off course." She looked around. "I think Little Lake is behind us. It connects to Big Lake, if we need to keep moving, and I think it also connects to the bayou if help is slow arriving."

"Do you think our distress signal got through?" He had not seen signs of signal blocking, but that was because the skimmer lacked the technology to know if its signal was being blocked. "We must assume we are on our own, until assistance does arrive."

Vi made a grimace he assumed was agreement. She glanced at Benson, then lowered her voice to say, "If this a move by you know who, at least it has reduced the collateral damage to our two uniforms."

Joe was not so sure. "It seems unlike it to be so altruistic." But who else would attack them so brazenly? Afoniki? The MITSC? "Whoever it is, they will not wish to leave behind witnesses."

"But they don't seem to be concerned about questions," Vi pointed out, looking at the smoking hole that had been the skimmer.

"No." Joe scanned the seemingly empty landscape. If their attackers went airborne—which he had to assume they would—Vi was right. They needed to move. "In any case, this location is what you would call hot. Let us move to this little lake and reassess."

⚜

"Couldn't we wait there?" Benson asked, as they drew level with the Pavilion of the Two Sisters.

Vi felt the same pull. But it had been thoroughly locked down ahead of WTF. Those hurricane shutters hadn't moved for the storm. Had a feeling they'd resist them to their last bolt. They could probably shoot their way in—and announce where they were as loudly as possible while doing it. Besides, she'd gone to a wedding there. Once inside there weren't that many places to hide.

"First place I'd look," she said, rather than waste

energy on a list of bad reasons to try it. Would the bad whoever-it-was after them think of Little Lake? Hard to know what an unknown assailant would do. So all they could do was try to keep moving and thinking. If the search for them did go airborne, which it would, it would up their level of difficulty by quite a bit. Though their attackers had to know they'd be armed. Wasn't that hard to find out the standard armament for a police skimmer.

Speaking of standard, Vi kinda wished she'd grabbed the parachutes. Though she wasn't sure there'd been time. And if that would have been a good move or piling on stupid. They were pretty old school, and she hadn't used one since her police training. Of course, whoever was after them could probably pick them off as they drifted down to —Vi considered dirt side and decided she'd rather die up here. At least there weren't gators up here—there had been critters here in the old days, but they were also holograms —and the suicide oak was offline. Was that symbolic or ironic? She wouldn't have minded a few more real bushes to hide behind.

Even though it was an illusion, it was relief to drop down into the shallow base of the lake. The water wasn't deep, but it did cover her boots. Mud sucked at the soles, then her knees as she crouched next to Joe, with Jack on her other side. She couldn't decide if it smelled better or worse than her last adventure in mud. Stagnant water went bad so fast, but it seemed like this smell predated the storm. The city probably didn't clean them that often when it was all hidden by holograms anyway. She tried to tell herself that no critters would have been able to move up and in, but herself wasn't entirely convinced.

So far there'd been no sign of pursuit, either on the ground or in the air. That was a puzzler. At least it gave them time to regroup, consider their options.

That didn't take long.

Beside her, Joe dug his hand into the mud and let it slide off his fingers, his expression thoughtful. He must have sensed her gaze, because he met it, one brow lifted a bit.

"It couldn't hurt," Vi answered the unspoken question. Kept her sigh to herself. Hadn't they just been to the covered-in-smelly-mud party? Her post-storm shower was a highlight of the week, right after getting kissed by Joe.

"What couldn't hurt?" Benson asked. She looked like she'd replaced awe for shock. And some wary.

But not enough wary yet. Clearly Benson hadn't clued into how deep in the *crapeau* they were. Vi was gonna go out on a limb and declare the girl crush over. She extracted a handful of mud and held it up. "Mud facials. They're supposed to be great for your skin."

Jack allowed himself to look thoughtful. Dude would be breaking out in half a smile if he wasn't careful.

"It should mute our heat signatures." Without losing any laconic, he placed his weapons on the lake bank, lay down and rolled in the mud. And while on his stomach, smeared the stuff liberally over his face and head.

"You missed a spot," Vi said, slapping some on his crown. It dripped down over his face, which made him blink. And yup, there it was. The half smile. He was out of control.

"We should expedite mud application," Joe said, a bit of something in his voice, that turned Vi his way.

Could a purple dude turn green? She grinned at him, then threw a handful of mud at him. Before he could retaliate, assuming he would, she took off her weapons and went down in the mud. If she'd been a pig, she'd have been as happy as one. She wasn't, but it did help to know she'd blend into the scant landscape better. And it made the armpit odor moot. One had to find ones positives where one could.

Benson was the last one to do the mud application. Her reluctance was interesting, but ultimately irrelevant. Jack might have been a little too helpful there. A little friction in the partnership? If she was annoying, Captain Uncle had picked her a good partner.

The mud might have helped, but they needed to keep moving. To where? And then what? She wanted to believe that help was on the way, but what if the call had been a fake? What if their transmissions had been blocked? Someone out there could have seen the fireworks over the Park. Might even have called it in. What priority would it get? Hard to say on that one. Would depend on who took the call and how it was reported. Which left her with a possible worst-case scenario that they were on their own for an unspecified amount of time. Now if the shooting ramped up into a firefight, that bumped up chances that lots of someones around the Park would notice and report.

Eventually there would be a tipping point that would trigger official attention.

They just needed to live that long. And make enough noise to make it happen. Which would expose their position and put them at higher risk of not living that long.

Yeah, more worst-case scenarios than not.

"We should split up." Jack's voice sounded as calm as if he were talking about picking where to eat lunch. He carefully holstered his hand weapon and picked up his long gun. Checked it for power pack and then assumed a defensive posture.

Clearly he'd been thinking, too. And not about lunch. Which Vi wished she hadn't missed. She'd even take an MRE right now.

"I concur," Joe said.

Not a surprise.

"The idea has...merit," she admitted reluctantly, pretty sure she knew where he was going to go with this. To head him off, she pointed out, "If whoever is after us didn't see us leave the councilman's place, they won't know we picked up these two," Vi pointed. "That might give us an advantage?" They needed the thin edges of even thin wedges, since that seemed like that's all they had. "You and I could go one way, these two could go another...."

Joe frowned. Also not a surprise. He was cut out of the heroic mold, and his people still had a "protect the women and children at all costs" code of conduct. The truth was, she and Joe were probably hosed, but it was possible that Benson and Jack could get clear. Tell their sad tale. It was easy to think noble thoughts, much harder to do noble things. Not that she minded Jack and Benson surviving. She just wanted to survive, too, if only to kiss the boy once more. When Joe didn't speak, she went on making her case like he had objected.

"We could draw pursuit off these two." She tried to sound, if not enthusiastic, at least wise. "Jack and Benson could make their way to one of the buildings and just lie low until help comes."

Benson looked horrified. Jack looked like, well, Jack.

"If you followed the lake bed, you could could head for the stadium. Might even get high enough to see something." Give us some cover fire, she almost said, but it undermined her "they don't know you're here" point.

"We won't leave you," Benson said stubbornly.

"Well, that's not your call, now is it? I kind of outrank you." Vi softened the rank pulling with a smile.

"You won't stand a chance." The line of her mouth was mutinous.

"If we stick together, no one will have a chance. Jack's right about that," Vi said. "We have to split up. And Joe and I seem to be the problem, the target, if you will. You can be collateral damage, or you can be witnesses for the prosecution."

There was a short silence.

"Yes, ma'am." She sounded subdued. As she should.

Funny how quick the "wow, it's so amazing to be a cop," turned into "holy freaking *crapeau*."

"Joe?" He'd been quiet, even by his standards.

"I believe that Jack and I should attempt to draw off the pursuit, while you and Benson make for the stadium. You can provide us cover when you have achieved the high ground."

He didn't seem to mind outing the witnesses. His people were also eminently practical.

"They are after us," Vi pointed out again.

"It is possible they know were are four, not two. We do not know what they know, why they have not acted." He blew out his breath. "We must balance our strengths, minimize our weaknesses. You and I both have experience."

In wallowing around in the mud? He was right about that. And he was hoping she wouldn't notice he'd put the girls together.

"They'll be looking for a guy and a girl, Joe."

He held up a muddy hand. "They are looking for a purple alien and someone with him. In our uniforms were are not gender specific. Identification will require close range. And covered in mud? Even close range will take time. Jack will provide, we can hope, an element of surprise if they do get close enough to ascertain our gender."

"It is the best configuration for success," Jack agreed. Maybe he liked the idea of being an element of surprise. Or he was cut out the heroic mold, too.

I don't want to split up. If she couldn't whine to Joe, she'd whine to Wynken.

Nor do I, but it does mean that there is also a nanite in each pairing.

But I'm stuck with Benson.

As you noted, her girl crush is on the wane.

Vi had to choke down the chuckle. A nanite with a sense of humor. *You're good—well, people, Wynken. I'm sorry about this, but glad to have you along.*

Like you, I would rather go down fighting.

"All right." Vi had to force the words out through teeth that wanted to clench. There wouldn't even be a chance for a kiss before parting. Her gaze held Joe's, hoping he got all she couldn't say from that look. She wasn't hopeful he would. He was a guy. And she had evidence he wasn't fluent in reading looks.

Amidst the debris she found a stick. "Here's basic layout of the park, at least as much as I remember." She sketched in the outline. X'd in the fixed landmarks. "We're around here. The NOMA is here. It's big. Has rooms. Might be locked down tight like the Pavilion, though. There is more cover that direction. At least, more buildings. We could cover you better if you mess around Storyland and the carousel, but that might be risky. From any of those places, we should be able to," she added, because there were two of them, "make it to Gormley Stadium and get high enough to get eyes on the Park."

She tried to remember what she knew about the stadium, but it had been a while since she'd been to a game there. And the date hadn't been that memorable. But it was a stadium. Shouldn't be that hard to get high. She looked at her watch.

"If no one stops us, we should be able to make the

stadium in—worst case—thirty. Let's hope for better than that." If the baddies went airborne, they wouldn't last that long without cover fire. She tapped her com, but it was dead. Or blocked?

Joe looked at his watch. "Once you are in position, we will attempt to draw them out. If—"

"Well, if the party starts without us, we'll join in as soon as we can." They should be able to move faster if the baddies were distracted. "If it hasn't started, I'll figure out a way to signal you to get it going."

"Jack and I will move out first."

"All right. Everyone mark the time." She met his gaze again. "Good luck."

"You as well."

Joe turned, keeping his body close to the edge of the lake and began to belly crawl away from them. From her.

I hope...

As do I.

CHAPTER FIVE

They were able to stay in the lake bed almost all the way to the NOMA. Nothing moved, on land or in the sky. Down in the mud, it felt as if things slithered away from them. Joe tried not to think about these things as there was nothing he could do about them, since screaming and jumping up and down would result in death. He'd always hated slithery slide-y creatures.

To distract himself, he and Lurch tried out various theories on each other for why the silence. Neither of them liked any of the theories that much, but they did keep his mind off what was moving in the mud. Hard to postulate when the opposition appeared to be acting without discernible logic. Despite his efforts to stay loose—whatever Lurch meant by that—Joe's muscles tightened and the back of his neck tingled, though that could have been because of the mud. He did not like to think what its component elements might be.

What were their enemies waiting for? Had they failed to draw them away from the women? Were they even now being—

That is not productive.

It wasn't. While he didn't like the internal circling of his thoughts, he was not happy to have them interrupted by having gone as far as they could in the lake bed. Suddenly down in the mud had much appeal, since getting out might result in getting blown to pieces.

Without speaking, they both paused, studied their surroundings, then looked at each other. From their location, both the NOMA and the pavilion that Vi had called Two Sisters, were visible, sitting there like choice A and choice B. Either would result in leaving the mud and moving into the open. Jack didn't appear eager to move, but then Joe had yet to see him exhibit any emotion.

Lurch had provided him with a mental map of the Park. Vi was correct in her assessment. There were more structures if they went left, taking a course parallel to their crash site. Structures in between open spaces where they would be visible to hostile forces. He'd been thinking about something else, but it would be equally...challenging to execute. Possibly more dangerous. "I have this idea...."

Out of his muddy face, Jack regarded Joe with his blank, patient gaze. His eyebrows might have risen in inquiry. It was hard to tell since the mud retained its flexibility.

"If they do have transport, and we have to assume they do, we will be—"

"Sitting, well, moving ducks," Jack finished for him.

"We won't last long, even covered in mud," Joe agreed. "I've been thinking about the missile launcher. If it really is mounted," he paused but Jack didn't speak. "What if it's still there where they left it?"

Jack's eyes widened and a grin broke the muddy expanse of his face. "I like the way you think, sir."

"Call me Joe."

Being called "sir" made him feel old. He'd like to achieve old before feeling old.

❧

THEY MADE IT TO THE STADIUM FASTER THAN VI HAD figured. Emboldened by the silence, she'd legged it, with Benson a few paces behind. They hadn't spoken at all during the dash. Silence was golden and speech wasn't that possible, even with Wynken helping her out—though it made sure she was enough winded to be believable without being embarrassed in front of the girl. It had a nice attention to detail.

Flattened against the side of the stadium, Vi let her breathing slow naturally and tried to extend her hearing. Not that she needed to strain. The silence was not golden or reassuring. Almost eerie in its depth and breadth. There should have been something to hear, even if it was just birds. She needed to get up where she could see. She needed to have been there ten minutes ago. She looked at Benson—couldn't keep calling her that, she decided.

"You gotta a first name, Benson?"

"Gladys, ma'am."

That's right. Frank had called her that. She didn't look like a Gladys, but what baby would? "If we're going to die together, we should be on first name basis, don't you think? Save the ma'am for the big *if* we survive."

"We're going to make it, ma—Vi."

Vi was glad she was optimistic. Someone should be. "I wonder what they're waiting for?"

"They?"

"The baddies. Why aren't they looking? Shooting?"

"Perhaps Jack and, er, your alien...partner, haven't broken cover yet."

That was a bit odd. Vi glanced at her. How had she kept that wide-eyed innocent look through training? To call her a baby cop seemed too much, but fetus cop sounded a bit weird. The hairs on the back of her neck rose, jerking her back to threat scanning. Something was wrong, but what? Joe and Jack had a much shorter distance to cover, even if they had to do it on their bellies. And why would the baddies let them scatter and make the search harder? It was crazy. No connecting thread to follow, to plan, and defend against.

"Or..." Benson's voice trailed off, possibly because of a fierce, don't-say-it from Vi. "Where do you think they are then, ma—Vi? Which way do you think they went?"

Vi gazed into the distance, but in her mind she studied her mental map of the park. "If it were me, I'd make for that cluster of buildings by the casino. There's a sanitation station and some other buildings that could give some nice cover. Maybe even provide ops for some crossfire action. Yeah, that's where I'd be."

Joe would have a better map than she had because he had Lurch. Wynken wasn't as up-to-date, it had said, with a soft *sorry*. So she hoped he'd figured that out. The NOMA was big, but they could get trapped in there. Of course, he'd need to respond to what he could see, too. Because that crossfire could be turned on them if the baddies were using the buildings for cover. She turned, catching an odd expression on Benson's face. There was something different about her, but Vi couldn't put her finger on what. Didn't have time for fingers on stuff anyway.

Perhaps she is afraid.

Vi should have thought of that herself. "It's okay."

Benson blinked. "What's okay, ma—" She pressed her lips together.

"To be afraid."

"I am not afeard." Her tone was defensive, verging on outraged.

Vi blinked this time. "O...kay."

Benson's cheek flushed. "My grandma used to say that." She grimaced. "I guess I must be a little nervous. Haven't said that since I was a kid."

Vi grinned. "No worries." She eased away from the stadium and scanned it. "Let's see if we can find a way inside this bad boy."

❧

THEY WERE SNEAKING THROUGH STORYLAND, ON target for the carousel, when Joe heard the sound of a skimmer starting up. He and Jack hit the ground, but its occupants showed no interest in them as it rose from behind something that he believed was the Garden Study, whatever that was. It headed across the great lawn toward the cluster of buildings that Vi had mentioned as possibly offering more cover. He exchanged a puzzled look with Jack, then turned to watch it circle the area. After a couple of circuits, another skimmer rose from the same area and flew that way. But it did not join the vulture-like circling. It settled in an open area, disgorging several armed men who began a systematic—and ruthless search of the buildings. They approached each with the skill of a SWAT team. One guy kicked the door open, another tossed in explosive grenades. It appeared that taking prisoners was not on the agenda for them.

"I am glad we changed the plan," Jack observed.

"As am I—" Their actions indicated they believed that's where the pair had gone. Why would they demonstrate such certainty— Joe's thoughts slowed, but his mind completed the thought —unless someone in their group was—passing on intel.

But incorrect intel.

The nanite was correct. That appeared to clear Jack.

Appeared. But I agree he is not our mole.

That left—*Benson*—

This time Joe's thoughts froze. Ice forming in big, painful chunks in his veins. It hurt to breathe, to think. But...she hadn't tried to manipulate events. Nor had Jack. She hadn't wanted to split up. *Are we bugged? The MITSC?* But why would they want them dead?

Trying to sound casual, Joe asked, "How did you end up getting the call to the MEC?"

"We were already there. Crowd control duty." Jack's lack of inflection seemed to increase. "Been there all night."

Benson. It has to be her.

You need to find that launcher. Without its fire power...

It was correct. There was a risk, but...

"If you found a missile launcher, would you know how to fire it?" He was following his gut. This was a surprise, but he felt most strongly that the place he needed to be was where Vi and Wynken were.

* * * * *

The sound of the skimmer firing up helped cover any noise they made breaking inside. Vi kicked or shot her way through each barrier, until they burst into the open field. Above them, the sky was calmly blue, indifferent to their plight. She looked around, trying to get her bearings. The sound of explosive detonations helped her with that. If she hadn't been so worried, she'd have enjoyed the lightness, the lift provided by Wynken. She jumped the barrier, and headed up the bleachers, like she had Wynken-fueled wings. As she closed on the top level, she slowed and crouched, unslinging her long gun. She eased up and stared through her gun sight at the men so ruthlessly clearing the buildings. Smoke drifted out the shattered windows of the buildings they'd already visited.

"They don't stand a chance," she muttered. She sighted in on one face. One of Afoniki's goons, the "receptionist." But why would he come after them? She took a breath. It hurt, the next one helped, though this pain was not something Wynken could help with. She used her sight to scan the area, tried to be systematic—was that movement over by Storyland? What had prompted them to head over—her sight picked up a gleam by the carousel. The missile launcher. But only one figure was darting that direction. She could tell by the way he moved it was Jack.

Was Joe trying to draw attention away from him? Where was Joe? Had to love a guy who was both brave and smart. She'd totally forgotten the missile launcher—hold it. Had she just thought the word love? It wasn't that she was *in* love, she explained to herself, but she did, well, love brains. On principle. Did the nanite give a little snort? Vi decided she didn't want to know. Thinking started again, though a bit slow after the sidetrack into, well...Jack had made it to the Wynken, Blynken and Nod ride—*sorry*. Not very tactful of her. She offered a mental apology.

It is okay. We picked the poem from Robert-oh-my-darling's brain for our identities when we were new. It was a metaphor. It is from the poem. We also set sail and 'Never afeard are we.'

Vi stiffened. And for some reason, that aligned her sight on a figure heading their way. *Joe.* Joe was smart. He'd wondered what she should have wondered. How had the baddies known right where to look? The skimmer had started up a minute or so after she told Benson—

"Why aren't you shooting them?" Benson asked from behind her.

Vi heard her take the last two steps and sensed Benson crouching down next to her.

"How did they know to look there?" Vi asked, though she knew the answer. Probably shouldn't have asked it out loud, but she had. She tensed, preparing to bring her weapon around.

"You told me that's where they'd be."

Vi began her turn, turned but found herself nose-to-nose with Benson's service weapon. Now she knew what had changed. Benson's injury had healed. As Vi stared, her eyes changed. Eerie lights formed around overlarge pupils. Sparks of light, like miniature lightning flashed on her skin.

It is pleased with itself.

Vi was surprised to note that Wynken didn't feel that afeared.

Nod tried to warn us. I was slow. I am sorry.

Nod. Tried to warn us. That means—

It still exists in there somewhere.

Nod isn't dead. We have to—

"They haven't found them yet." Benson's face creased in a frown, sending sparks of light dancing across the surface of her face. "Oh well. Shoot them."

"What?"

"Shoot them."

"Shoot...who?"

"Afoniki's men. Do it now."

Getting them talking always worked in the vids, so Vi went for it now. She didn't have that much to lose. "Why would you want me to shoot them? They seem to be working for you."

"They are surplus to requirements now that I have you." The lights glowed brighter in her...its eyes, a hint of green in there now.

Could it know that Wynken was in her? And if it did, how?

"Why would you want...me?" Seemed like Joe—

"I knew you would not find pleasure in Jimbo. He was an unattractive specimen with dubious hygiene habits. Though he was not as stupid as he looked. He suspected me. Almost got away." It frowned at the memory.

Jimbo suspected the...dog. He *was* smarter than he'd looked.

"This body is more pleasing. It has many elements of human attraction. Young. Fit. Pleasing to other humans. I observed this at both crime scenes."

"You picked Benson...for me?"

It seems we were wrong about the girl crush. It has a crush crush.

Joe was used to Lurch downloading programs into his head to help him adapt to the different situations in which they'd found themselves, programs that were really people skills acquired from others who had hosted it through many years. Sometimes it asked. Sometimes it acted. This time it was Joe who asked. *I'm going to need a lot more than me to get there in time.* If 'it' was inhabiting Benson's body, then Vi was in mortal danger. Hopefully the searchers would be distracted—

The skimmer's engine sounds changed.

They have spotted us. You will need to make random, evasive moves.

How...?

Joe felt the new program come online inside his brain. Felt it in every cell in his body as it sharpened his senses, gave him access to knowledge that made the impossible suddenly feel entirely possible— *Doc?*

She was a most remarkable human. If she can't get us there, it is not possible.

The doc program didn't take him over. The nanite would never do that, though Joe didn't think that in this instance he would have minded. He needed all the help he could get. But it did send new knowledge to limbs and to muscles, gave him a new agility and strength. It improved his instincts, too. He dodged, he rolled and fired at his pursuers, then dodged again. He survived despite the explosions striking the ground all around him.

This is impossible.

Doc did the impossible regularly.

But he knew, even with this Doc's extra skills, this was a battle he would lose if something didn't change and fast. His attackers had the high ground, something this doc deplored, according to her program. He needed Jack to get that missile launcher located and fired up. Assuming it had a missile ready to go. And that Jack could figure out how to fire it.

He heard the whine of incoming and leapt impossibly high in the air, his lift getting extra boost from the shock-wave when the weapon impacted on the ground. He spun in the air. Felt like it took a long time to hit the ground. He rolled a couple of times, firing each time his weapon pointed in the right direction. One of the shots did some damage. The skimmer veered off, trailing smoke. It circled around, coming back in. The doc program concluded that they were trying to cut him off from the stadium.

They must be watching from atop the stadium, Joe postulated.

Lurch did not respond to this. *How curious. I wonder...*

Joe did not have time to deal with what it wondered. Multiple impacts kicked up chunks of mud and metal sizzled against metal as some of hits drilled down to the platform, adding a heated metal scent to that of dirt and sweat. And yes, fear. He was not afraid to die, but he was afraid he would fail Vi.

In some strange way, it was as if he could anticipate the enemies' moves, but he could not stop them, something the doc program deplored—

I would have liked to meet this doc. There was a

complexity to the program that the scientist in him found fascinating.

I could arrange a meeting, but then she'd probably kill you. Lurch sounded amused, but Joe sensed it might not be joking.

The second skimmer rose to join the fight, but a high, rushing whine, a smoke trail, and an explosion knocked it out of the sky.

His chances of surviving went from none to slim.

Any chance is better than none. This voice was not Lurch's, which might have been distracting, but the doc program kept him on target....

❧

Vi let her held-in breath out in a whoosh. *Nice shot, Jack.* Joe looked like he was made of wings and wires. That level of loose had to be Lurch helping him—

The other skimmer circled him, firing so fast, she lost sight of him in a roiling mist of smoke and dust.

"I rather like your Joe, though I've never cared much for purple. Garradians think they are just so all that, too." The tone was petulant and oddly young.

Vi could not argue with this, not with Joe's *we try not to have emergencies* still stinging in her ears. Still, something about her—it—made her brain twitch. But there was no time to follow this thought. Since Vi rather more than liked Joe—though *not* to the point of love—she needed to help him. And Nod. They had to save Nod, which might help save Joe. And her. And Wynken. This wasn't all about her, even though it kind of sounded like it inside her head.

How do we appeal to Nod? How do we save it?

I am not certain we can. Blynken and I tried and now I am the only one.

But this time Nod's in there trying to help.

One word is a warning. It is not, technically, help. It is possible it is a remnant of his programming.

But it is fighting back. Okay, not visibly fighting, but if she could figure out how to help it fight. With all her programming and nanite experience, she castigated herself wryly. Despite this dash of reality, she kept up the pressure on her brain. The inability to give up was preprogrammed in her genes.

A figure briefly appeared out of a plume, then dodged into another. Nice moves. But he couldn't hold out forever. Each shot seemed closer than the last, like they were learning him. She looked at Benson. Was it controlling the skimmer? Controlling the people in it? *Can you jam its signal? Or tap into it?*

Lurch and I can connect, but we feared it would sense the connection.

Well, I think it knows you're here now.

Lurch is closer—with Lurch's assistance, we might be able to help....

Give it a shot. I'll try to distract Benson...it.

How...?

You do not want to know.

"Why don't you help him? Why don't you shoot them?"

Because that's what you want me to do. "I'm an officer of the law. It is my job to serve and protect. To do the right thing. You wouldn't want me to do the wrong thing—if you really like me?"

"Boring." Benson made a face, but Vi thought she saw uncertainty, too. "I mean, I get your law thing, that's why I gave you Jimbo and Bubba, but," She frowned, "They didn't assign you to Bubba. I thought they would."

They were a...present? "Can you read Benson's thoughts? She's an officer, too, you know. Do traces of them...linger?"

"Most humans are so boring, I don't bother poking around in their brains that much. And they don't even try —But I guess I can look—" Benson blinked, the lights in her eyes getting brighter, greener. "How strange. Seriously? That's how you feel?"

Vi nodded, a bit cautiously.

"I guess figuring out stuff isn't so bad, but all that 'punish the bad guys' deal is so, so, ugh. I like killing. When I move in, it is hard to wait. It's just so, well, so *so*. Every now and then someone fights back. That's the boss." Maybe something in Vi's expression penetrated its self absorption. "I guess if you like this body, I can keep it for a while. That's not very fun, though. I get so bored, but I can try—" Her head turned sharply, as if it sensed a threat and was searching for it.

It only seemed to use the information from a host that it needed. Surely this could help?

"So what's all this," she asked quickly, gesturing around her. "Why bring us here? You could have been hurt in the crash." Not to mention Vi could have.

"I was okay," she said, with all the self-centered-ness of a particularly young thirteen year old. "As for why, duh, so we could be together. And I was tired of all the going here, going there, talk, talk, talk. Ugh."

"Oh, right," Vi said, her thoughts circling around an idea. So it didn't *know* Nod, didn't seem to really be aware it was there.

Benson's head started turn toward the faltering battle again.

How could she use—not sure where the idea came from, her or Wynken, but Vi went with it, using a soft, soothing tone. "...one night they sailed off in a wooden shoe. Sailed on a river of crystal light, into a sea of dew. Where are you going, and what do you wish?"

Benson's head jerked back her direction, the lights in the eyes acquiring flecks of purple in the green. "What's that?"

"It's called a poem." Vi continued, "We—I like poems. It's a...gift. You gave me Jimbo, so it's for you..." She didn't wait for it to approve or disapprove of the gift. "We have come to fish for the herring, that live in this beautiful sea; nets of silver and gold have we."

Vi didn't actually know the poem that well, but Wynken fed her the lines, and she picked the parts that sounded the most soothing. Even though she felt Wynken's uncertainty and hope, felt it straining in that other direction, trying to disrupt the connection with the skimmer through Lurch, or maybe by providing extra boost. Would hope kill them? Or save them? She didn't dare look Joe's direction, but it sounded as if the attack had faltered some more. Or they were closing in for the kill—

Benson's mouth opened. Closed. Worked and then she said, in the sing-song voice of a child, "The old moon laughed and sang a song, as they rocked in the... wooden...shoe—"

It seemed to Vi that it fought the words, because the last few came out in spurts. The color of the lights crackling on her skin and hair changed.

Vi picked it up, "—and the wind that sped them all night long ruffled the waves of dew."

Benson's shoulders twitched and then her body jerked, as if it had received an electric charge. The lightning storm on her skin and hair filled the air with the smell of singed hair. And flashes of over-bright light.

"Never afeard are we, so cried the stars to the fishermen three: Wynken, Blynken, and..." Benson's eyes opened wide, and instead of the last name, she shrieked like an animal in pain.

JOE HEARD THE BANSHEE SHRIEK. HE DIDN'T KNOW why the skimmer's attack had faltered. But he—and the doc program—grabbed the chance offered. He found the broken door and surged through it, following Vi's trail by following that endless, eerie sound. He burst into the open. The large oval was surrounded by rows of seats that rose toward the sky. The building had no roof—there they were. An unmoving Benson, covered in lightning. Vi also not moving, but standing.

Alive. She was still alive.

For now.

Benson held a weapon and it was pointed at Vi's heart, the hands holding it twitching as flashes of light ran up and down her arms.

The doc program still aided him, plotting his approach. He made no sound as he raced toward them, though it only mattered when the scream abruptly shut off, like a flipped switch. The storm continued its dance across and around her body. Slowly the storm calmed some, but what it meant he did not know.

He crept closer and saw Vi make a tiny stopping motion with her hand. He nodded, to show he understood, but still closed on their position, coming in on Benson's six. He blinked at the phrasing, then attributed it to the doc program.

Into the sudden silence, Vi spoke, her words puzzling to Joe.

"So shut your eyes while mother sings of wonderful sights that be, and you shall see the beautiful things as you rock in the misty sea." She paused, though Joe was not sure why, then said, "...where the old shoe rocked the fishermen three: Wynken, Blynken, and *Nod*."

Benson twitched, her finger tightening on the weapon trigger.

Joe felt his heart freeze with fear, enough that it almost took the doc program offline. Lurch seemed to still inside him, too.

Slowly, very slowly, Vi held out her hand, the palm up. "Take my hand."

Benson shuddered. "Why?"

"When humans...like each other...they hold hands."

What was she doing? Her gaze never left Benson's, but Joe felt her willing him to hold position. Slowly, but not slowly enough for Joe, Benson's hand—still sparking with the remnants of the storm—moved toward Vi's. Just shy of contact, it stopped.

"You want to trick me." But she did not sound certain. Perhaps even somewhat lost. Like a child almost.

"I want to help you." She licked her lips. "You shall see the beautiful things as you rock in the misty sea."

Prepare yourself, Lurch warned.

🙚✦🙛

BENSON'S EYES FLICKERED BETWEEN GREEN AND purple and small twitches shook her frame.

"Just take my hand, and we'll rock in the wooden shoe. Aren't you tired? Wouldn't you like to rest?"

Benson gave a slight nod, the mouth drooping.

"Tired..." Her hand moved, but not enough. Her lashes drifted down. So did her hand.

Vi felt the heat of it, smelled singed flesh and hair and something metallic lingering in the still hot air. The lashes jerked up. The eyes were all green. Her mouth curved up in sneer.

"Yes, let's hold hands."

Her fingers closed around Vi's hand with crushing force, but the cry in her throat didn't make it out as her insides lit up with pain and images.

Of death.

Faces twisted in fear. Tormented as they died. Horror in death. So many of them.

And places and things. She tried to look past the faces to those things. They weren't as bad. There was something about them—a blow came from one direction. Then another.

The images twisted, curled into a sphere and began to spin and writhe.

Hot. Cold. Lava gold, mixed with green and purple.

Mardi Gras on steroids, she thought vaguely, wondering if this was what it felt like to burn from the inside out. Though she kinda thought her head would explode first. Not that she'd mind exploding. Seemed better than burning....

The whirling sphere seemed to change, slowing some, or perhaps forming into multiple spheres within the larger. Each was a face or place....

She leaned in. Felt like she reached toward one, though how...?

Then all the spheres began to pulse and throb.

This is where I die, isn't it?

But there was no response. Was Wynken already dead?

I don't want to burn....

She heard a sound and looked up. It was a hammer. A big one. It came down.

⚜

LURCH BLED, NOT BLOOD BUT DATA, MEMORIES... knowledge. It spilled everywhere, stinging, burning, aching with loss. He felt a whirling, a sinking, like he swirled down a vast, deep, bowl-shaped funnel, going down, down, down on sea of data....

Out of the depths, clinging to consciousness, Joe reached for the doc program....

He stopped sinking, but did not rise. Around him orbs spun, spilling faces and places into his brain. Filling it up. Pain, so much pain. Burning, turning...

Wait...

Was that...Vi's face? How was that possible?

WYNKEN, BLYNKEN, AND NOD ONE NIGHT
   Sailed off in a wooden shoe —
   Sailed on a river of crystal light,

Into a sea of dew.

THE WORDS ECHOED IN HIS MIND, MIXED WITH memories. So many memories. Meeting Lurch. Leaving his lab to hunt. Crossing distance, traveling through time....

...traveling...hunting...burning...

Am I dying? He'd thought it would be different. He'd hoped...he'd wanted...

Vi. He wanted Vi, but more than want, he'd hoped to save her....

There was the bitter taste of failure on his tongue. When the blow came he did not fight it....

CHAPTER SIX

S he was cold. It was freaking August. August was always hot...must be inside, because August inside was colder than an arctic blast....only that didn't seem right either. It felt as if the cold came from her...

Voices called her. *Voices in the deep.* No, one voice. And she wasn't a hobbit, so no deep. There was no deep in NON....

"Detective Baker?" Sounds, thumps on metal, regular enough to be steps or something, then, "Joe? Can you hear me? Joe?"

Warmth trickled through her, starting in her midsection and creeping out like slow-moving goo. The cold faded as warmth moved in. Sun, she felt heat from the sun now. She tried a finger. Thought it moved. Her brain said it moved, but she didn't see it move. Eyes wouldn't open yet. She tried more fingers. Felt like they moved. Lids so heavy. Like a hammer—

Her lids popped up. The hammer. It had come down. Dang, that hurt. Was glad to go lights out. Thought that was it. The light—the sun—hurt her eyes, but at least there wasn't a hammer up there anymore. Okay, that was a seriously crazy thought. Of course there wasn't a hammer hanging in the air overhead. Did she imagine it? She dragged a hand up and touched her head. It throbbed like she hadn't imagined it. Her skin felt clammy as the shock eased from the sun's heat.

That was most painful.

Wynken?

Yes.

We're not...dead?

I am also surprised to not be dead.

She laboriously began to piece together the random memories floating inside her head. They drifted around like a really messed up jigsaw puzzle. Evil nanite infesting Benson here. Wynken there. Joe—he'd been there. Nod— Nod! *Is it...did it—?*

There was a sensation of unfurling, like when Wynken moved in.

How did I get here? A pause. *This brain is aching badly.*

The voice was new, distinctly different from Wynken's.

I am sorry. I lack the ability to mitigate the pain. I am not fully online.

Okay, that was Wynken. There was joy in the words, though. Vi felt it, a bubbling up, like millions of bubbles darting around in her tummy. Was a bit disorienting, and it tickled. But it was better than all that other crap.

Wynken? Where are we? Who are we in? How did I get here? Why don't I remember?

I will explain later.

Um, I can hear you both. Vi thought it apologetically.

Sorry.

Sorry.

A moment of silence, then it came.

Wynken, where is Blynken?

I'm just going to see how Joe is. You two probably need to, um, talk, um, by yourselves.

Vi struggled into sitting position, trying to ignore the whispers in her brain. The sudden stab of grief. Didn't need the nanite heartburn added to the mix. Poor Nod.

In the meantime, she had a situation to assess. And she needed to get up off her assess, because it hurt like a son-of-a-gun. Okay, sit-rep based on available external data. She'd landed on the deck between two sets of benches. It was still August, so it was still hot and humid and yes, she smelled worse than before. Based on throbbing in elbows, hips and head, the landing hadn't been pretty. At least she hadn't gone over the edge. Physically gone over the edge. Mentally, yeah, she'd gone over. She rubbed her aching noodle, then expanded her assessment.

Benson...her laconic partner...Joe! Where was Joe?

Down a row...Jack—she pulled the name painfully out of the morass inside her head—crouched by Joe, who had landed crosswise the benches in an untidy sprawl. She got her elbows on the benches on either side and struggled to her feet. Yeah, that hurt. Even her eyeballs were whining. She wanted to rush to his side and smooth his pale purple brow. Not gonna happen for a few minutes though. She sank onto the higher bench and rubbed her face.

"How is he?"

Jack turned at the sound of her voice. "He's got a pulse."

Vi spotted Benson. She'd been tossed backwards like a discarded doll. At least it hadn't burned her face off. "What about Benson?"

Hard to believe any of them had survived that—whatever had happened. Was it gone? Dead? Hiding in one of them?

"She's got a pulse, too." Jack sat back as Joe stirred.

Jack got his hands under Joe's arm and helped him into sitting position. Joe didn't complain. His chest heaved, and he opened his eyes as if he dreaded what he'd see. Wary turned to pleased when he saw her. He attempted a smile. Vi attempted one back. Dang that hurt. Felt like the hairs on her skin throbbed.

"You are—"

"—not dead."

Jack looked at Joe, then at Vi. "What happened?"

Joe's expression turned wary beneath the dried mud. Small smoke trails still rose from him and Benson, now that her vision came into better focus.

You are smoking, too. This came from Wynken.

Good to know. She smoothed a hand down her hair, which also seemed to have acquired nerve endings.

That did not actually stop the smoking. Nod added this, a hint of pain still in its voice.

Let's pretend it did. In high school, she'd wished she were smoking hot. Which just went to show you should be careful what you wish for. *Is that singed smell coming from me?* It felt like both nanites looked away and whistled.

When Joe didn't answer, Jack looked at her.

"I feel like I got hit by lightning." And apparently looked like it, too.

Jack frowned, then half nodded. "There was a big flash. I've heard lightning can travel pretty far, but wow. It got all three of you?"

Vi's gaze met, and slid away, from Joe's. "Apparently. We were...standing kinda close together." She looked down. Looked like metal. "Metal conducts electricity." Bet they'd made an interesting circuit. She quit trying to stand up. "What about the skimmer? What happened to you?"

"I was trying to load another missile when they crashed into the playground. Blew up some swings."

Vi thought about this for a few seconds. "So no ride?"

"The missile launcher is actually some kind of tank. I can go try to fly it here. If you're okay?" He looked doubtful and excited.

She got that. He was hoping to fly a tank. Another time she might have arm wrestled him for the chance. Because who didn't want to fly a tank? She waved a hand. "Fetch it. Don't crash it though!" she called after him, and quickly regretted it. If there was a molecule of her body that didn't hurt, she hadn't found it.

She and Joe watched Jack until he was out of sight, then looked at each other. In novels and vids, this was the moment for the relief-driven clinch. The kiss. Man, did she want that kiss. Movement wasn't possible at the moment, which was *crapeau* plus. And if what she'd seen during the —whatever that was—well it raised some big questions, which meant that Joe had some explaining to do. And then she'd kiss him. Even if she had to shoot him later, she was getting that kiss. She'd earned it. And not even a huge pile of misunderstanding was doing her out of it.

Benson began to stir. Quickly, Vi asked, "How is Lurch?"

"He is...not himself yet, but he is not dead."

"Same for Wynken and Nod."

Joe's eyes widened. "Nod is with you?" She nodded. He swallowed. "Lurch is...very pleased by this news."

She rubbed at the dried mud on her face. She needed a shower so bad she did not have a metaphor for it. "We need to talk."

Benson chose that moment to open her eyes. She groaned. "What the—where am I?"

⚘

JACK FOUND A FEMA PHONE IN THE TANK AND called in, so their backup finally showed up. There were lucky. No messages, no black box signal, no one had known they were missing. Hadn't even been a 911 call about the explosions. Somehow 'it' had managed a total lockdown. The evil little sucker had been good. Crazy—there was the crush and the creepy love of killing—but she had to give it that much. It was good at being bad.

She'd gotten way more insight into the bad 'it' during their connected time. It had felt like being in the head of an out of control teen. Unlike Wynken and what she was learning from Nod, this one hadn't tried to learn anything from any humans—or the dog—before killing them. Just the fact it hadn't noticed gender differences was...

...nanite puberty... Nod told her. *It was young and had no moral center, no values. It was not sentient the way we are. It was...flawed.*

Seriously. Vi was glad she hadn't known just how on their own they were and what they were up against. She'd needed the hope.

Captain Uncle swallowed the lightning story, though it looked like it got stuck halfway down his throat. And tasted nasty. Benson was in bad shape. Her last memory was of being on duty at the FEMA camp. Something about someone sick in a tent. She went in—then blank. Everyone seemed to think it was an effect of the lightning. Vi had no desire to stop them from thinking that. It's not like there were a lot of options for alternate theories.

Someone had logged Charity Hospital into the database about the time the evil it was trying to fry them, so that's where Captain Uncle ordered Benson, Vi and Joe. Benson got the ambulance skimmer. She and Joe climbed in the back of the SWAT transport, since they were semi-ambulatory. Nothing for them to kick down or shoot, so the SWAT team didn't want to stick around.

Jack looked like he wished he could go with them. Vi didn't blame him. It was a confusing mess. And being the only bird in the skimmer headlights of Captain Uncle's glare? Yeah, not sorry to leave that party even though she wasn't eager to get checked out at Charity either.

Her only hope was the confusion of WTF would muddy the edges of this mess. It sure had muddied them. Joe looked like a zombie. A really cute zombie. Wished she knew how he did that. Couldn't all be Lurch.

If Joe knew why it had failed to kill them or Benson, well, he wasn't talking, and Wynken and Nod had figured out how to mute her out of their conversation. The SWAT skimmer touched down long enough to offload them at Charity's ER entrance. They watched Benson's stretcher port her inside.

Vi wasn't in a hurry to follow. There'd just be more questions they didn't have answers for. Neither, it seemed was Joe.

"You must be, well, relieved. I mean, it's over, isn't it?" This seemed safer than the "what the *crapeau*" semi-relationship talk they needed to have.

"It...appears to be over." Joe managed part of a smile on one side of his mouth. "I think I am still in the processing, feeling disbelief stage."

She could understand that, since she was still there, too. And she hadn't been in on the 'it' hunt for as long as they had. Which was a lot longer than she'd realized. Ire tried to get a foothold, but there still wasn't anywhere that didn't hurt. And she didn't have the energy for mild ire, let alone the serious stuff.

"We should go in—" She said this without enthusiasm, but before Joe could respond, a sleek, black skimmer landed between them and the entrance. The MITSC. The rear hatch popped up and one of the Smiths slid out, holding a weapon that looked incredibly cool. And dangerous. But very cool. Apparently she had just enough energy to feel jealous.

"Please, join us."

"*Crapeau.*"

"On a cracker," Joe agreed.

⚜

THE MITSC SKIMMER APPEARED TO BE PILOTING itself, as it rose swiftly above NON. Vi had been directed to one bench, next to a Smith, and the other Smith had directed Joe to sit next to him. It seemed an odd choice to Joe.

Indeed.

And it was troubling that they'd last been seen the pair with Afoniki, whose goons had been co-opted by 'it' for the attack at City Park. The hairs on his neck rose. Joe was pleased to note that this did not hurt. Lurch was gradually dialing back the pain level, though neither of them approached normal yet. He felt his muscles flex, though not noticeably, as the doc program came to the forefront once more. It felt as if the doc program overrode the tired program. Or perhaps kicked it to the curb.

She always trusted her gut.

I lack her gut, Joe felt compelled to point out.

Relax and maybe you will find it.

Vi appeared relaxed and apparently unconcerned, but Joe knew her well enough to know that she was also on high alert. Her color was better, though she still showed signs of lingering pain beneath the crusted mud. She shifted and the Smith next to him made a minute adjustment in how he held the weapon—that he'd already had pointed at her. The Smith next to Vi had his weapon pointed at Joe.

"Chill, dude. I've got some serious pain issues," she said, adding some winces to her small movements. "Some of them concentrated in the area currently stuck on this less-than-comfortable bench."

Joe noticed that her adjustments put both feet more solidly under her, the knees bent just in case leaping were required. Her gaze met his, and he gave a slight, very slight shake of his head. They needed some kind of distraction, and he had a feeling that it wouldn't be easy to distract these two.

They want us kept apart. Not touching. What do they fear? You? Joe asked Lurch.

It is possible. If they were controlled by 'it,' if they were drone infested, then they should have reverted to normal. Or died. I wonder...

"What is the old nanite telling you about us?" the Smith next to Vi asked. "It really is past time it died."

"Excuse me?" Vi looked at her Smith, then at his.

"Doesn't she know?" the Smith next to Joe considered her. "She might be a good host for more offspring."

Do it. Attack now while they are still young. Lurch's tone was the sharpest, most urgent Joe had ever heard.

Joe dove for the one across from him, hoping it wouldn't expect that. He was aware of a blur of motion as Vi leapt, too. The nanite must have found a way to signal her—

Offspring. He didn't have time to think about it. Didn't have time to wonder. He was back in the vortex, though it was not as deep as the last one. He was still present in the outerworld this time, staring into the maddened eyes of his Smith.

"You can't win. You are one. We are more."

"You should have waited," Vi gritted out. "We are more, too."

His Smith's eyes widened. Realization stealing its focus for a microsecond.

Take them into the time stream, Lurch ordered.

"Didn't we just leave this party?" Vi panted, though it wasn't the same party. There were differences. For one thing, she was still present, looking at Smith and his color swirling eyes. Lightning was back. So was the pain. The burning, but no spheres, no images, thank goodness. There was ground beneath her feet.

The color deepened in the eyes when it realized Vi hadn't come to the party without a nanite. She didn't know if Nod was strong enough to help. Just hoped that the offspring—and Lurch's sudden call to action—meant these were young enough to take down without quite so much drama.

Young makes them both easier and harder. Do not look away from its eyes.

Wasn't sure she could.

Hang on.

For what—?

The sudden yank to her midsection felt like it bent her back until her head brushed her heels. This wasn't the place of horrors and pain. More like a freaky ocean of lights and colors. Like being dragged through a storm with a writhing, fighting offspring of evil.

And no more solid ground beneath her feet. Wasn't sure she had feet in this place.

The time stream. Nod felt happy to be here.

Of course it is. Vi knew she sounded wry because she felt wry.

It fought her, like something from a bad *SyFy* flick. Seemed to have thousands of arms, with fingers that clawed and stung and slapped and ripped. She kept her head down, well, it felt like that, though her body didn't feel like her body anymore. She felt a bit like a writhing mass, too, but whatever it was, she hung onto like her life depended on it. Because she was pretty sure it did.

Knew the battle mattered, though couldn't remember why anymore. Only she was losing....

The harder she clung, the more it seemed to slide away...*can't do it*....

The thought had barely formed when she felt...something...a surge of strength flowed through—whatever she was right now. The mass got smaller and smaller....

I got this. That thought surprised her. And then she saw it again.

Stupid *crapeau* hammer. Looked a bit different. But it still came down.

CHAPTER SEVEN

Soft whispers and the gentle, healing touch brought her slowly back to consciousness. It smelled lovely, like, she didn't have a word for how great it smelled. Except for this tiny bit of something. If it hadn't been so nice, she'd have said something rude, because waking up lately hadn't been that great for her, particularly when she factored in what happened before the hammers.

There was no gathering together of scattered memories this time. She remembered everything up to the hammer. The boys in drab, the offspring, the squirmy, squicky battle in the...time stream...

How did she know what something was called when she didn't know what it was? Okay, she probably did know why she knew the word.

Everyone okay?

Yes.

Yes.

Yes.

Wait a minute. She sat up with a jerk. It did not change the sense she had three, counting again, *three* nanites swirling around in there. And she identified the something taking the edge off lovely. Her. She sniffed an armpit. Oh yeah, she was the stinky in the nice.

Really need an explanation.

I believed that Nod had erased Blynken because it was gone.

Okay that was Wynken. She'd know its voice anywhere now.

Blynken was wounded, badly wounded. The only way to save it was to hide it in me.

That had to be Nod, because it wasn't Wynken...

But... That was Vi, she meant that was her. She blinked and gave her head a little shake.

I did not remember what I'd done until the offspring attacked us. Blynken was still somewhat damaged but was able to fight well enough to tip the balance before the offspring could escape into the time stream again.

That was Nod again. Starting to recognize its voice now, too. *So, hail, hail, the gang's all here.* Inside her—Joe! And Lurch!

They are both well. If you wish to see him, we will show you the way.

That had to be Blynken. She felt like she ought to say howdy, but did one, when one had fought a battle almost to the death with it? Since she wasn't sure, she looked around. She was in a sort of bedroom. It was very sci-fi vid—sleek and new. And pink. Lots of pink that swirled from pale to intense. She blinked, feeling a bit pink-sick.

"Why is it moving?"

We are still in the time stream, Blynken told her.

They helped settle her stomach, because the view wasn't doing that. Sliding off the bed—comfortable, but also pink—onto a moving floor was almost as unnerving as Afoniki's transparent one. Her legs held and nothing hurt, which was a nice bonus. Her brain, which wanted to ache on account of the shock and awe, couldn't.

She didn't need to ask the way. She knew it, even though that knowledge felt separate. New. She approached a wavy wall and the wave parted for her, allowing her to exit into corridor that wasn't pink, but still moving, or flowing. It was a rainbow ribbon that bent and curved and flowed so that it reminded her of a crazy, old school vid game that her Grand Paw Paw talked her into playing with him every now and again. Mario something or other.

She was kind of embarrassed to be struggling with the weird overload. She was a NON-ian, for Pete's sake. Weird was supposed to be her wheelhouse. She followed the rainbow until another opening appeared. This room was weird on steroids, like mad scientist steroids. Could have been the vid set for *Frankenstein*—she tried to remember how many times it had been remade and couldn't. The Frankenstein vibes were boosted when she spotted Smith and Smith floating in tubes of golden goo. Their eyes were open, but she didn't get the feeling they were conscious.

Until their eyes followed her. If the role of Igor wasn't taken, she didn't want it.

They are in a sort of semi-stasis. They will not remember, Wynken said.

You didn't put me in goo, did you?

You had us, Nod pointed out

Oh right. So it's...helping them?

Healing and repairing their minds and bodies, Blynken finished.

She went past the tubes of MITSC boys—no longer in any color but the goo managed to be strategically placed—and rounded a sort of corner that rippled and changed color like her passage disturbed it. There she found Joe. A very shiny Joe.

Vi touched her still gritty cheek. *You didn't tell me there was a shower in mad scientist land.*

Sorry, all three of them said in a sort of echo.

"I forgot to look for the shower." And the bathroom.

His eyes glowed. "You look...well."

"I am...well." Looked like *crapeau* though. And she was freaked to the eyeballs, but sure, let's go with well. "Where am I? And don't say the time stream."

He closed his mouth, considered for a moment. "You are in my laboratory."

Vi blinked, not sure how she felt about finding out Joe was the mad scientist, but yet not surprised, now that she considered things. "Oh."

"Please sit down and I will attempt to explain."

"Where—" she looked behind and realized that some

of the wavy goo extended out from the gooey counter. She tested it, found it held and sank slowly down. It was actually pretty comfortable. For goo.

Joe sat down opposite her and a silence formed that felt a bit wavy like the goo. A wry smile flickered on his mouth, then he sighed.

"I am not sure where to begin."

"Why didn't you tell me the evil 'it' could make little its?" Seemed kind of need-to-know. She'd have been less cocky after taking down, um, daddy? Mommy? Itty?

"Lurch was still processing the remnants of 'it' when we got picked up by the MITSC." Joe rubbed his face. "I knew nanites reproduced. I did not know it knew that. Or that it could. It is... a process that leaves a nanite...reduced for a while. It was weakened during our encounter with it. Lurch believes that is why it was not able to kill Benson before it was destroyed." He gave a look that was wry and annoyed. "It was brave—and foolhardy—of you to try to save Nod. It is...most grateful."

Vi shifted on her goo seat. Decided to change the subject. "The kids were pretty bad-A."

"We are fortunate they were still...processing. They could have been much worse."

Vi made a face. "How did they get into the boys in drab?"

Joe frowned. "They were on site at the MEC, if you recall. They must have had contact with Benson there."

"Jack's lucky it didn't pick him."

"It will be interesting to study the data. Perhaps there will be clues in there as to how and why it picked its hosts."

Vi could have told him why it picked Benson, but instead she looked around. "Which brings us back to this place. How did you get from here to NON?"

He looked around, too, then gave her a rueful look, one that asked questions she wasn't sure she understood. Or maybe she wasn't ready to understand.

He leaned back in his goo chair, his gaze considering, or perhaps he consulted with Lurch. "My family has always been able to traverse the time stream. I am not sure how or when this happened. It is, of necessity, a most well-kept secret, even within the family. Not all possess it, but there are signs—and then training occurs to prevent —accidents."

"Who wants to lose their kid in a time stream."

Joe didn't smile, just nodded. *Okay....*

"And there is always the risk of imperiling one's own timeline."

Vi kind of knew about the grandfather paradox. Her people had always believed in time travel, even though they kind of didn't. Believed it was possible, just not proba-ble, she amended. And honestly, if Joe were telling her this back on NON...

"With a nanite, the ability is enhanced. I did not have a nanite, until, well, Nod's programming was overridden and it disappeared—"

"In time? It time traveled to—" She didn't want to finish that question. Even though she'd had inklings from what she'd seen during 'its' attack at City Park. She'd seen...places...the past...and what looked like the future. "So you've been looking for 'it' longer than six months in the Big Easy. How...long?"

"In your time, I have not yet started looking for it. All of it is—the distant future for you." He hesitated. "For me, it is the distant past. You are—"

"Long dead. Gone." Vi tried not to show her shock. So she was like seriously older than Joe?

He flinched. "In here, neither the past nor the future..." he stopped, as if searching for a way to describe it. "We are buffered from time's changes. I created this lab to track disruptions in the timeline and to make tracking of changes and people possible. In the beginning, there were time trackers, but they were...not precise. Because the stream is an imprecise place. There was a battle that almost wiped the trackers out. They went...offline at some point or became less visible. I am not sure which. I knew the technology had existed and I'd heard stories. Some of my family continued to use the stream. Damage was done. But still they used it."

Vi looked around her. "I would imagine it is somewhat...addictive."

He nodded. "I never planned to do more than study the time stream—but Lurch came to me. His human host was damaged, dying, from the battle with that evil it. He had saved Wynken, but it was wounded as well. It did not know Nod survived. And Blynken was lost—"

"Actually, Blynken is back. Apparently Nod hid it—

and well it can probably tell the story better." Because they were in her, she knew their story. Had seen it play out from decanting inside someone called Robert, through the trio's breakup to explore, and the first battle with it. There was a lot about their story, their past that would have made her head ache from emphatic scoffing, but she could "see" it inside her head.

Joe's eyes widened, then he smiled with so much delight that Vi's toes curled in her truly nasty shoes, and she almost forgot he was a future mad scientist dude who was both younger and cleaner than she was.

"This is very good news indeed."

Vi waited a minute before asking, "So how long have you and Lurch been hunting it?"

"It feels long, but there is no way to know. We have been to many planets, in many different times. I am," he swallowed, "still struggling to process that our hunt is complete. That we have succeeded."

"A happy ending then." As long as the happy ending didn't include hugs and kisses and, well, happy endings, then this was one. She'd worried about him going back to his planet, but if he went back to his time...

His troubled gaze met hers. "I have given you much to process. If you would like to return to your sleeping chamber and sanitize...?"

She rubbed a cheek. Had she really thought he'd want to kiss her muddy face? Almost felt like she heard a mighty crack from her heart. But it couldn't be breaking. She hadn't fallen in love with the purple alien. She'd promised herself she wouldn't do that. No way, no how.

"That would be...good." Was that her voice sounding so husky and near tears? It couldn't be. Bakers didn't cry. It was programmed into their DNA....

❧

HE DIDN'T WANT TO LOSE HER, BUT HOW DID ONE LOSE something that one never had? That one did not have the right to have? He was out of his time. He'd taken her out of hers. Put her life at risk.

When he embarked on this hunt with Lurch, he had not expected this...these...feelings. His family, for the most part, did not like feelings. Oh, there'd been stories he'd heard from his grandmother. Stories his father scoffed and derided. Love? Messy and embarrassing. Results in reduction in intelligence. Emotions were to be avoided at all costs. Emotions, love had turned the family purple skinned. Don't give into it. Self control. Discipline. Science. He'd believed he was that person. Had lived as that person. He'd loved his grandmother but thought he didn't believe in love. A scientist with a huge blind spot.

And then came the day he'd looked in the eyes of an Earth woman named Violet. Then he'd understood what his grandmother meant when he'd asked her what love was.

"You'll know it when it happens to you." She'd smiled,

her gaze going to the image of his grandfather as a young man.

"I hope it never happens to me," he'd said, imitating his father's shudder.

"You'll be a better man if it does, but you must follow your own path. That is love, too."

"What is?" He'd been puzzled, confused by the contradictory nature of this. He'd always liked things clear. Concise.

"Letting go. Seeking not your own. Caring more about what someone wants, than what you want for them or from them. I love you enough to...let you find your own path."

He had been satisfied at the time, had felt safe and content with her love. But now, now he knew. He understood. Because he loved...he wanted what was best for Vi, even though the thought of losing her made his heart flinch. Made his insides die a little. He had to let her go.

I am not certain that is what your grandmother meant.

She said love lets go.

But not without giving the object of your affection a choice. You are trying to decide for her. That is arrogance, not love.

Joe considered this, not sure he could believe it, since it gave him hope.

If she did not like you, at least a little, she would have knocked you on your, er, backside.

Joe frowned. *Why would she want to knock me down?*

You lied to her about who you are and yanked her

through time. And you are younger than she is. Trust me. She likes you or you would be dead.

Oh. Joe considered this. That was just the tip of ice mass, he realized, she had many reasons to be angry with him. *Perhaps I should apologize to her?*

Perhaps you should tell her how you feel. And then apologize. And tell her how you feel again.

Joe did not know why this seemed more terrifying than facing down the evil nanite.

But it did.

⚜

Vi had to admit that, even knowing the-massively-younger-than-her Joe had suggested the shower, it was epically fabulous. She could even sniff her own armpits without fear. It had helped that the nanites promised to turn their bytes around so they couldn't see her starkers.

She knew, on some level, that their future in her was tied to what happened next. She had a lot of questions about what Joe had told her, but one thing she got. Nanites were special. Hosting one was an honor and benefit. Having three...had to be unusual. And reserved for people who needed to travel through time.

We would miss you.

Their happiness, that had tickled her insides pretty much since she woke, lost some of its steam.

I would miss you, too. All of them. They seemed more,

felt more now that they were reunited. She felt their distinctness, but yeah, more.

Which was pretty mind boggling, so she didn't dwell on it. It wasn't like she had a lot of say in it if...she tried to circle the thought, but it refused to be circled.

If Joe didn't ask her—didn't want her—then she'd be going home soon. Alone. Might even be cycled through the goo so she wouldn't remember all this. Could she forget Joe? Her heart said, nope, never going to happen. But this place...only...

Home.

She missed it. Of course she did. She'd missed it before the jump into the time stream. It wasn't just the evil nanite that had hosed her. WTF had done a number on home, too. Her parents—they'd be so worried. Some...when? Joe hadn't been real clear on *when* it was right now. If she was out of time, maybe there wasn't a when.

She knew what it meant to miss NON, to miss family. She'd gone away for college. No question the surfeit of family drove her crazy, but she loved them—and Joe? Here inside her head she could admit she might, though she still couldn't quite think it.

Assuming they didn't try, how would it feel to miss the man who hadn't been born yet? The clench of her heart stopped her breath for almost a minute. At least it felt that long. Could she have spent the last six months falling—she circled the thought, but eventually had to land on it—in love with Joe? She looked at the fluid pink walls. Could she give up NON, in all its gritty glory, for this? For her guy?

This was pretty crazy, over-the-top mad scientist. Did he live somewhere? Did his family pop in for visits while cruising the time stream? How would they feel about their boy and the earth girl?

The pink walls started to close in on her, so she left them for the rainbow hallway. Instead of right, she went left, away from Joe's lab. The rainbow appeared to extend into infinity, but when she stopped, it opened onto a kitchen—one straight out of the 1950's on Earth. Was Joe a secret fan of vintage style? Vi peered in, then stepped in. There was pink, but it had been toned down. The vibrant green...was kind of cool. Loved the touches of flamingo dotted here and there. It was such an unexpected, non-mad scientist side. Where had this come from?

She turned in a circle and when she reached where she'd started, Joe stood there.

"My grandmother loved that period in your country's history. This was how her kitchen looked when I was small, so I replicated it during, well, during our travels." He half shrugged. "It...helped."

"My Grand Maw Maw swears we still don't know the whole truth about Roswell." Vi gave him a tentative grin.

Instead of laughing, he nodded.

Vi's eyes widened. "You're not, it wasn't—"

He looked a bit embarrassed. "We did not start it, but there was an...incident. Or two."

Vi chuckled. "I'd like to take a gander at your family history. Bet that makes some interesting reading."

He nodded, but she sensed he was distracted. He looked up.

"Lurch was wondering how...they are. The nanites."

He is the father, the first. Wynken had said. "They're having a regular party in there." She glanced away, but managed to watch him through her lashes when she added, "I'm going to miss them."

He made an involuntary movement, one he checked. Vi leaned a hip against the counter. He'd kissed her a couple of times, and hauled her tush through time. Seemed fair to make him start if, if they were going to have the relationship talk. Only she'd never had it before and was pretty sure he hadn't either. If he even wanted to...if he could have it.

"You—"

"Yes?" Vi tried not to sound too hopeful. She thought she wasn't sure about Joe, but looking at him? Pretty sure she wanted to kiss him and keep kissing him. Might even cook him something in this pretty kitchen. She liked him that much. It was stupid really, but even after all these years and the end of the gender wars, a girl kinda wanted the guy to do the asking.

You could give him a nudge.

Oh great, their great inarticulate moment had an audience.

Will you really miss us? Nod asked hopefully.

Do not interrupt them. We can talk about it later. Wynken said this.

Can you pass the nutrients? This is getting very good.

That had to be Blynken.

She must have had an odd look, because Joe asked, "Are you all right?"

"I am. I am fine."

The silence felt painful and prolonged. Vi turned and looked around, then nodded at the refrigerator. "Mind if I have something to drink?"

"Of course, but..."

Vi pulled open the door. It was empty. Really clean, too. Didn't it work?

He moved to the wall and tapped some buttons, then turned and handed her a glass of water. "It is not programmed for drinks more common to you yet."

Yet? Vi perked up at this very minute bit of encouragement. "Cool." She took a sip. "Tastes good." She gave him an encouraging smile and a hopeful look. He just stood there. Yeah, not very schooled in reading looks. She licked her lips. "So, now that your Quest is done, what's next?"

He looked a bit like a bug stuck on a board with a pin, but still cute. "Um, Vi..."

"Yes?"

"My grandmother..."

Okay, not sure where he was going with this.

"...the one who...this...this kitchen..."

Still not sure.

"...she told me I'd know when it happened."

Vi blinked. "When what happened?"

He flushed. "I am doing this all wrong. It is very difficult."

That didn't sound good. Might be the Garradian version of "it's not you, it's me."

"You see, my family is, for the most part, uncomfortable with these things, but my grandmother, well, you see, she was from Earth."

"She was?" That was a bit something. So some of his family liked earth girls.

"The men in my family, well, some of them, my father was, but that is not relevant." He looked at her with a hint of desperation. "Some of us find, we fall for...my grandmother's story was a love story, you see."

Okay, this was a little better. Vi took a step toward him. "I like love stories. If they have happy endings. Did she have a happy ending?"

Some of the tension eased from his face. "She did. When you come to my home, I will show images of them and you will know."

"What will I know, Joe?"

"That she loved him. And he loved her."

"That's really sweet." Was he going so slow because they were in the time stream? Because she was getting older by the minute.

"I asked her about love, how you know it, and she told me you know it when it happens."

He'd used it. The "L" word. Hope surged again.

He looked at her and now Vi saw the longing there. She gave him another step, but he needed to move, too. His feet weren't nailed to the moving, yet somehow 50's patterned floor.

"And do you...recognize it? Somewhere?"

Finally he moved. A step but progress. "I see it in myself. It is harder to believe that someone else..."

"...would love you back?"

His eyes widened. "But surely you can't doubt—"

"I think...uncertainty...rides along...with love."

Vi was not sure who moved this time. It was enough to be close. He smelled wonderful. Thankfully she did, too. His hands, warm and strong, clasped hers and tugged her until they were chest to chest, but not yet mouth to mouth. It was an oversight, but she'd give him some slack. For now.

"It feels wrong to ask, to want. My grandmother told me that love seeks not its own, so I believed I shouldn't."

"A girl likes to have a choice." He really was cut in the heroic mold. A girl, even one who could save herself and a few nanites, might not be opposed to having a hero in her life. And there were other things a girl could do with her own hero....

"That is what Lurch said. It is wiser than I am, I think."

Yeah. And still no kiss. And only half a declaration.

"Joe."

"Yes?"

"Ask already. So we can get to the kissing part. And then the 'when did you,' and 'when did I' and more kissing..."

He cut to the chase by stopping her words with his mouth, which she did not mind, actually. He'd come a long way since their first kiss in the heart of WTF. A long way...

CHAPTER EIGHT

"So what happens now?" Vi rested her chin on her hands and regarded Joe from across the table. He did not care for the distance, but it had been necessary for eating to occur. The kissing was more addictive than time travel.

Joe put his fork down. He knew what he wished to happen next, but he knew what convention and tradition decreed. Fortunately, they could travel in time and accelerate the journey to what her people called the honeymoon. He may have already have done the calculations...

"I need to meet your parents, and you will need to meet mine." He said that without enthusiasm. His father would be disappointed his son had fallen for an earth woman. And that he'd fallen in love. But his grandmother would love her.

Vi grinned. "I'd kind of figured that part out. I meant

the-rest-of-our-lives stuff? Do we live here?" She gave a dubious look around. "What do I do?"

"Oh. Lurch had an idea about that. If you don't mind continuing to host the nanites? They will not wish to be separated now." He felt a stab of worry. If she didn't—

"I like them. It's kind of like having puppies. Puppies you don't have to walk or take out in the snow to do their business—" she stopped, looked about to ask something and then shook her head. "I'd rather not know that. So what's this idea?"

Joe blinked, but was willing to move on, since he did not know what she did not want to know. "I set this laboratory up to monitor time, to track movement within the stream. I did not think past that, but Lurch has pointed out that my family are messing with time, have done for a very long time, so it is only right that I try to correct the more egregious time disruptions. And we are not the only ones who move through time. We could be..."

"Time detectives?"

He smiled. "Time detectives."

Vi looked thoughtful. "Could I have one of those cool guns the men in drab were carrying?"

"See, that is a problem right there? Where did they get advanced technology?"

"Is that a yes?"

The way she looked at him? He'd have given her her own planet. He nodded.

"Speaking of the dudes in drab, what are you going to do about them?"

Joe gave her a wary look. "Well, we might need additional teams. There is a lot going on out there. For all we know, we already hired them, and they were there at our direction. That might explain why they had the technology." Where had he seen those particular weapons?

"I think I just got a headache."

"Time paradoxes can do that to you."

"And that's another reason to have nanites?"

"It does help."

She smiled at him, reached a hand to him. He clasped it, feeling the warmth of the contact steal up his arm. And lit some things in his mid-section that were hard to control. Mentally he reworked the calculations that would get him to the honeymoon faster.

"So, that's it. The Baker and—" she stopped. "I still can't say your name. Unless—"

"No, it is not my real name, though I would prefer to stay Joe to you. It is the moment I felt my heart change."

"Okay, that earns you a hug and a kiss." She shifted from her chair to his lap and delivered both. To his extreme disappointment she pulled back to ask, "So what is your real name, in case I like it better than Joe?"

"I was named after one of my more illustrious ancestors." He hesitated. "A Leader. The Leader during our first contact with Earth."

"That's kind of cool."

"Helfron Giddioni."

She blinked. Then grinned. "So Joe it is."

He tightened his hold on her. "What if I told you there

was a way to travel through time to our honeymoon? Right now. We could have the wedding and the family meetings later..."

She studied him, heat flaring in her amazing eyes. "I would say, talk is cheap."

He stood, holding her tight against him. "Don't let go," he said. And pulled her into the time stream....

THANK YOU FOR READING *SUCKER PUNCH*. I HOPE YOU enjoyed it. And look for more Vi and Joe adventures in *An Uneasy Future*.

To find out about all my releases, be sure to sign up for my New Release eZine and get a free eBook!

Or hop over to my website and check out my series:

Project Enterprise The Big Uneasy Lonesome Lawmen

Browse my complete backlist by visiting my website. :-) I have some stand alone novels, too.

And if you want to talk books, you can find me here:

My Blog Facebook Fan Page Twitter Google+ Pinterest Linked In Goodreads

If you enjoyed this book, I hope you'll consider leaving a review. It's not just because I'm needy (even though I try not to be!). Reviews help other readers decide which books to buy.

Out of Time (World War II Time Travel Romance)

An Uneasy Future

(A science fiction romance mystery series set in future New Orleans)

Core Punch (1.0)

Sucker Punch (2.0)

One Two Punch: An Uneasy Future Bundle

Short Story Collections

Project Enterprise: The Short Stories

Do Wah Diddy Delete

Let's Fall in Love

The Real Dragon and other short stories

Romantic Suspense

The Big Uneasy Series:

Relatively Risky (1)

Family Treed (A Big Uneasy Short Story)

Dead Spaces (2.0)

Louisiana Lagniappe (3.0)

Worry Beads (4.0), 2018

The Big Uneasy Bundle

Lonesome Lawmen Series:

The Last Enemy

Byte Me

Missing You

Lonesome Mama (Bonus short story)

(The *Lonesome Lawmen* is also available as a digital bundle)

Do Wah Diddy Die

The Spy Who Kissed Me

Perilously Fun Fiction Bundle (includes *The Spy Who Kissed Me* and *Do Wah Diddy Die*. Bonus: *Do Wah Diddy Delete Short Story Collection*)

A Dangerous Dance

ABOUT THE AUTHOR

Award-winning, *USA Today* Bestselling author Pauline never liked reality, so she writes books. She likes to wander among the genres, rampaging like Godzilla, because she does love peril mixed in her romance.

To find out more about Pauline or her books:
http://paulinebjones.com

ACKNOWLEDGMENTS

I'd like to acknowledge the assistance —both as an editor and for her world-building/flight dynamics insights—of Alexis Glynn Latner. Her invaluable assistance has made this book possible. Her help was much appreciated.

I'd also like to acknowledge my son, Nathan, who was my weather/How New Orleans Might Be in the Future consultant for this novel. His ideas on how to make my characters suffer were spot on and oddly cathartic.

My thanks to Ana Baird for her keen copyediting eye and unfailing support. :-)

I'd also like to thank Elizabeth Vargas for her innovative cover design. No project is complete without great packaging. :-)

I would be remiss if I also didn't acknowledge my family—who suffers through my flights of fancy—and my readers—who stick with me through my flights of fancy. :-)